The Diary of Amy

The 14-Year-Old Girl Who Saved the Earth

Also by Scott Erickson

The Best of Reality Ranch

The Diary of Amy

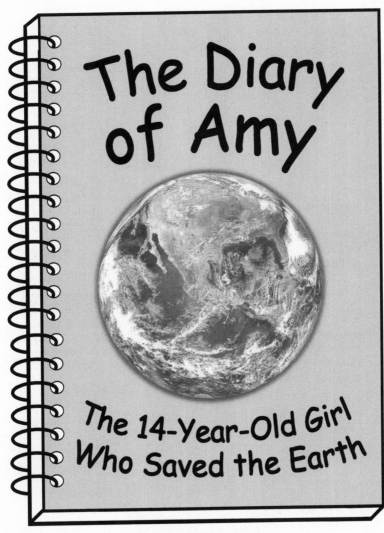

The 14-Year-Old Girl Who Saved the Earth

Scott Erickson

This is a work of fiction. All names, characters and incidents are the products of the authors' imagination. Where the names of actual locations or corporate entities appear, they are for fictional purposes and do not constitute assertions of fact. Any resemblance to real events or persons, living or dead, is coincidental.

ISBN: 978-0-9898311-0-9

Published in the United States of America
by Azaria Press

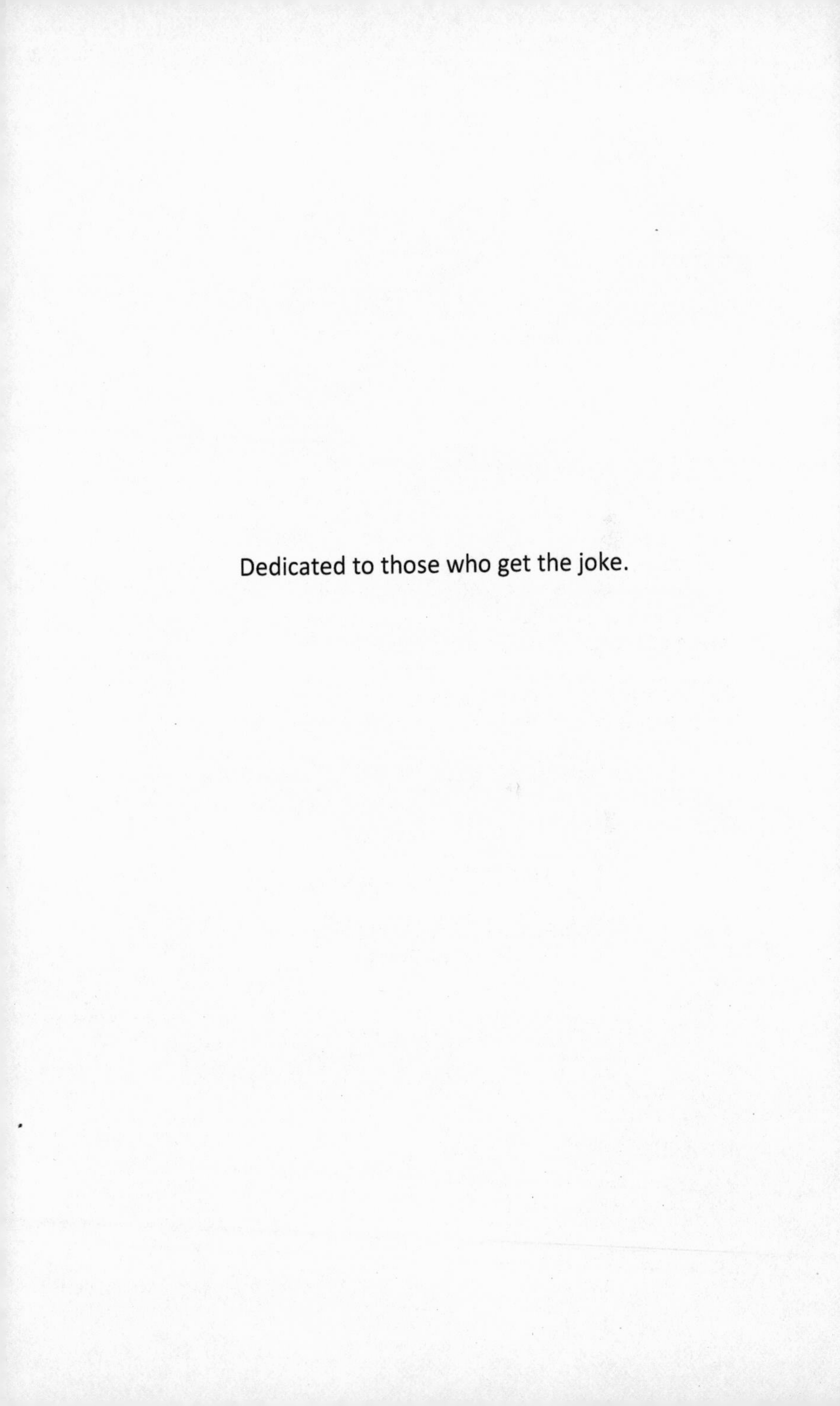

Dedicated to those who get the joke.

This diary is made from paper that contains 100% post-consumer fiber, is processed chlorine-free, is Forest Stewardship Council Certified, is made with green energy, and before the trees were harvested we said a prayer of thanks and the trees were cut respectfully and pushed over gently after we made sure there were no animals underneath that might get crushed.

June 15

I CAN'T BELIEVE IT! I MET JUVIE STARR, MY FAVORITE ACTRESS OF ALL TIME!!! I didn't even recognize her at first. She came over and asked me, "Are you the 14-year-old girl that's saving the earth?" and I said "Yup, that's me!" and I told her she looked a lot like Juvie Starr and she said, "That's because I am!"

Good thing the TV cameras didn't catch me falling over!

I told her I'm her BIGGEST fan and she's such an inspiration for her strong female roles. Then she said no, it's people like ME who are an inspiration for HER!

WHAT AN INCREDIBLE DAY!!! I can NOT believe that all that happened just a few hours ago, right before the announcement that the governor was stepping in to stop the condo development. So Juvie got to be there during the big announcement, when the governor came to deliver the news. Oh yes, I can't forget the news:

THE WETLAND IS SAVED!!!

I think a lot of the people that showed up were celebrities, but I don't know since I don't watch TV. But the crowds of people sure went crazy when they showed up.

Juvie gave me her private cell phone number! She said, "Call me any time if you need advice or support."

I think my favorite "guest" (besides Juvie Starr, of course!) was that hip-hop group (forgot their name) that did a rap song about my activism.

That reminds me that I must be CAREFUL what I say to the media. I got all excited talking to one of the reporters about wetland protection and said, "We need to keep the wetlands wet!" which I now realize sounds kinda silly. But it was live TV so I couldn't ask them to edit it out. Which is why the rap song included the lines:

This girl Amy I just met
Says to keep the wetlands wet

Oops! Be more careful what you say, Amy, especially when a microphone is in front of your face!

June 16

I'm getting a TON of mail! How will I have the time to answer it all? The letters congratulated me on "sticking it to the greedy developers" and other revolutionary sayings. (Am I a revolutionary?)

But there was one thing that got me kind of weirded out. Many of the letters were from teenage boys who said I was "cute." Maybe I'll write them back and say, "Thanks, but instead of calling me 'cute' please follow my example and do something to save the earth."

June 17

Dad just brought me today's Oregonian, which included an EXCELLENT interview with a certain 14-year-old girl!

> *Ms. Johnson-Martinez, what motivated you to camp in a wetland for five days?*
>
> First of all, please call me Amy! As for wetlands, they are very important and need to be saved. Wetlands are among the most fertile and productive ecosystems on earth. Half of all North American bird species nest or feed in wetlands. Over half of the fish eaten in the whole world are dependent on coastal wetlands. Wetlands are also beneficial to human society, by filtering pollution and excess nutrients, improving water quality, and offering flood protection.
>
> *Well, that's probably enough about wetlands.*
>
> In fact, one study estimated the value of all the wetlands on earth to be 14 trillion dollars. Wetlands are very important!
>
> *Amy, how long have you lived in Sellwood?*
>
> Since I was 11. Before that I lived in Hillsboro, where I was born. I just graduated from Sellwood Middle School, at the top of my class!

Did you have a history of activism leading up to your "Wetland Camp"?

Well, mostly just volunteering for HomeEarth's "GreenKids" program for the past two years. I help lead trips of grade-school kids to expose them to nature. And you know something that's really funny?

What?

A lot of these kids are actually scared of nature! One time I was leading a group of third-graders on a hike in Oaks Bottom and they were scared that alligators were going to eat them. Alligators! In Oregon!

Who was the biggest inspiration in your activism?

My mom was a famous activist, Sara Johnson – before she became Sara Johnson-Martinez. Her activism was in the civil rights area. She was shocked by the working conditions of the farm workers in Hillsboro. That's how she met my dad – Alfonso – when she was working on worker's rights. That was back before he got a job building houses.

She never worked on environmental issues?

She only worked on an environmental cause one time. There was a beautiful forest of old-growth oak trees near where we lived. But they tore it down to put up a stupid Hooters restaurant.

Were your Sellwood neighbors supportive of your activism?

They were totally supportive! They were against the development because of all the extra crowds and noise and traffic. When they found out about my wetland camp, they came by with food and water and blankets!

It seems that environmental issues are becoming very popular.

I think the GloboChem spill is really making people realize that we have to stop putting poison on the food we eat. And people are starting to see that drilling for oil in the Arctic National Wildlife Refuge was a huge mistake. It's not even very much oil, and now the media is publishing photographs of dead caribou and polar bears.

How long did you plan your "Wetland Camp"?

Actually, it wasn't planned at all. I was finishing up a GreenKids hike and we were going back to the van, and suddenly I couldn't leave. I had to ask the co-leader to go to my house and get my camping stuff. I didn't even think about it being illegal until later, but I guess the police didn't want the publicity of dragging away a teenage girl in handcuffs.

It sounds kind of like what happened to Rosa Parks, when one day she reached her limit and refused to go to the back of the bus.

Exactly! And maybe my action can be a trigger, like Rosa Parks was for the civil rights movement. I mean, it's totally important to save this wetland – but also to save *all* wetlands. And all rivers, and all forests. My goal is to get to the roots of why all natural areas are being destroyed. I feel certain there is a root cause, and I want more than anything to figure it out.
I want to save the earth!

Why not a 14-year-old girl saving the earth?

Exactly! Why not!

June 18

I went through the mail and found some letters from magazines and TV shows. They want to interview me!
I showed them to Dad, and he noticed that none of them mentioned "financial compensation." I replied that my activism is about saving the earth, and how can you put a price on saving the earth? He asked, "How does being broke save the earth?" I couldn't think of an answer for that.

Unfortunately, summer is the super-busy time for the construction business so Dad is very limited in how much he can help. But I promised that I would check with him before accepting any interview offers.

I said to Dad that maybe he needs to hire me an agent. He gave me his "Do you think I'm made out of money?" expression.

I found a very disturbing news item:

> *Chicago, Ill.* – In last week's news conference in the aftermath of the disastrous GloboChem accident, spokesperson Thomas Chan appeared in a press conference expressing his deepest apologies for the accident. The tearful Mr. Chan expressed his desire to do "whatever is necessary" to repair the environmental damage and take care of "all those poor suffering babies."
>
> In a surprise announcement, GloboChem CEO Lionel Hovercraft issued an official denial of Mr. Chan's statements. He stated that he personally fired Mr. Chan because his excessive compassion is a serious threat to the company's profitability.
>
> "If Mr. Chan really cared about those babies," said Hovercraft, "he would have focused his attention on growing the company in order to provide jobs for them, assuming they live to become adults." A replacement for Mr. Chan has not yet been found.

This seems to imply that "profit" and "compassion" are opposites. This is a very disturbing idea and I'm going to assume this was an isolated incident.

Hey Mom, wherever you are. Are you proud of me? I feel like I'm finally honoring your example. I will NEVER forget that time you told me, "Every time you do good in the world I am alive in you helping you to do good in the world."
I WILL NEVER FORGET! Even though I have to admit sometimes your sayings to me were sort of "wordy," I will never edit them, because it would feel like I'm editing your memory.

I saw some YouTube clips of me being interviewed at my wetland camp. So weird! I noticed that when I get excited I wave my arms around a lot. I have to remember to not do that. Besides not looking very mature, I might hurt somebody.

June 19

SO FUNNY! Today I got a letter from Hooters, Inc. expressing their "extreme displeasure" regarding my comments in the Oregonian interview. The letter said: "Hooters, Inc. is very concerned about creating a natural workplace. For example, we refuse to hire waitresses with silicone implants."

But then the letter got less "funny" when it said: "Any future negative comments concerning Hooters, Inc. will be referred to our legal department."

Is Hooters my enemy? I MADE AN ENEMY! Mom told me that's a good sign, it means you're standing up for something. She also said, "If you want to make an omelet you have to ruffle some feathers."

I got a call from Katherine Bliss, president of HomeEarth!!! She said she would like to meet me in her office tomorrow to discuss an "opportunity." I asked her what kind of opportunity, and she said she'd rather discuss it in person. HOW IN HECK AM I SUPPOSED TO SLEEP TONIGHT???

June 20

I can't believe it! HomeEarth wants me to be their spokesperson! After seeing my TV interviews they think I would be a GREAT representative for HomeEarth! I deeply agree 100% with their motto: "No Compromise in Defense of Mother Earth!"

But ME??? I'm just a girl! Isn't that an adult job? Do they really think I can do it? Do I MYSELF think I can do it? CAN I? Are they crazy? AM I CRAZY? ("Don't answer that question!" "Okay, I won't." "Hey are you talking to yourself again?" Haha!)

Being Serious: The official title of the position is "Communications Manager." Katherine said it would mostly involve giving talks about saving the earth, such as to schools and organizations.

Katherine said my "appeal" is that I come across as "genuine and unpolished, as if I'm telling the truth." Of course! What else would I tell?

Because of child labor laws (technically I'm a "minor") it can only be a "summer job."

But if High School is going to be the same stupid stuff as Middle School, I would not mind at all if I could skip it and go right to college. The students in Middle School were SO immature. For some reason they thought it was "cool" to be stupid. All they cared about was TV shows and music stars and making out.

I told Katherine that I need to talk it over with Dad before I can accept the job, but I think he'll approve because it's a FULL-TIME PAID POSITION.

Katherine told me to take my time, that this is a big decision for me. Obviously! Probably the biggest decision of my life in my whole 14 years of living.

Too much to think about. So instead of thinking, I'm going to plant some tomatoes. Working in the garden is so good for forgetting about mental craziness.

June 21

The totally nice neighbor Carol left me a note with a recipe. Into the diary you go!

Dear Amy, I see that your garden is growing very well, especially your beets and radishes. I want to share an old family recipe with you. Just combine the following ingredients and press into a greased casserole dish, bake 350 degrees for 50 minutes. Enjoy! ~Carol

ROOTS 'N' NOODLES CASSEROLE

2 cups egg noodles (cooked)
1 cup beets (sliced)
1 cup radishes (sliced)
½ cup swiss cheese (grated)
2 tsp salt

P.S. – Thanks for saving the neighborhood!

Talking with Dad I got so excited he had to keep telling me to slow down and to repeat things. He asked me what the salary was and I had to admit I was so excited about the incredible opportunity that I didn't ask. Then he started talking in Spanish as he does when he's upset.

His biggest concern was how this would impact my plans for a law degree. He felt that competition for legal jobs is tough and a resume with something like "Gave speeches about saving the whales" would give law firms the idea that "I'm not serious about my career."

GRRRRR!!! I felt like BREAKING something but I held my emotions in control. I said (very calmly, I think) "If we don't save the earth then there won't BE any careers," but he said I was exaggerating. He said he didn't think environmental problems were serious! He went to the window and pointed outside and said, "I don't see the earth being destroyed."

I could not believe those words came out of my very own father! A million things were in my mind but they all smashed into each other and nothing came out. He thinks I'm just a melodramatic teenager! Then I slammed the door and ran outside, which I suppose made me look like a melodramatic teenager.

I just had a "heart to heart" talk with Dad. He said he was sorry for being mad at me before. He said it wasn't easy watching me become a famous activist and it wasn't what he expected or wanted in a daughter. But he told me, "You take after your headstrong mother, and I was very proud of her." He said I was like her, in the sense that when either of us gets an idea there's no way to talk us out of it.

Whenever Dad gets talking like this it gets sad, because sooner or later he starts talking about Mom, and about how she sacrificed to make our lives better. And if he gets REALLY sad, he'll say how he felt so guilty using the insurance money to buy a nice house and start my college fund. Then he won't be able to talk anymore and has to be alone for a long time.

June 22

I had lunch with Tiffany, the office manager at HomeEarth, so we could talk before I "officially" accept the position. It's very important that we get along because I'll mostly be working with her.

I expressed my concerns that Katherine doesn't seem very "warm" or "friendly." But Tiffany explained that Katherine is an OK person, and she's a great boss to work for. Just don't expect too much hugging, or any hugging.

I asked Tiffany why she's so cheerful and positive, and she got all excited telling me about her "personal growth stuff." She showed me a book she got from New Renaissance, the "New Age" bookstore. The book was called something like, "Keys to Unleashing Hidden Energies and Emerging Consciousness and Life is Sacred."

She said she's sure we'll be total friends. She said "everything happens for a reason" which got me very curious but we didn't have time to discuss further.

But the important thing is: I ACCEPTED THE POSITION!!! After lunch we went back to the HomeEarth office and I told Katherine that I gladly and proudly accept the position of Communications Manager for the fourth-largest environmental organization in the United States of America!

June 23

Dad came home late, very tired. I told him I'd make him dinner, the "Roots 'n' Noodles Casserole" recipe so kindly given to be by the totally nice neighbor Carol. Unfortunately it was not quite so "delicious" as described. Dad added lots of ketchup and at least we were able to finish it.

Random Thought: I was at Fred Meyers and they have a small part of the grocery store section (maybe 10%) called "Healthy and Organic" which implies that the other 90% is "Unhealthy and Poisoned with Agricultural Chemicals." Wouldn't it be funny if they labeled it like that? They probably won't, though.

June 26

I'M WRITING FROM MY OFFICE AT MY JOB! It started off very exciting, but then it got boring. For 2 days all I've done is read tons of HomeEarth stuff and decorated my office. Tiffany gave me a "present" of an inspirational saying in a nice frame:

> Our deepest fear is not that we are inadequate. Our deepest fear is that we are powerful beyond measure.

Is that true? I never felt powerful at all until my wetland camp saved Oaks Bottom, but at the time I didn't feel like it was a "powerful" thing at all. I just had to do it. Now I feel a little powerful, but definitely not "beyond measure."

June 27

I gave my first HomeEarth presentation! Unfortunately I must report it was a mixed success. I totally understand Katherine's point that we must reach the "unformed minds of youth" before non-environmental thoughts get in there. I totally agree but I'm thinking that the minds of pre-schoolers should maybe stay un-formed for a while longer. They were NOT interested in my presentation - a HomeEarth KidsTalk entitled "The Earth is Fun." They were getting bored and fidgety until I brought out the little foam rubber earths (nerf balls painted to look like miniature earths).

I guess they were having fun, but unfortunately they started taking bites out of the earths. I feel bad that 2 of the children had to go to the emergency room. On the bright side, it seems like the message of "The Earth is Fun!" was received, except maybe for the 2 kids who had their stomachs pumped.

I expressed my disappointment to Katherine about the pre-school talk. I told her I thought I was going to have more "substantial" responsibilities such as speaking to an audience that doesn't try to eat the presentation materials.

Finally I was able to talk to Tiffany about the whole "everything happens for a reason" thing. She said everybody has a destiny, and that the important events in your life all contribute to your destiny - even if you don't know exactly what it is until later. I asked her if my wetland camp was part of my destiny, even though it felt totally spontaneous. She told me, "Listen to your heart," which I guess means "yes."

I was remembering in the interview when I said, "I want to save the earth!" I didn't really think about that before I said it. But now that I'm thinking about it, it sounds SCARY! Is that actually my "destiny"?

June 28

Dear diary, I've been not looking forward to this, but I've been putting if off and I need to just do it and get it over with. It is vitally important for my job (and maybe also for my destiny) to focus on the TRUTH because... I can't remember. I knew before but then I forgot.

Oh, I remember: Because if I avoid the full truth of the problems then how can I find the full solutions? So that means sometimes I have to honestly and with my eyes fully open and not blinking LOOK at the truth even if it's hard. So as a result, dear diary, I'm going to put some "bad" news into you, some news articles I've been saving up.

New "Dust Bowl" Leads to Sale of State

Pierre, S.D. – The catastrophic drought in South Dakota has led to a new "dust bowl" in which the fertile topsoil formerly occupying the state has been blown into Nebraska.

As happened previously with the dust bowl of the 1930s, environmental refugees have been forced to migrate to other states as did the "Oakies" of the original dust bowl. These new refugees, informally dubbed "Northies," are migrating south in search of employment as fast-food migrant workers.

GloboChem has offered to buy the entire state of South Dakota to use a test site for an experimental variety of wheat. The experimental grain includes portions of the genetic code of the kangaroo rat, a species which never needs to drink due to its ability to synthesize water from food.

Drought Relief for Arizona

Phoenix, Ariz. – Due to the continuing drought, the Arizona Department of Hydrology declared that the state must choose to either stop drinking water or stop watering Arizona's 421 golf courses.

Declaring both options "untenable," the governor announced that before the end of the year construction will begin on a 2,000-mile pipeline linking Phoenix to Duluth, Minnesota. "Think of the pipeline as a very long straw," said the governor, "allowing Arizona to suck water from Lake Superior."

The governor added that since Lake Superior contains 10 percent of all fresh water on earth, "Arizona can continue to suck for a long time."

America's New "National Sacrifice Area"

Carson City, Nev. – America's growing landfill problem has been solved, thanks to the generous offer of the State of Nevada to become America's official "National Sacrifice Area." In exchange for extremely reasonable disposal fees, Nevada has agreed to accept "anything and everything" that the rest of the country doesn't want, including toxic chemicals and radioactive waste.

As for concerns that these materials will contaminate underground aquifers, the governor explained that wastes will be confined to immense pits lined with weather-resistant plastic sheeting guaranteed to last until it wears out.

Global Warming Solved, Stop Worrying

New Haven, Conn. – Researchers at Yale University have released a report announcing a "Plan B" emergency strategy to counteract global warming. "Only one strategy was deemed both affordable and effective," stated head researcher Blondie Belle, "which is sun-reflecting sulfates distributed into the upper atmosphere by high-altitude balloons."

The scientists stressed this is strictly an emergency plan with enormous risks and should be used only as a desperation measure when every other conceivable option has been exhausted. "We hesitate to make this plan public," explained Ms. Belle, "for fear that some people may think technology has solved the problem and eliminated the need to drastically reduce carbon dioxide emissions."

When asked for comment on the report, U.S. Secretary of Energy Federico O'Leary released a statement saying, "This is great news because it means now we don't need to drastically reduce carbon dioxide emissions."

Another Slurry Spill in Tennessee

Kingston, Tenn. – The Kingston coal-burning power plant beat its own record of 1.1 billion gallons of toxic slurry, set in 2008, with a new record of 2.3 billion gallons. "This should stop any other state from trying to beat us," said Tennessee Governor Luke Duke.

No fatalities were reported, except for the people that died. "But they would have died anyway," reasoned the governor.

According to the Environmental Protection Agency, the slurry contained especially high amounts of lead. Plant manager Bo Duke conceded that excessive lead causes brain damage. But he reasoned that brain damage is not that bad because, "One result of brain damage is it makes it really hard to sue power plants."

Navajos Report Alarming Birth Trends

Tuba City, Ariz. – The Navajo Nation is demanding an end to industrial uses of its land, claiming that decades of uranium mining have resulted in abnormal birth rates.

The journal *Environmental Health Perspectives* reports that normal gender-based birth rates are approximately 51 percent girls and 49 percent boys. However, the most recent statistics from the Navajo Nation indicate a rate of 33 percent "both" and 67 percent "neither."

The Navajo Nation is demanding an immediate end to all uranium mining and $100 million for gender assignment surgery. Bureau of Indian Affairs head Bruce Lohan reacted to the demands by saying he needs to see the results of an official investigation into the cause of the abnormal birthrates before he can deny them.

Florida Announces Plan for Protective Seawall

Miami Beach, Fla. – The Florida Legislature announced a plan to begin building a massive 1,000-mile seawall to protect the coast from rising sea levels.

The continuing loss of Florida's beaches has caused a dramatic drop in tourism which is responsible for approximately all of Florida's annual revenue. The loss has been especially dramatic for beach communities dependent on spring break vacations for America's college students.

"Environmentalists should be helping us out on this," said the governor. "Since they're so concerned with preserving habitat for endangered species, why aren't they concerned with preserving habitat for endangered partying?"

Hungry Grizzlies Invade Montana Supermarkets

Missoula, Mont. – Continued encroachment and degradation of their habitat has resulted in hordes of hungry grizzly bears raiding supermarkets throughout the Northern Rockies.

"They head right to the meat department," stated Montana Wildlife Biologist Shawn Redline "It's kind of pathetic," says Missoula resident and Safeway employee Wilma Butters. "The bears want to feel like they caught the meat, so before they eat it they kind of wrestle around with it. This morning I saw a grizzly fighting a slab of porterhouse steak, which by the way is on sale this week."

The grizzlies pose little threat to humans. "If you see a grizzly while grocery shopping," stated Redline, "just head to the produce department."

June 29

My next presentation will be to adults! It will be to an insurance company here in downtown Portland.

I read an article by Toastmasters that says humor is very important in giving successful presentations: "Well-executed humor can enliven dull topics and help the speaker connect with the audience." So I took a few minutes and came up with some environmental jokes:

Q - What's blue and green and we should save it?
A - The earth!

Q - What kind of vehicle gets 32 miles per burrito?
A - A bicycle being ridden by YOU as one way of saving the earth!

Q - What are the 3 "R's" of living ecologically?
A - Reduce, Reuse, and SAVE THE EARTH!
(The joke is that people are expecting the 3rd one to be "Recycle")

July 1

My "Greening Your Corporation" presentation basically went fine, but at the Q&A section at the end I guess I panicked. Somebody asked me if re-usable coffee cozies really make that much of a difference, and I might have exaggerated a little. I said that if everybody in the country stopped using disposable coffee cozies then each year we would save "all the trees in Oregon" when I think the actual answer is "a tree in Oregon."

P.S. - I tried one of my new jokes at the presentation, and for some weird reason nobody laughed. But then the truth occurred to me: People are so devastated by the destruction of the earth that they can't laugh about it. Even though my jokes are very hilarious, the destruction of the earth is no laughing matter.

July 2

I had an amazing brainstorm and told Katherine my idea: How about if at our presentations we provide FREE re-usable coffee cozies printed with something like I'M DOING MY PART TO SAVE THE EARTH BY USING A RE-USABLE COFFEE COZY INSTEAD OF A DISPOSABLE COFFEE COZY. Katherine made an unhappy face and started talking about "budget constraints." But then I said: How about if they also have the HomeEarth logo and website? Then her eyes got all big and she almost smiled. She said she would discuss the idea with the Marketing Coordinator! But she said they would probably have to shorten the message to make it fit on a coffee cozy.

July 6

I can't believe I haven't written for THREE WHOLE DAYS! (Sorry diary!) I've been SO BUSY. My office wall is covered with artistic drawings from the 2nd grade presentation about "The Value of Wetlands." One of them is SO CUTE! It's a crayon drawing of a little boy (labeled "Carlos") holding hands with me (labeled "Miss Martinez") and between us is a frog with a huge smile. On the bottom he wrote, "Will you marry me?" which I assume refers to me and not the frog. Haha!

July 7

It was so awesome to go back to Sellwood Middle School to give a presentation to the summer school students! It's weird that now I'm popular, but when I was a student there they ignored me and called me "intellectual" for thinking that being stupid is dumb.

A lot of the students stayed for the Q&A part, which went on for a long time. Actually it was all boys for some reason. They were very excited to hear me talk. I couldn't figure out why a lot of them were looking at my chest, until I realized I was wearing my "I HEART WETLANDS" t-shirt with the beautiful glue-green dragonfly.

July 9

The HomeEarth re-usable coffee cozies just arrived - thousands of them - and I was SHOCKED to discover they include a picture of MY FACE! I showed Tiffany and she said my hair looked nice in the photo, which was NOT what I was concerned about! I showed Katherine and she said it must have been a decision by the marketing people. She also said that my hair looked nice.

I just found out that the "Greening Your Lifestyle" presentation is being changed to add proper tire inflation as a simple change that "is good for the earth as well as for your wallet." According to the Department of Energy, underinflated tires waste more than 1.25 billion gallons of gas per year.

July 10

Katherine just told me some awesome news: I'm getting my own web page! She says I've become much more than a regular Communications Manager, I'm also a "celebrity." (!!!)

So the HomeEarth website will contain a link to "Amy's Page" so I can save the earth via the Internet! There will be a blog so I can give opinions on environmental issues and communicate with what Katherine calls my "fans" but I call my "fellow earth-savers."

July 11

Katherine assigned me to HomeEarth's "top priority issue" of sustainable agriculture! She says it is excellent timing to really push this issue for 3 reasons:

1. The GloboChem spill of agricultural chemicals with all the pictures of sick babies has shown to be bad publicity for chemical agriculture.
2. With the economy finally on an upswing, more people can afford organic foods.
3. Food is important to people because they eat it. Katherine told me, "People might not care too much about saving the Albuquerque Swamp Worm, but they sure as heck care about pesticide on their spinach."

I did some research into GloboChem because I didn't really know exactly what spilled except that it was really BAD stuff. Turns out it was what they call "GrowMagic" but is actually ONE OF THE MOST POISONOUS AGRICULTURAL CHEMICALS EVER MADE. I looked at the GloboChem website and it is UNBELIEVABLE what they do. This is from the "About Us" page:

> Our main product is HappySeeds™ which grow 73% of the world's vegetables and grains. Most of those seeds are Magic-Ready HappySeeds™ that are genetically engineered to accompany GrowMagic™ "agricultural helper." As happy farmers around the world say, "I need the miraculous GrowMagic™ to keep my Magic-Ready HappySeeds™ happy!" And since Magic-Ready HappySeeds™ are genetically designed to grow plants that don't produce seed, farmers around the world are happy to come back and buy more HappySeeds™ year after year – which keeps GloboChem shareholders happy! GloboChem: Spreading happiness wherever it touches.

I can NOT believe how crazy this is! They're not spreading happiness, they're spreading POISON! I searched their site and found a page called "The GloboChem Commitment to Environmental Stewardship" which is kind of hilarious (but not really).

> GloboChem has dedicated a portion of our profits toward planting a tree in Oregon. It is a totally natural tree that absorbs carbon dioxide and creates the oxygen you are breathing right now, otherwise you would be dead. GloboChem: 100% committed to preserving our planetary home.

Does anybody actually BELIEVE this stuff???

P.S. - I did an internet search, and there's no such thing as an "Albuquerque Swamp Worm."

July 12

I had another High School presentation, and once again ended up for a long time with a group of excited boys. Like the last time I noticed they were looking at my chest a lot, but when I looked down I realized I was wearing a plain shirt. Weird.

Katherine found a local organic farm that wants to "partner" with us on HomeEarth's "Stop Putting Poison on the Food That We Eat" initiative. It's called "Laughing Ladybug Farm" and I'll be visiting them soon so I can become an expert on the subject.

She said lots of people will be asking me, "Why is organic food so expensive?" so I need to make sure I have a good answer.

Good question! Why does organic food cost more? I mean, chemical fertilizers and pesticides and herbicides must cost a LOT of money so why wouldn't it be cheaper to NOT use them?

Anyway... she gave me this big speech about how nobody wants to hear a "gloom and doom" message. She said don't EVER mention the word "sacrifice" because people do NOT like that word. It makes them unhappy and not likely to renew their membership.

I just had a strange and interesting idea. I wonder: What would it be like to live 100% sustainably? Would it feel like a "sacrifice"? Is it possible? Has it ever been tried, as a sort of "experiment"?

July 13

Exciting discovery! I did a bunch of web searching to see if there are people trying to live as sustainably as possible. There are a LOT of places - all over the country and even the world.

I found a place not hugely far away that looks REALLY interesting. It's in the Central Oregon high desert and is called "EarthSage Institute." They're doing experiments in how to "exist in harmony with living ecosystems" and stuff like that which is EXACTLY WHAT I WAS LOOKING FOR!

I'm going to contact them about doing a weekend visit. Since I can't drive, I'll ask Tiffany if she'd be interested in going. (I don't think I'd want to go with Dad because I'm pretty sure he would freak out.)

I got invited to be part of a panel discussion at the coast (in Lincoln City). There's a wetland out there that's being threatened and the pro-environmental people could really use some help. Maybe I can help save another wetland?

July 14

GloboChem found a new spokesperson. Katherine told me the person is a guy called Anthony Iron who I never heard of but apparently is legendary and INFAMOUS in the business world. He has made a career out of representing the most terrible companies and organizations in the world, such as LibertyWork Corp. (nerve gas and land mines) and KiddieSmokes, Inc. (children's cigarettes).

She called him a "snake" which is not complimentary to amphibians which are an important part of the spectrum of earthly life. I told Katherine I would feel better if she

to deny them for Little Billy because he's usually depressed and sugar drinks are about the only thing that makes him happy, except for cheeseburgers.

Then Anthony Iron said, "Mothers have the hardest job in the world, but does anybody really appreciate it?" Then she started crying into his shoulder and the audience was going "Awww!"

Then she promised that she'd do her best to encourage Little Billy to consider possibly cutting down on the sugar drinks but that even discussing the cheeseburgers would be pretty much impossible.

Then he announced his plan to visit Little Billy after the show and take him out for a soft drink and cheeseburger. "And if anybody tries to call him 'fatso' or any other derogatory comment, they'll have to deal with me!"

He summed up by saying, "Ladies and Gentlemen, if we banned everything that could possibly be misused, what would be left?" There was total silence, and then he said, "Exactly!" and the audience actually stood up and gave him a standing ovation. Which is really weird for someone representing a product that last year contributed to heart disease, kidney failure, and blindness in 25 million people.

I'm having serious second-thoughts about wanting to debate this Anthony Iron person. Perhaps I was a little overconfident in my abilities.

July 15

Just got back from my visit to "Laughing Ladybug," the organic farm that HomeEarth is partnering with. The couple that run the farm are John and Linda.

They explained the ways they control bugs without poisons, such using ladybugs to eat aphids, which are a major problem in the Pacific Northwest. She said they named the farm "Laughing Ladybug" because of imagining ladybugs happy with full tummies after eating a bunch of aphids.

It was a little weird when Linda went into the refrigerator and showed me a box full of ladybugs - hundreds of them!

Another thing they do that's kinda weird is they plant fennel which attracts beneficial wasps. The wasps lay their eggs inside of other bugs, and when the eggs hatch the larva eat the bugs from the inside and kill them. GROSS!

I'm thinking that when I do media stuff for organic farms it might be best not to mention the wasps.

I was finally able to find out the answer to my question of why organically-grown food costs more than industrial agriculture.

The main reason is that organic farming is much more labor intensive. It's true that chemicals are expensive, but they are fast and easy to use. Spraying a huge field with herbicide takes only a few hours to kill the weeds, but not spraying means it takes lots of time to constantly weed them by hand.

Linda explained to me that farmers who try to "do the right thing" are at an unfair disadvantage, because the economy favors what's cheaper but doesn't account for the effects - such as soil erosion and chemicals in the water.

Linda said, "In organic farming, everything is based on healthy soil." She said that healthy soil is alive. But industrial agriculture KILLS the soil, and makes up for the lack of fertility with chemical fertilizers. And since the soil isn't healthy the plants aren't healthy, which means they aren't strong enough to withstand bugs and diseases. And that's why industrial agriculture needs all the pesticides and other chemicals.

John explained how the chemicals kill off most of the bugs and diseases, but always a few develop immunity and multiply. So the chemical companies have to invent stronger chemicals. And this leads to things like the GloboChem accident, with just one spill making all those sick babies.

I told John and Linda that this all ties in perfectly with an idea I had: Hurting nature also hurts us because WE ARE NATURE. John and Linda totally agreed!

July 16

I just watched the GloboChem press conference on TV. I can't believe it! Anthony Iron acted like the offended one! And he said the problem isn't GloboChem; the problem is ENVIRONMENTALISTS!

He started off saying that of course GloboChem is saddened by the accident. He said the company is reimbursing the families for medical costs, but "no amount of money will ever dry up the tears of babies." (Ugh!)

Hey said, "Yes, you can blame GloboChem for this spill. But consider: If you get burned by a light bulb, do you blame Thomas Edison for inventing the light bulb? You might as well blame Western Civilization for dragging itself up out of the muck of darkness and ignorance."

He explained that all technologies have pros and cons. For example, automobile accidents are bad, but we have decided as a civilization that the cost of a few accidents is worth the benefits and advantages of automobiles.

He said, "Why not ban cars? Why not go further back and ban the wheel? Because we, as a civilization, have no desire to go back to the Stone Age. Yes, you can blame us for this spill - but I hope you also thank us for helping to keep food prices as low as possible."

He asked the audience, "You all like low food prices, right?" and a lot of people nodded "yes." Then he started blaming ENVIRONMENTALISTS! He said, "Well, the 'environmentalists' (he said 'environmentalists' like it was a dirty word) want you to pay more of your hard-earned money for food with holes in it where bugs ate. And maybe those bugs left a little bug spit."

A lot of the audience was kinda grossed-out by this, but it got even worse. He said, "They want you to pay more money for vegetables fertilized not with nice clean chemicals, but with something 'organic.'" He said, "You pay an organic farmer 12 dollars for a carrot, and you notice there's some brown stuff on it. Could be dirt. But it could be something else. In other words: Poop." And the audience was like, "Ewwww!"

Yes, organic farmers use manure as one source of fertilizer but it's aged for a long time and then dug into the soil so it can break down before the seeds are even planted! He made it sound like farmers plant seeds right into fresh poop!

He said, "Environmentalists are attacking the good people of GloboChem for putting America's food where it belongs: In the mouths of Americans and not into the mouths of beetles and snakes."

That's CRAZY! Snakes are carnivores and don't eat vegetables!

Then he got himself all optimistic-looking and said, "Ladies and Gentlemen, some people would suggest that GloboChem has gone too far. I put it to you that we haven't gone far enough. I am proud to announce that GloboChem has developed an innovative new product that will absolutely end all problems with human exposure to agricultural chemicals."

Then music started playing. Patriotic music.

He said, "Our new product is a highly-advanced version of our famous 'HappySeed' technology. As you surely know, 'Magic-Ready HappySeeds' are genetically engineered to go with our 'GrowMagic' agricultural helper. I am proud to announce GloboChem's brand-new product, which we call 'HappyHuman.' It will make human beings - people like you and me - able to withstand the 'GrowMagic' that brings us the clean and inexpensive food you serve to your loved ones. 'HappyHuman' will be available in capsule form - just one dose per month is all you'll need to stay healthy and prosperous."

Somebody asked, "How does this 'HappyHuman' product work?"

He said, "Each capsule contains specially-engineered radioactive isotopes that go throughout the body, miraculously altering the genetic code to change the cell chemistry in each and every cell. Then, our bodies can withstand the 'GrowMagic' that brings us attractive pest-free food at a reasonable price. In other words, it will make us able to withstand 'GrowMagic' 100 percent naturally!"

The audience was pretty shocked! I mean, he was suggesting that WE SWALLOW RADIOACTIVE ISOTOPES TO ALTER OUR GENETIC CODE AND CHANGE OUR CELL CHEMISTRY!!!

Then he said, "I know what you're all thinking. You're thinking, 'What about our household pets, our fuzzy kittens and puppies?'"

I'm pretty sure this is NOT what people were thinking!

He said, "I'm pleased to assure you that GloboChem will offer our supplement in a pet-friendly form, because GloboChem cares about your pets. In fact, we love them more than you do."

Then he said, "However there are certain regressive laws currently on the books which halt human progress. But we are confident the good and wise people of America will enthusiastically support the quick passage of Congressional Bill H.R. 5873 to be introduced next week, so this great country can become even greater."

I told Katherine that I MUST do something about this and she told me to write a press release (my first press release!) to give HomeEarth's "official statement." It will have to be reviewed by Katherine before being released, which is good because all I want to write is GLOBOCHEM IS EVIL! over and over, which is probably not the best "official statement."

July 17

My first press release has been sent to the media. I also posted it on my blog, and the comments have been 100% supportive and are 100% OUTRAGED. But even though people were 100% supportive, a lot of them asked me if there was any truth to the stuff about bug spit.

This weekend is the visit to EarthSage Institute. I'm so excited! I'm sure I'll learn a lot.

July 18

Saturday morning (very early) and we're on the road to EarthSage Institute! Tiffany told me, "When we get there, I'm going straight to the bar!" I thought that was HILARIOUS because it's an ecological institute and not a vacation resort.

We just listened to an interview on NPR with an author of a book called: "Soil: The Ground on Which Civilization is Built So We Better Take Care of It." VERY interesting! The author did research into the health of civilizations compared to the health of their soil - and it corresponded almost exactly! I was amazed to discover that many civilizations collapsed because of destroying their soil.

It's sad that most people think of soil only as something that gets your clothes dirty if you fall on it. Without soil there would be no people!

Question: Since our soil is eroding, does that mean our civilization is eroding?

July 19

Sunday evening (very late) driving back to Portland and I have SO MUCH to write about! Where do I begin?

I'll start with the setting of EarthSage which is BEAUTIFUL. It's in the high desert with lots of sagebrush.

I couldn't stop picking sagebrush leaves and rolling them between my fingers. Sagebrush smells SO GOOD!

EarthSage was founded by a guy named "Coyote" (who I'll get to later) who was described to me as a "mysterious figure." The vision is to be "a living example of ecological living" to show people that living sustainably is not "going back to the Stone Age."

EarthSage is almost totally self-sufficient. They produce all their own energy - burning wood (juniper) for heat and using solar panels for electricity. They aren't depriving themselves of treats (ice cream!) or modern technology, such as computers or DVD players to watch movies.

I found out their land philosophy is based on "permaculture" which means:

> A philosophy of working with, rather than against nature; of protracted and thoughtful observation rather than protracted and thoughtless labor; and of looking at plants and animals in all their functions.

For example, let's say you have chickens. The chickens eat grubs and other yucky things as well as leftover food scraps, and in return they provide valuable protein (eggs) and their manure helps fertilize the garden. The idea is to design everything so there's no waste and everything supports everything else and there's as little work as possible.

I was surprised that they aren't strictly vegetarians. Somebody explained that "vegetarianism is a luxury for the affluent." One advantage of the high desert is lots of rabbits, which were explained to be "an abundant source of protein that is self-sustaining and not very smart."

A teenage girl got all offended and said, "How can you eat a living thing?" and the guide said, "What about the potatoes you had for lunch?" She said, "Well that seems different somehow," and the guide said "How?" And she said, "Well, the potatoes can't look at me," which made a lot of people laugh.

The high desert climate makes gardening very challenging. So they are experimenting with adapting native edible plants for gardening - plants such as wild celery and desert parsley, and wild roots such as bitterroot and camus. Since they are adapted for this exact climate they're much easier to grow. It makes total sense when you think about it!

Tiffany said she found EarthSage "fascinating" and I was very glad she was so open-minded. But there were a few times she sort of "embarrassed" me. She is so non-shy she'll ask anybody ANYTHING, and she sort of treated the people that lived there like animals in a zoo.

Such as this one family living in a yurt, she asked, "Do you people wear underwear?" which is when I pretended I didn't know her. The guy said, "We are explorers on the leading edge of consciousness evolution." Tiffany said "Totally!" since she's into anything with the words "consciousness" and "evolution." I left because I was more interested in practical things, but I ran into them three hours later and they were discussing whether molecules have consciousness.

I thought it was going to be another "Tiffany embarrassing herself" moment during the tour when she suddenly said (very loudly) "So where's the bar?" and a lot of people laughed. But the tour guide said they don't exactly have a "bar" but they do have a "spirit processing project" (alcohol still) where they make vodka and gin. A lot of their income is from selling it.

So Tiffany got a couple bottles of vodka and disappeared, and I'm assuming she invited herself to someplace to talk about conscious molecules. But the tour of the spirit processing project was very interesting since I didn't use nature metaphors for negative things, because nothing in nature is "bad." Yes, things like mosquitos are totally a nuisance from a human point of view, but they are important food for bats. But that's not the best example because I realize that some people hate bats.

I sure wish I could debate this Anthony Iron person! Yes, maybe it would be a LITTLE scary facing a spokesperson representing a huge multinational company that made something like a thousand billion dollars last year and sort of controls agricultural policy. Katherine says "they have the Department of Agriculture by the short hairs" (whatever that means).

Katherine gave me a link to a video of a panel discussion he did last year, and I'll watch it later on.

WOW! What I don't understand is: How did he do it? He was part of a TV panel discussion about childhood diabetes. He was representing Ultra-Sugar Soft Drinks, Inc., and the other people were leading doctors and the president of a group against childhood diabetes. I thought: How does he have a chance?

His main message was about personal freedom. He asked the audience, "Are we in such bad shape as a nation that we need the government to make our decisions for us?" Then he got on this thing about the "dumbing down" of America and said he does not want to live in a country that requires labels on sidewalks that say, "Caution: Hard Surface," in case people fall on it.

But then I thought he was doomed when a mom in the audience stood up and showed pictures of "Little Billy my poor fat baby." (She called him "my baby" even though he was 12.) She said he weighs 400 pounds and the doctors told him if he doesn't stop drinking so many sugar drinks he won't live to be 20.

The mom said it was easier for her to have the government ban sugar drinks. She said it was hard for her knew nothing about "spirits" (booze) but I learned many interesting things:

- The "alcohol" in spirits is ethanol - which can also be used for fuel for heaters or stoves or lanterns.
- EarthSage is best known for its gin, which is their specialty, since gin gets its flavor from juniper berries which grow in abundance here.
- Gin also has medicinal uses, in addition to getting drunk.

The guide said that gin and vodka will be very important for bartering when society collapses. I'm pretty sure she was joking except that nobody was laughing.

I thought one of the neatest things was that instead of a refrigerator they have a "cool box." It's a frame covered with screen, outside the kitchen on the North side (which is shady and cool). This acts as a "refrigerator" for most of the year. Why use electricity to power a refrigerator inside of a warm room when it's cool outside? If you think about it, it makes no sense at all.

Actually, that's true for a LOT of things. Such as: Why do we spray poison on the food we eat? How did that idea ever become thought of as "normal"?

A funny incident: Tiffany was VERY nervous about going to the bathroom when she found out there are no "regular" flush toilets. The only option was a "clivus multrum" (a very advanced composting toilet invented in Sweden). She did NOT like the instructions, such as after you poop you have to throw in twigs and leaves (to add carbon) instead of flushing.

I asked her later how it was, and she said, "I barely survived." I tried very hard not to laugh but her expression was HILARIOUS and she was totally pale when she told me.

(She just now asked me what I'm laughing about, and I said "clivus multrum" and she got pale again!)

They do a lot of their cooking on something called a "Rocket Stove" which makes a very hot fire that shoots up like a rocket. I got to use it while helping to cook dinner and it brought a huge pot of beans to a boil in only 5 minutes using only a handful of wood scraps! Just imagine if all our energy use was so efficient!

The MOST EXCITING PROJECT is the "natural building project" that makes "alternative" homes out of local materials. They are very energy efficient and very affordable, only a few thousand dollars for materials. (This is for homes that are very small by most people's standards.)

One home was made out of "cob" which is a mixture of mud and straw and sand. It looked like a cute little adobe house. It reminded me of the little houses in the "Lord of the Rings" movie! I found out later they call it the "Hobbit House"!

But the one that got me REALLY excited was a strawbale home. Here are the reasons why I liked it so much:

- VERY simple to build, anybody could build one. It's mostly just stacking straw bales like huge bricks.
- Super-fast: The straw bale part can be put up in ONE DAY!
- VERY inexpensive! Straw bales only cost a few dollars each and it doesn't take a huge number of them.
- No wooden frame is required - the straw bales are the frame AND the insulation. The roof is strapped to the top with cables that anchor it to the ground which also makes it very solid.
- It looks more "normal" than a yurt or tipi, so less chance of people thinking that the people who live inside are hippies.

- Very energy efficient. The straw bales are over a foot thick so it's better insulation than even the most expensive manufactured insulation (which is VERY polluting to make).

The mysterious "Coyote" is in charge of the natural building project, and gave the tour. Some of the stuff he said was kind of "out there," such as: "Homes as currently built are a crime against nature and human nature."

I sort of understood the anti-nature aspect (waste of resources and energy) but asked him to explain the anti-human-nature aspect. He said that partly it's because of the "mass-produced, soul-less" quality of homes (especially suburban sprawl homes). But mostly his point was about the extremely high cost of homes. He said the 30-year mortgage forces people into working full-time for their entire lives at jobs they might not even like very much.

He said building codes are un-American because they stifle individual expression and are possibly against the 5th Amendment of the Constitution. I said that I thought building codes were about safety. He laughed and said that's true if you consider the "safety" as being to protect the big profits for the construction industry.

He called building codes "mandatory consumption laws" and had a bunch of statistics about the waste of a typical American home:

- Causes 18 tons of greenhouse gasses per year
- Creates 7 tons of construction waste
- Uses $\frac{1}{4}$ acre of trees for the wood

Oh - he also said there was a more basic question of: Why do we have to pay money for land to live on, which should be considered another "crime against humanity." He asked, "Who decided that we need to earn the privilege to occupy a portion of the planet of which we are made? Shouldn't it be a natural right to occupy our planetary home?"

Coyote said it's not necessary for everybody to live like they do at EarthSage to be a sustainable culture. But one HUGE advantage of the rural location for EarthSage is that there's more freedom (such as from building codes) which gives them the ability to live ecologically.

Something like EarthSage would not be legal in Portland which is REALLY WEIRD. Portland likes to think of itself as very ecological and progressive and everything, but Portland doesn't allow inexpensive natural homes such as strawbale homes.

I asked Coyote "Are you saying that it's illegal to build a home that's in harmony with nature?" and he said, "Of course, didn't you know that?" and I said "No, I didn't know that! That's crazy!"

I need to write this out again because I can't believe it: IT'S ILLEGAL TO BUILD A HOME THAT'S IN HARMONY WITH NATURE.

Oh - I almost forgot to write about one of the BEST things at EarthSage. They have a huge outdoor hot tub. It doesn't need electricity since it's heated by a wood-burning stove!

It was my first hot tub experience! The night was very clear with no moon so it was totally dark and if you looked up you could see the universe! The stars were incredibly bright (some of them were even different colors) and there were MILLIONS of them and the Milky Way was bright across the entire sky.

I'm not exactly comfortable being naked around other people. I don't think nudity is "bad," I just have very little experience with it, or actually no experience. But I felt OK because it was so totally dark, and anyway we were all looking at the universe and there was almost no talking. Even Tiffany (I forgot to say that Tiffany came with) was impressed enough that she didn't talk, which if you know Tiffany is kind of miraculous.

People came and went, sometimes with no talking so you didn't even know who was there. Eventually it was just me and one other person. I didn't know who it was until he said "Beautiful night" and I knew it was Coyote! I started feeling "fuzzy" for some reason (maybe I was in the hot tub for too long?) so that's when I finally left the tub and went back to the yurt to go to sleep. I was in the water so long I was shriveled up like a raisin!

As for Coyote... I should say that when I met him the first time it was kind of shocking. I can't say exactly what I was expecting, but I can definitely say that what I was NOT expecting was a guy wearing a loincloth.
A LOINCLOTH! Like he was Tarzan or something!

Anyway, later on I had a chance to talk to him. I tried to be encouraging and said, "It's so awesome that there are places like EarthSage to be an example for other people to follow and save the earth!" He was very quiet for a while and looked far into the distance. Then suddenly he looked into my eyes with his large blue eyes which was kind of scary.

He said, "That was the original vision, yes. But it is increasingly obvious that collapse is inevitable. Therefore our original goal of a 'living example' has now become a 'lifeboat for survival.' I'm afraid we have become reluctant survivalists. Coyote did not see this before, but Coyote sees it now."

I don't know what bothered me more: Hearing such pessimism, or hearing him talk about himself in the third-person (kind of pretentious, I thought).

I am NOT ready to give up on the earth so I told him that I know for a FACT that it's possible to save the earth because I saved Oaks Bottom wetland which happens to be part of the earth, so all we have to do is save all the other parts. Very logical!

He said, "Coyote is familiar with that place," but then he went back to his off-in-the-distance looking again.

It didn't seem like he was going to say any more (a man of few words!) so I sort of filled in the silence and talked about my career at HomeEarth as the Communications Manager and how I make a difference by encouraging proper tire inflation and re-usable coffee cozies.

But then he interrupted me and said, "Coyote is familiar with the organization. Their motto should be, 'Slightly Less Unsustainable.'"

I didn't know if should defend HomeEarth or say something snarky like, "What do you know, Mr. Tarzan?" (my mind was going crazy) but I said something calmer about there are all kinds of ways to save the earth. I said we should work together instead of fighting, and some people get scared off if you try to be too radical.

When I said the word "radical" he looked VERY interested and looked at me again with his eyes. He asked me, "Do you know what the word RADICAL means?"

I was surprised that I didn't really know. He said, "Everybody confuses the word 'radical' with the word 'extremist' and thinks they mean the same thing, but I will tell you the difference." (Suddenly he was VERY interested in talking.) He said an extremist takes one position to the extreme, and therefore must oppose all other positions. For example, a left-wing extremist ends up opposing a right-wing extremist, even though a reasonable person sees that politically the left and right both have legitimate points. Therefore, "Extremism is the enemy of truth."

I said that was very interesting, I'd never thought about it that way. He seemed surprised that I was interested, so he went on to say that a radical is not that at all. He said that the word RADICAL is a Latin word which translates as "going to the roots," which means to go for the truth underneath extreme views. He said, "To be an extremist is easy but to be a radical is the ultimate challenge."

I guess I thought being a "radical" meant being a person that goes to protests and yells and gets arrested.

I told him about my idea of "going to the roots" of environmental destruction. Suddenly I asked (out loud) "Am I a radical?"

Then he got quiet for a minute and said (all seriously) "Very few people have the commitment to be a true radical." Then he went back into distant gazing again (what is he looking at when he does that?) and I realized he was finished talking.

Was he implying that I did NOT have such commitment?

I figured I'd probably never see him again so I might as well ask a "risky" question. I asked why he refers to himself in the third-person, and he got all pretentious and said, "It's a way to avoid pretension." He said if you listen to people talk, the word they use most is "I" which reinforces the idea that we are the center of the universe. So by referring to himself in the third-person he "keeps things in perspective."

But I pointed out that maybe he isn't aware of how pretentious it sounds. I said it seems to me that a person's attitude is what's important, and that I knew lots of nice and helpful people that refer to themselves as "I."

I was going to say more, but I stopped when I saw the expression on Coyote's face. It was a strange expression, like a combination of "shocked" and "humbled." He got quiet for a LONG time and I could tell he was thinking about it. Then finally he said (very quietly) "Yes – you're right. Thank you for calling me on it. Very few people have the courage to stand up to me."

This gave me real respect for him, that he's willing to question himself.

I'm asking myself: "Amy, what was the most important thing you learned this weekend?" And I answer myself: "Wow, Amy, that's hard to say. I learned SO MUCH!"

But (seriously now) I think the most important thing is that I saw with my own eyes that it's possible to live in harmony with nature, and that it's NOT a sacrifice (well maybe a little) and in many ways is better. Probably some people would say there is definitely sacrifice, such as many modern conveniences aren't there. But I would say that those "conveniences" are mostly things we don't really need, and the "natural" ways aren't always as convenient but they're more meaningful, which makes up for it. As far as "conveniences" like television, people would be better off if they read books or played music or did basically any other thing besides watching television.

But how many people actually think about this kind of thing? And then make a decision based on what makes sense?

Actually... this makes me think that the REAL most important thing I learned is how our lives are based on ideas in our mind. For example, if your idea is "shopping malls are awesome" then when you see a shopping mall your emotions get a "happy" feeling and you go inside and buy junk you don't need. This is the opposite of me, who has the idea "shopping malls are stupid" in which case my emotions make me want to run away or burn it down.

In addition to deciding not to watch television or go to shopping malls, we can make up our mind to live in harmony with nature or to not live in harmony with nature. I mean, not just as individual people, but as a whole country.

July 22

The panel discussion in Lincoln City went great! But there was something about it that I don't understand at all. The main people opposed to saving the wetland was a group from a church. I'm confused, because I've heard religious people refer to natural areas as "God's Country."

I guess "God's Country" mostly refers to beautiful areas, such as forests. But if the forest is "God's Country" then how can it be okay to clearcut the forest?

I've never heard of a religious group trying to protect forests from clearcutting.

Is a wetland also "God's Country"? Logically it seems like it would have to be, since according to religion God is supposed to be everywhere. Is God even in mosquitos?

Since it was the weekend, Dad was able to drive me there. On the drive home I asked Dad about these questions, and his reply was that I ask too many questions.

The totally nice neighbor Carol came over and said she was so sorry about the recipe because she accidently left out a vital ingredient. So she gave me a new recipe and told me to throw away the other one.

ROOTS 'N' NOODLES CASSEROLE

2 cups egg noodles (cooked)
1 cup beets (sliced)
1 cup radishes (sliced)
½ cup swiss cheese (grated)
2 tsp salt
Ketchup (lots)

July 23

I was talking to Tiffany about EarthSage and somehow I got talking about Coyote and how frustrating he was yet also fascinating in some weird way. I figured this would be interesting for Tiffany and maybe she would understand it because of her knowledge of personal growth stuff. My talking about Coyote might have gone on for a long time (although Tiffany is exaggerating that it was over an hour) until Tiffany finally said, "Amy! I'm glad you have a boyfriend!"

I was very quick to point out HE IS NOT MY BOYFRIEND! I told her that I don't even like him and she said, "Well you sure seem obsessed with him." I said I felt the correct word was "interested," and she said, "Then why have you been talking about him for over an hour?" (Exaggerating!)

I said mostly I was ANNOYED by him, and she said something about "a thin line between love and hate." I said, "How did you get to 'love' because I don't 'hate' him either, he just drives me crazy." I reminded Tiffany that he wears a loincloth.

So now I was annoyed at Tiffany because of the implications that she was implying. She asked me, all "suggestive," that when I was alone with Coyote did I ever have a "warm and fuzzy feeling"? I replied about that one time in the hot tub, but the warmth was logically explained by the hot tub and the fuzzy feeling could be explained by looking at the universe.

July 24

I finally had a chance to talk to Katherine about EarthSage. I mentioned Coyote several times and she asked if I knew his "real" name. I had no idea but I showed her a picture of him I took when he was demonstrating eco homes.

After a while of being shocked, she said, "So that's what happened to him!" I told Katherine she had to tell me EVERYTHING (which doesn't mean I'm "obsessed" like a certain person suggests).

I can't believe it but Coyote used to work for HomeEarth! His name was not Coyote then, it was - I can NOT believe this! - it was Edward Nothwang Wormwood!

He was a sort of "childhood prodigy" that was the youngest-ever winner of the MacArthur Grant (the one people call the "Genius Grant"). He was hired to analyze incredibly complex environmental issues. Katherine said he was a "one-person think tank."

Oh, and his name! It indicates that he is from a very wealthy aristocratic family (possibly from Boston, Katherine wasn't sure) but apparently there was a "falling out" but Katherine didn't know exactly why. Katherine said trying to get him to talk about his past was like "pulling teeth."

NOW I understand where all his money came from to start EarthSage, which is very admirable. I mean, he could have built a big mansion and had fancy cars, but he must have seen all that as meaningless and rejected it (but kept the money). And instead of a mansion, he lives in... Actually I don't what kind of home he lives in. All I know is that he calls it as "his lair" and he keeps it private and away from visitors. That makes sense when there are people like Tiffany poking around asking personal questions about underwear.

But back to the story: When he came to HomeEarth at first he was their "boy wonder" but apparently there came to be controversy or disagreements with Coyote's conclusions - Katherine wouldn't go into details. But one day he was just "gone" - no notice, no forwarding address. And they never saw or heard from him again.

Now I understand why Katherine looked so shocked when she saw the picture!

July 25

I was invited to be a guest on "Late Night with Lindsay"! Katherine had to explain to me that this is a local TV talk show (since I don't watch TV).

One result of the EarthSage visit is realizing that I can be much more ecological in my life. It's especially important to "set an example" since I'm not just a private individual, I'm a spokesperson for the most important cause on earth which is to save it. Here are things I can do:

- Expand the garden
- Plant LOTS of blueberry bushes (easy to grow, native to this region, and VERY healthy. The berries contain lots of vitamin C and antioxidants which help against many diseases including cancer)
- Build a cool box - maybe not to replace our refrigerator (I don't think Dad would be OK with that) but to mostly be a "demonstration" item)
- Get chickens (legal in Portland as long as it's not too many and NO roosters)
- Put a clothesline in the yard (electric dryers use TONS of energy which it wasteful when you can dry clothes for FREE on dry days - which in Portland is about 10 days per year. Haha!)

July 26

I just got done talking to Dad about my proposed ideas, which I'm going to call my "household ecology project." I suppose I shouldn't have been surprised that he was not enthusiastic.

He's concerned about what the neighbors will think, and he doesn't want to "stand out." He reminded me that unfortunately a lot of people are still prejudiced against people from Mexico and the prejudice is less if people think he's "just like them."

Even though he's not crazy about the ideas, he'll let me try them out. But the one thing he will NOT allow is the chickens because he says they would be too much trouble.

WEIRD! I just saw an article about public reaction to the GloboChem plan. The environmental community is 100%

opposed (Yay environmental community!) but the general public is NOT. Here are the survey results:

Strongly Opposed: 80%

Moderately Opposed: 9%

Need More Information: 11%

HOW COULD ANYONE POSSIBLY "NEED MORE INFORMATION"??? They want to alter our genetic code to tolerate toxic chemicals, HOW COULD YOU WANT "MORE INFORMATION"??

Very excited because tomorrow is my appearance on "Late Night with Lindsay"!

July 27

The show went GREAT!!! The only thing that was a little annoying is that Lindsay made a big deal about my age. She said I was probably "the youngest spokesperson in the history of the universe" (as if she knows the ages of all spokespersons in the history of the universe). She asked me over and over, "How does it feel to be a 14-year-old environmental leader?" After about the millionth time I finally said, "How does it feel being a middle-age talk show host?" This made the audience CRACK UP but Lindsay didn't laugh for some reason.

After the commercial break she (unfortunately) brought up my silly old comment about "We need to keep the wetlands wet!" complete with a film clip. Embarrassing! She asked me a question, but as a joke: "Should we also keep the deserts dry?" At first I thought I would answer "seriously" (that all ecosystems should be kept natural). But I decided to make my point as a joke and said, "I also believe that damp places should be kept damp!"

The audience laughed like CRAZY but then I blushed and got VERY embarrassed because I realized maybe they thought I was making a reference to sex. I'm thinking maybe they didn't understand the serious point underneath the joke.

I think my appearance was very popular. After the show, Lindsay even congratulated me and said, "Good job, although 34 isn't middle-age."

Katherine is very pleased with my TV appearance. The office has been getting all kinds of positive comments plus the website (including my blog) is getting HUGE traffic! The technical people are going to put my appearance on YouTube so I can link it to my blog! I asked them if they could edit out my "damp" comment, but they said, "Why would you want to?"

July 28

INTELLECTUAL BREAKTHROUGH! I did some research. Here's the definition of "nature":

> A collective abstract term for the entire universe, and embracing all its existence, forces and laws.

Then I looked up "natural":

> Agreeing with the course or system of nature. Not forced or artificial, without affectation or exaggeration, unaffected, hence, according to life.

ACCORDING TO LIFE! EXACTLY!

Being "for" nature is the same as being "for" life because

THEY ARE THE SAME THING.

So to make a culture that supports LIFE we should make a culture that follows nature as closely as possible.

Let's form A PHILOSOPHY OF LIFE BASED ON LIFE.

What ELSE would you base a philosophy of life on besides life? Duh!

I just realized that my diary is becoming (among many other things) a record of my intellectual journey.

What's frustrating is that I would REALLY like to discuss this kind of stuff with someone, but I don't know ANYBODY that's interested. Are there any intellectuals left anymore?

I wonder if Coyote is interested in this kind of stuff? I think I'll ask him. Yes, it's true that our last conversation wasn't 100% smooth, but I felt like we were having a great intellectual conversation.

He doesn't have email, so I'll have to resort to snail mail which takes FOREVER. How did people survive before email?

I just got a message from People magazine! Their managing editor saw me on "Late Night with Lindsay" and they want to do a profile of me! Because of my heritage they can feature me in the regular magazine and also in "People en Español." Dad will be so proud!

July 30

I HELPED SAVE ANOTHER WETLAND!

The city council of Lincoln City voted to give permanent protection to the wetland! I got a call from the mayor with the BIG NEWS: They're naming the wetland after me! He emailed me a copy of the press release.

FOR IMMEDIATE RELEASE:

Lincoln City Votes to Preserve Historic Wetland

Lincoln City – After months of contentious meetings and lots of finger-pointing, City Council voted unanimously to give permanent protection to the wetland informally referred to as "Ebenezer's Bottom".

City Council was pleased with the participant of Portland activist and HomeEarth spokesperson Amy Johnson-Martinez, famous for her courageous "wetland camp." City Council

> considers the participation of Ms. Johnson-Martinez good for publicity and will hopefully result in more tourists from Portland.
>
> In honor of her participation, City Council has decided to change the name of the wetland from "Ebenezer's Bottom" to "Amy's Bottom."
>
> The renaming was initially opposed by historical preservationists, until Historical Society President Miranda Hall was asked the reason for the name "Ebenezer's Bottom" and replied, "I have no idea."

I can't wait until Dad comes home. I want him to be the FIRST to know the good news.

July 31

I was talking to Tiffany about how I'm starting to feel like some people (meaning BOYS) were less interested in my "Save the Earth" message and more interested in thinking they could go on dates with me or something. I said how they often are looking at my chest for way longer than it takes to read the message, and sometimes there's no message. I'm beginning to suspect they're looking at my femininity.

At first Tiffany said, "If you got it, flaunt it!" But I pointed out there's not much to flaunt because my femininity is "humble" at this point.

But the more important thing is that I don't want this to detract from my important message. Then Tiffany got serious and asked me if I've ever heard of "the curse of beauty." She said, "Of course, I'm very familiar with this curse myself."

She explained that the advantage (or "blessing") of beauty is that you can accomplish things easier. But the drawback (or "curse") of beauty is that you don't always get taken seriously.

This is VERY DISTURBING to me because I am 100% sincere about my message. I didn't ask to be born attractive (actually I didn't ask to be born at all, but that's a whole other discussion.)

It doesn't feel "right" to try to make myself un-attractive on purpose, which seems to be un-natural and would contradict my pro-nature philosophy and message. But is it okay to have my natural beauty contribute to the success of my message?

August 2

It has been a loooong weekend but I am proud to say that I finished my "household ecology project." I started early yesterday and finished late tonight when I could barely see, it was so dark. I am now MUCH more sustainable!

As for the stuff I needed to build, Dad said I did "pretty good" but fixed a few places such as for example where nails were sticking out. He got upset when he saw what I did to my thumb (a result of hitting it a LOT of times with the hammer and accidentally almost drilling a hole in it). He started saying cuss words in Spanish (as if I couldn't understand). But overall he was so proud of me he treated me to a frozen yogurt at that place next to Kay's Bar.

August 3

CRAZY DAY! I was followed around by the writer from People magazine (whose name is pronounced like mine but she spells it "Aimee"). I was also followed about by a photographer, a Korean guy named Chang.

Aimee met us at the HomeEarth office, but Tiffany trapped her and had to know all about the famous celebrities that she's met. We all went out to lunch (Aimee paid!) but mostly it was me listening to stories about celebrities.

I am NOT surprised that Tiffany was flirting with the Korean photographer. She said to me, "I've never tasted Korean before" which was silly because the other day we went out to a Korean food cart. She probably just forgot.

Finally we got home and Aimee talked to Dad for a while, about the history with Mom being a human rights activist. This excited Aimee because it had "genuine human interest."

Unfortunately, Chang drove us crazy with his photography. He wanted a picture of me and Dad behind a photo of Mom, and told us to have expressions of "sorrow combined with hope mixed with pride touched by sadness." After he got us all posed he said, "Okay, just act natural." This made me want to say (yell): "HOW CAN WE ACT NATURAL AFTER YOU TOLD US EXACTLY HOW TO ACT?"

Aimee wanted to go to Oaks Bottom because it was a "critical piece of the narrative." On our way there she wanted to visit the Sellwood mayor to talk about my wetland camp, but mostly he seemed interested in saying that the homeless people are up in Portland so Sellwood is a good place to start a business and everybody should visit the quaint antique stores. Eventually he said that he was in agreement with saving the earth since "we live on it."

When we got to Oaks Bottom, Aimee had me stand right where my camp was. I realized she wanted me to say something profound, and Chang was getting his camera all focused on me to catch an expression of me looking profound. I felt totally under pressure, and I said something like, "I have thought hard and deeply upon our fate and have concluded that the relationship of humanity to the earth is the biggest ethical issue that faces us."

Yes, I realize that this isn't how I normally talk. But what could I do when my real feelings were, "What am I supposed to say with this reporter writing down everything I say and a photographer pointing a camera at me?"

Okay... this was the end of the interview, and Aimee and Chang left. Then I turned around to walk home and there was COYOTE!!!

Arghhh!!!

I asked him how he knew I was here, and he said he didn't. He had to visit Portland for supplies, and he always visits Oaks Bottom when he comes to Portland. But he was planning on visiting me later so he could reply to my letter.

He said he doesn't exactly have "answers" to my concerns, but he said that "answers" are misleading, and that the appropriate attitude to life is not so much to seek answers but to "savor the process of questioning which keeps our eyes open and our minds engaged."

Oh, and I should point out that he was NOT wearing a loincloth. He was wearing regular jeans. It's like he was reading my mind, because even though I didn't say anything about it he said, "Oh, I only wear the loincloth at EarthSage."

So anyway... He said he had something to tell me that had to do with my idea of a philosophy of life based on life. He asked if I had read anything by Aldo Leopold, which I hadn't. Coyote said there is a very important idea he developed called the "land ethic" which goes like this (I looked it up online to make sure I got it right):

> A thing is right when it tends to preserve the integrity, stability, and beauty of the biotic community. It is wrong when it tends otherwise.

Coyote said that if we adopted that as our ethics it would totally revolutionize the entire world.

Then Coyote's "cynical side" started to come out. He said that we're doing the exact opposite of the land ethic. We're destroying the integrity and stability and beauty for short-term profit and calling that "right."

He said that the philosopher John Locke summed up the philosophy of Western Civilization when he wrote: "The negation of nature is the way to happiness." Coyote said everything about our civilization is based on this philosophy. Therefore, trying to oppose the "negation" (destruction) of nature is to oppose the very roots of our civilization. He said, "Nothing will save the earth except for a total cultural revolution. And that will never happen in time."

I started to come up with positive environmental things, such as 50 years ago ecology wasn't even an issue but now everybody knows about it. But Coyote very patiently explained that even though the environmental movement has grown large it hasn't kept up with the speed of the destruction. I pointed out that there has been huge progress, such as most places now have recycling, and pretty much everybody knows about "buying green."

But that REALLY got him going about how a lot of "buying green" makes us feel good, but isn't really much more ecological. He gave the example of electric cars that don't use gas, but use just as much resources to build, and they use electricity from burning coal, and their batteries have to be treated like toxic waste.

I finally got fed up and said, "If everything is so hopeless why don't you just jump off a bridge?" I realized that this was not incredibly mature, so I added, "What I mean is: Why do you still do things like teaching workshops and demonstrating sustainable living?"

He said, "That's a good question," and it took him awhile to answer. Finally he said, "The only answer that works for me is: It's less painful to keep trying than to stop trying."

Then it got very quiet and felt awkward. Somebody had to say something, and I didn't think it was going to be Coyote.

So I told him how glad I was that he shared the "land ethic" idea, because he was right that it relates very much to my philosophy of we should do whatever preserves nature's patterns because it preserves LIFE.

And then I said (this was an idea that came to me all of a sudden) that it was the ethic of native cultures because they lived very close to the land. Therefore, the effects of their actions were obvious. For example, let's say you eat too many of the wild ducks that nest by the lake next to you. Right away you realize there's less duck eggs for you to steal. But the problem with modern civilization is that the effects of our actions usually happen far away and we never see them.

Coyote just thought for a minute and said, "Interesting." That's it: "Interesting." And not with any emotion or anything. Ugh!

And then he said very casually, "Thanks for saving Oaks Bottom." Then he told me why he comes here whenever he visits Portland.

Oaks Bottom is where he changed his name to Coyote. He said it was a "spiritual experience." He had just left HomeEarth and had no idea what to do with his life. He was at a point where his "old self" had to die, and right at that moment an actual coyote walked right up to him and looked right into his eyes. He told me, "When the student is ready, the teacher appears."

What could I possibly say after that? So we started walking to my house while my mind was thinking all kinds of things, such as how can your "teacher" be an animal? And this is when we were walking along residential houses in Sellwood. It felt really weird to be having all these deep and possibly "mystical" thoughts on an ordinary street with people doing ordinary things.

We got to my house, and I showed him my "household ecology project." He asked me, "Are you going to be more radical?" I said I didn't know what else I could do. He asked me what was my favorite thing about EarthSage, and I said that I really liked the strawbale home. Then he asked, "Well, when are you going to build one?"

That totally shocked me, because I never even thought about actually doing that for myself. Would it even be possible?

He said that in Portland (as in basically every city or town in America) you can't build a strawbale home because of "criminally restrictive building codes." But I could legally build a strawbale building as long as it was no bigger than 100 square feet and had no plumbing. It couldn't officially be a "full-time permanent residence." (But if nobody complained, you could get away with living in it "unofficially" - in other words, illegally).

He said he could arrange to build it as an EarthSage workshop, and all I'd have to do is pay for the materials. He said it would cost about $1,000 for the straw bales and some other materials, mostly for the roof. If I wanted electricity, it would cost extra. The home would need a concrete foundation, but he noticed we already had a small concrete pad next to the house.

I'm not sure what I was thinking, but instead of just saying no, I said I would think about it. He said he would have to know soon, because the workshop will take time to organize, and it's important to finish the construction before the rain starts in the fall. He would need to know in one week.

ONE WEEK??? Ack!!!

And right then Dad came home, and he had an expression that was not warm and supportive.

I guess I was nervous and said something about Coyote being an "old friend" but I don't think he believed me. Coyote was starting to introduce himself, and I thought, "Oh no! Don't say that your name is 'Coyote'!" so I quickly said, "This is Edward Wormwood." Then Coyote looked at me with the WEIRDEST expression!

I told Dad, "I met him on that trip I did to the East Coast with Mom." Finally Dad relaxed and smiled. I thought it would be a good time to introduce the idea of a strawbale home. I said that Edward was my "natural building consultant" and we were discussing a demonstration project. Dad said, "We'll discuss it later."

Then Coyote said he had to go, and he gave me a weird look. I'm sure he was SHOCKED that I found out his "secret identity"!

I'm SO MAD at Dad! As soon as he sat down for dinner, he said "I forbid it." And I hadn't even told him about the project yet! It wasn't like, "Hey Amy, tell me what your project is so we can discuss it."

I said, "That's it? No discussion with your daughter who is trying to save the earth?"

He didn't say anything. He just sat there with a stubborn expression and wouldn't look at me. I said, "It will only cost $1,000." This was a good idea because he finally looked at me, but a bad idea because he started yelling, "¿Estás loco?" and "No tenemos mucho dinero!"

I said that $1,000 would just be a small part of my college fund, and with my HomeEarth job I'll pay it back eventually.

I am NOT going to write down what Dad said to that, but it included a lot of Spanish cuss words.

Then I did something I vowed I would NEVER do. I said how Mom would have been so proud to see all the good I've done, and if she was here right now she would have encouraged me to follow my beliefs.

Of course I knew what would happen. He got all choked up and I felt pretty terrible for doing it. Then finally he asked what my project was, so I explained the strawbale home idea.

Before he went away to be alone for a while, he said to me really quiet, "I can't forbid you from doing this, but I want you to know I think it's foolish."

August 4

I explained the whole fight with Dad to Tiffany. She didn't take it very seriously. She said, "It's just like one of those teen angst movies. That was the 'fight with the parent' scene. Later on you'll both say you're sorry, and it will be the 'we both learned an important lesson' scene."

I just saw something about an upcoming book reading at Powell's Books. It's for a book that claims to "get to the root of all social problems." Of course this got me VERY interested, since that's very close to my own mission. The book is called: "MONEY FIXES EVERYTHING; Economic Growth is the Solution to all of Our Problems." I wonder if that includes environmental destruction?

August 6

This has been THE WEIRDEST DAY OF MY LIFE. I am officially giving this day a title:

"The Day of Weird Random Visitors"

I was in my office and Tiffany called me and said, "Amy, you have a special visitor." I asked, "Is it Juvie Starr?" She said, "It's a guy carrying a bicycle wheel and he won't stop talking about geese."

Katherine had warned me that my public position would mean sometimes dealing with "crazies" so I figured this was my first one.

He was very excited and I was afraid he was going to knock something over with the bicycle wheel. He was saying something about a bus had almost ran over a goose, and there must be a law against that because animals are people too, only smaller, except for the ones that are bigger. He asked Tiffany if geese are an endangered species, but before she could answer he started talking about how he fully supports a universal single-payer national health insurance plan. And then for some reason he said, "I like tofu!"

Then he noticed I was there, and said, "AMY! THE TEENAGE GIRL WHO'S SAVING THE EARTH!" I held out my hand to shake hands, but he held out the bicycle wheel so I ended up shaking the rim of the bicycle wheel. He didn't seem to notice that was TOTALLY BIZARRE. Then he started talking about how America had a so-called "Department of Defense" which was really the "War Department" but we should have a "Peace Department," and he could have SWORN that geese were an endangered species.

I was already exhausted and I hadn't even said a word. Then Tiffany said, "You're Lester Bozzio, the congressperson that represents Northwest Oregon!" and he said, "I already know that."

I was a little amazed that Tiffany would know ANYTHING about politics (she mostly seems to know about dating and metaphysics). But it turns out she recognized him from a time he was on "Late Night with Lindsay."

I said, "Pleased to meet you Representative Bozzio." He said that he wanted to thank me for saving Oaks Bottom, and by any chance had I seen his intern Montia who keeps track of his appointments? She was supposed to meet him here, unless he forgot to tell her, which she is always accusing him of.

He started talking about geese again, which somehow led to how in Eastern Oregon he once saw a badger. While he was talking it occurred to me that I hope he never visits a mental institution, because they might accidentally keep him there.

I asked Katherine later how such a "scattered" person can possibly be a congressperson. She told me he has an amazing sort of "split personality." She said that sometime he's a "semi-genius" but most of the time "the only thing that keeps him on earth is gravity." Katherine said it was kind of like Einstein who developed the Theory of Relativity but couldn't remember to wear socks.

But the purpose of his visit (which he finally got to) was that he wants to work with me to save the earth! He wants my support on his plan to introduce a "Ban Lawn Blowers Act." He said, "I'm absolutely against lawn blowers. I'm also against nuclear weapons."

I said that I totally agreed with his position on lawn blowers, and also nuclear weapons. I said that lawn blowers are incredibly annoying. For example, every morning they're all over downtown and the noise echoes all over super loud, and they pollute the air, and all they're doing is blowing stuff off the sidewalk onto the street.

The only problem is that he doesn't exactly want to "ban" lawn blowers, because people don't like the idea of the government banning things.

I said instead of "banning" them, how about setting a noise limit that's incredibly low? Such as they can't be any louder than a cat purring.

He said that idea is brilliant!

I asked if he could make it apply not just to lawn blowers but to ALL yard things such as lawnmowers and weed-whackers. I explained that those machines are not only a problem because of noise pollution, but of other kinds of pollution. I told him I had facts about the pollution at home, and I would send them to him to use in his legislation.

He liked that he could change the name of the bill from a "negative-sounding" bill to a "positive-sounding" bill. He said, "How about calling it the 'Let's Stop Noisy Things and Bring Back Peace and Quiet Act?'" but before I could say anything he said, "Montia! Write that down!" even though Montia wasn't here.

I said, "I'll write it down for you, but isn't it kind of long? How about just calling it the 'Peace and Quiet Act'?" And he said that idea is extra brilliant!

He said it's not exactly a "Save the Earth Act," which is his long-term dream. But he needs more information before he can draft a "Save the Earth Act," because at this point it's too vague. It only consists of "stop destroying the earth." I told him about my intellectual journey to get to the roots of environmental destruction. He said if I find out, then let him know.

Oh – I almost forgot: I told Representative Bozzio about my plan to build a strawbale home. He'd never heard of anything like it, but thought it sounded like a great idea. I explained that unfortunately such buildings can't currently be used for "real" housing because of building codes.

I asked him, "Maybe that's something you can work on changing?"

He said, "Of course!" He said that might take years, but for now I should go ahead and use it for a home. He said that building inspectors only check if there are complaints, and who would complain about such a great thing?

That was Weird Random Visitor #1.

So... I was back at my desk too excited to do anything, and I got ANOTHER call from Tiffany who said, "Amy, you have another special visitor," and I said, "Oh no! I'm not calm enough to see Juvie Starr right now!" and she said "It's some guy who's very nervous and he's wearing a disguise."

I could see right away he was wearing one of those "Groucho Marx" glasses with the fake nose and moustache, but of course Tiffany didn't recognize it because she doesn't know who Groucho Marx. It makes me sad how so many people have never seen a Marx Brothers movie, or any good old movie, and when you suggest watching a black and white movie people are automatically against it. But I'm getting off-topic.

What's weird is that except for the weird disguise he looked totally normal.

The first thing he said (in a weird fake voice) was "No cameras!" I thought, "Oh right, I really want to take pictures of somebody wearing Groucho Marx glasses."

He said, "I have something very important to tell you, in private. Also, no recording devices." Then he said, "Oh, pleased to meet you."

I must have had a worried expression because Tiffany made an "I'll keep an eye on you" gesture so I knew I would be safe. I said I was very busy but I could meet him for ONE MINUTE in the conference room. But for approximately 59 seconds he couldn't figure out how to start (very nervous, kept looking out the windows). So to break the ice I pointed to his shirt (he was wearing a University of Oregon "Ducks" t-shirt) and said, "So, how about those Ducks, huh?"

And he sort of snapped back (in a regular voice now) "I just pretend to like sports because regular guys are supposed to like sports!"

I was thinking I better wrap things up, so I said, "Well, it's been great meeting you, whoever you are."

He said, "Oh, sorry about the disguise. But if I was spotted talking to an environmentalist, it could destroy my business."

I told him that was crazy talk! 93% of people identify themselves as environmentalists and what's the matter with those 7% of people who don't, because anybody who lives in the environment should be an environmentalist, and that's everybody. I said that being an environmentalist is something to be PROUD of.

He said, "Not in my line of work."

I said, "What line of work?"

He said to close the blinds, and then he looked down very sadly and took off the Groucho Marx glasses, or I guess technically they slid off his face. I was SHOCKED!

It was Doug Normalson!!! The developer who was going to build the condos in Oaks Bottom!

Now I realized why he was paranoid about cameras and recording devices and closing the blinds. Because obviously he was here to murder me!

But he didn't murder me at all. He just said, "Now do you understand why I can't be seen with you?" Then he said, kind of laughing, "Don't worry, I didn't come here to kill you!"

I said back, "Oh, I wasn't thinking that at all!" (Why did I say that?)

He said, "You might find this hard to believe, but actually I came here to thank you."

My mind was stunned, which allowed him to keep talking.

He said, "You might not believe it to look at me now, but I used to be a hippie." I couldn't believe it! If there's such a thing as the opposite of a hippie, he was it.

So basically I heard his whole life story, about how once he was a "typical hippie carpenter." He was a very good worker and everybody liked him, so he kept getting promoted until suddenly he was supervising a construction team. And "to make a long story short" he was now a respectable businessman who owned his own company, and was also a responsible husband and father.

Part of him would always be an earth-loving hippie. But that had to stay secret, because he is caught in a profession that sees environmentalists as "the enemy." He called himself a "closet environmentalist."

He still loves the earth, but has to be "sneaky" about it. For example, he goes fishing because fishing is seen as an acceptable way for men to enjoy nature because they're also killing something. But he doesn't actually "fish" - he just hangs out next to the river. If somebody is watching he'll cast a lure, but he cut off the hook so he can't catch anything. But one time he was forced to catch a very stubborn fish that wouldn't let go.

He said that "privately" he's glad I saved Oaks Bottom, even though "publicly" he has to rant and rave about "damn environmentalists."

I told him about some of the natural building projects I've seen, and asked, "Why can't you just build ecological homes?"

He said there's a "silent conspiracy" to make homes as expensive as possible. For one thing, homes have a "required minimum size." That means it's against the law to build a small home! For another thing, the building codes say you have to use expensive materials made by big companies. It's against the law to use materials that are inexpensive or free!

He also said it's hard to be an ecological builder because every "green" option costs more - for example, sustainably-harvested wood or natural materials or non-toxic paints. He showed me an ad for a new home that's "Earth Advantage & Earth Star Certified." It costs $475,000! We both thought it was crazy that a "green" house should cost MORE and a destructive house should cost LESS. It's like everything is "backwards" somehow!

He said, "The meaning of life is to leave the world better than when you found it. I want to do that with how I make a living, but I feel trapped."

I asked if there was any way I could help him, then he started getting all teary-eyed. I thought, "Please don't cry! I won't know what to do, you're a middle-age man and I'm a 14-year-old girl!"

So I thought it would be a good idea to talk FAST. I told him that I was already working on this, and that I have political support. Plus soon I would have a demonstration eco-home, and that I was sure that public demand would change the building codes that make it illegal to build naturally. I told him my belief that someday he could come out of the closet.

But he started crying anyway! I wished there was a transporter machine so I could transport myself to anyplace that wasn't there. But at least he didn't try to hug me, because I probably would have screamed.

He said he was sorry for crying but that I have no idea of his "inner conflict" and "the pain of living a lie."

FINALLY he stopped crying and said he had to get going. He picked up his Groucho Marx disguise and put it back on. I said the best Marx Brothers movie was "A Night at the Opera." He said it was "Duck Soup."

That was #2

Then Tiffany called me AGAIN to say I had a "surprise visitor." I didn't have huge hopes that it was Juvie Starr, but I just said I hoped it was NOT another "crazy."

She said, "Oh no, it's somebody that seems to be very evolved. We're having a very interesting conversation about the illusory nature of the material world."

I thought that was strange, because at an environmental organization like HomeEarth we take the material world pretty seriously, and in fact are trying to save it.

Then she said, "Nothing is permanent but change." A voice in the background (a male voice, therefore not Juvie Starr) said, "How perceptive of you, my dear," and there was giggling before the phone was hung up.

I definitely did NOT want to talk to some "New Age" friend of Tiffany's, or actually to talk to anybody on earth. But I thought, "Okay let's get this over with."

At Tiffany's desk I saw the back of an extremely sharp business-type man, and then he turned about and I saw THE FACE OF EVIL. In other words, the face of ANTHONY IRON!!! Right here in the office was the spokesperson for the evil GloboChem corporation that poisons the earth and babies.

So why was Tiffany just chatting with him like he was the cute bike courier or something?

Then the FACE OF EVIL smiled at me and I swear his eyes twinkled. He said, "Hi there beautiful, I was in the neighborhood so I thought I'd stop in to say hi."

I said, "How can I talk to you, the representative for GloboChem which is against everything I stand for?"

He said (smiling and twinkling again), "Despite what you think, we are not enemies. In the big picture, there is no reason to create more anger and negativity in this world."

Tiffany said, "Yes, you can't fix negative energy by adding more negative energy,"

He looked at her and said, "Just like how you can't fight fire with fire." But he said it in a flirty way, and Tiffany "swooned" (I think that's the right word, "swooned").

As if he was reading my mind (maybe he was?) he said, "I'm not an 'evil' person, and you will be much more effective if you can get beyond that sort of thinking."

I suddenly got this feeling of super-courage. Up until that moment, the idea of having a debate with him totally scared me. But with my feeling of super-courage, I suddenly looked him right in his eyes and said, "I want to debate you."

His answer was weird.

He said, "If you debate me, then I would win. You are no match for me and you know it. But what you probably will not be able to understand is that if I win against you, then I will lose."

As if he was reading my mind (again) he said, "You probably think I'm lying. But do your research. You will find that while I have emphasized certain truths to succeed at the task at hand, I have never lied. I never lie, and I never stay with a losing team."

Then he checked his watch and said, "It's been a pleasure, but I have another engagement." Then he said, smiling (and twinkling), "Perhaps someday we shall meet again," in a way that makes me think we definitely will.

After he left I was angry with Tiffany. I asked why she was flirting with THE FACE OF EVIL. She accused me of being melodramatic. She said it was just "fun flirting," and for her flirting is a lifestyle.

Today was WAY too crazy. I don't know if I can survive any more days like this.

August 7

I've been thinking about what Dad said about environmental problems not being "serious." It's hard for me to admit, but probably that's what a lot of people think. So it's very important to have facts for all the people who will be asking me if environmental problems are "serious" or "real."

Here's a bunch of stuff I collected from books and magazine articles that show how environmental problems are both real AND serious:

- Half of the world's forests and wetlands are gone.
- Forests are shrinking by 13 million acres per year.
- 4/5 of ocean fisheries are being fished at or over capacity.
- EPA estimates 50,000 leaking toxic dumps in U.S.
- Soil erosion exceeds soil formation on 1/3 of the world's croplands.
- Soil fertility is steadily decreasing, in many areas soil is essentially "dead" and only produces crops by use of chemical fertilizers.

- Species are going extinct 1,000 times faster than normal. Loss of biodiversity signals the decline of ecosystems on which all life on earth depends.
- 1 in 5 people don't have access to fresh drinking water.
- Climate Change/Global Warming: We're already seeing melting ice caps, higher sea levels, and more severe droughts and floods.
- Pollution (chemicals, toxins, heavy metals): EPA estimates 1,200 Superfund sites that will require approx. $200 billion to clean up.
- Ozone layer depletion (need to find stats)
- Agriculture: Industrial agriculture uses 16 calories of input to produce 1 calorie of grain, and 70 calories of input to produce 1 calorie of meat.
- Coral reefs are disappearing.
- Water shortages: Many aquifers being drained far faster than being replenished (especially Arizona & Texas), and some areas are dependent on "fossil aquifers" that will never be replenished. This is causing water tables to fall, wells to fail, sinkholes, water wars, etc.
- Desertification (need to find stats, but I know it's something like millions of acres of land converting to desert)
- Energy: Fossil fuels = stored solar energy, and every day we burn an amount of energy the earth took 10,000 days to store. (Might sound better to put it like this: Every day we burn 27 years of stored solar energy.)
- Agricultural pollution: Every year 6 billion pounds of pesticides, herbicides, and fungicides are added to the soil.

And what do all these facts add up to? UNSUSTAINABLE! Scientists can measure how the earth is doing by figuring out "biospheric productivity" and "net photosynthetic production." Here's something from a magazine article called "Earth in Trouble."

> A 2002 study by a team of scientists combined all of humanity's uses of the earth's natural assets into a single indicator – the ecological footprint. The authors concluded that humanity's collective demands first surpassed the earth's regenerative capacity in 1980. By 2000, the demands on the earth's natural systems exceeded sustainable yields by 20 percent. The latest calculations show the excess demand at 50 percent.
>
> In other words, we are no longer living off nature's "interest" but are now consuming the "capital" on which all life depends. Soon, earth's "capital" will be used up and a mass die-off of all earthly life will inevitably follow. Since humanity is one form of earthly life, the situation is problematic.

So we are 150% unsustainable, which is bad enough. But when Peak Oil really hits it's going to get so much worse, because we use oil for practically everything it seems like. Right now nobody cares because we're getting lots of oil from the Arctic National Wildlife Refuge, but that's not going to last forever. My fear is that when the oil runs out things are going to get VERY BAD.

There are natural substitutes for oil. We can grow seeds that can be used to make natural oil. For heat, we can "grow" firewood. Instead of plastic made from oil, soybeans can be used to make a natural kind of plastic. But the problem is there's not enough farmland to grow all these substitutes.

It makes NO sense to me that there are people out there that when you mention environmental problems they don't think it's serious.

But actually, Dad kind of had a point when he said you can't really "see" the problems. For a lot of things, that's true. You can't "see" toxic chemicals leaking into the aquifers, or the aquifers being drained unsustainably, or the shrinking ozone layer, or soil fertility decreasing, or extinct species (obviously), or dying coral reefs. I guess you could see dying coral reefs if you went on a trip to Australia, but they'll probably show you the non-dying ones. I mean, who wants to fly thousands of miles to see a dying coral reef?

August 8

Beautiful Saturday morning in Oaks Bottom Wildlife Refuge! I've been thinking more about the idea that we can't "see" environmental destruction. One reason is that it usually happens in places far away, and those places aren't really excited about advertising it. (Such as Australia doesn't advertise to come and visit their dying coral reefs.)

I totally thought about the example of the paper mill we saw on our vacation on the north shore of Lake Superior. All the pulp effluent (waste) goes into a creek. I think it's called "Blackbird Creek," but I bet there aren't any blackbirds there now! It turns the creek brown with white foam and it looks AWFUL and smells TERRIBLE. It's hard to believe it's legal, but I guess it is somehow.

But here's why this is such a good example of what I'm thinking about: There's a spot where the polluted creek runs under the Trans-Canada Highway. Many travellers on the highway saw it (and smelled it!) and complained.

And how did the company respond? If you guessed "Put in pollution controls and clean up the creek" you are WRONG. Because what they did was put these huge metal covers over the creek so you couldn't see it from the highway. (You can still smell it, but you don't know what causes the smell. You just think maybe a bunch of moose (mooses?) pooped on the road or something.)

The other example is from the redwood forests in Northern California, where we also went on a trip. The forests have mostly been clearcut, but people might get MAD if they saw the clearcuts. This is important because people come from all over the world and spend lots of tourist dollars to see these huge and majestic trees that seem so "wise."

So what did the timber companies do? You're right if you guessed that they did NOT stop clearcutting. What the timber companies did was leave what they called a "redwood curtain" of beautiful ancient redwoods along the highway. Then people couldn't see the ugly clearcuts.

This is a huge problem for environmental activists like me. People need to SEE the problems so they realize how serious they are. And since I'm the HomeEarth COMMUNICATIONS Manager, part of my mission could be to COMMUNICATE so people can see.

Maybe I can make a presentation, like the PowerPoint show Al Gore did with "An Inconvenient Truth" to spread awareness about Global Warming. SPREADING AWARENESS! That's what I need to do.

What would I call this show? "Out of Sight; Out of Mind"? How about, "In Your Sight; In Your Mind?" No, that doesn't sound very good.

Actually, the problem isn't just that we can't "see" the problems that are happening right now. Part of the problem is what I said to Coyote in Oaks Bottom, about how a lot of environmental problems have been going on for a long time. They're so gradual we don't notice them.

How about some way to show everything "speeded up"? Such as the nature show I saw that had an entire year of a forest squeezed into a few minutes.

But it would have to be many years - hundreds of years. It would have to show deforestation. And aquifers depleting. And soil erosion.

A lot of the stuff would be impossible to film. And most of it wasn't filmed, since it happened before film was invented.

Could there be a way to show all of it with computer animation?

I get so impatient! I want to save the earth RIGHT NOW! But I realize that it's not going to happen overnight. It will take months. Maybe even years.

August 9

I just got back from the book reading for: "Money Fixes Everything." The author is from some organization called "People for Economic Common Sense."

These are the main points of how (according to the book) economic growth is the solution to all of our problems:

- POVERTY - He said this was CLEARLY obvious, because if the problem is that people don't have enough money, then the problem is obviously more money. Someone in the audience suggested that people "on the top" can share with the people "on the bottom" but the author strongly disagreed and said we are Americans and not Communists.

- UNEMPLOYMENT - The only way to make more jobs is to grow the economy.

- CRIME - Since it's mostly poor people that commit crimes, if we grow the economy then people can buy a TV instead of stealing it.

- OVERPOPULATION - He said it's a proven fact that poor people have more children, so the only solution is to grow the economy.

- AFFORDABLE HOUSING - If the economy grows, then people have more money and can better afford housing. Someone said, "Can't we just make housing more affordable?" He laughed at that idea, and said it's not a "solution" to make people live in rat-infested shacks.
- HEALTHY FOOD - He said that people eat unhealthy food because it's cheap, which is why poor people fill up their shopping cart with cases of macaroni and cheese. Only with economic growth can people afford to eat healthy.
- ENVIRONMENTAL DESTRUCTION - He said that it's not just organic and local food that's more expensive, but organic and local EVERYTHING. He also said that if we want to clean up polluted areas it takes tons of money. So therefore the only way to save the earth is with more economic growth.

A woman in the audience had a very interesting question. She asked, "Economic growth creates environmental destruction, so are you saying that we have to destroy the earth so we can afford to save it?" The author answered, "How else can we afford to save it?"

That reminds me of something Katherine told me. She explained how saving the earth goes better when the economy is up. She said HomeEarth has been struggling for a while because the economy had been bad. But since the oil from the Arctic National Wildlife Refuge started this spring, the economy has finally got a boost - and so has the HomeEarth membership.

The oil has resulted in a lot of spills and dead wildlife, and of course all the pollution and global warming from burning fossil fuels. But one good thing is that HomeEarth is more able to do their good work.

Drilling for oil boosts the economy so we can afford to fight against drilling for oil? That seems to agree with what the book author is saying, but it makes NO sense.

August 10

The "Peace and Quiet Act" was introduced today!

FOR IMMEDIATE RELEASE:

Bozzio Introduces Bill to Discourage Noisy Lawn Machines

Washington, DC – Rep. Lester Bozzio (D-OR) has introduced the Peace and Quiet Act which, if passed, would strongly discourage noisy lawn maintenance equipment such as lawn mowers and those annoying lawn blowers.

"Doesn't it drive you crazy?" asked Bozzio. "They sound like giant monster robot mosquitos."

In addition to the noise, the machines cause substantial environmental damage. There are 30 million acres of lawn in the United States. Mowing this much lawn burns 800 million gallons of gas per year, which causes over five percent of urban air pollution.

The act would not explicitly ban such machines, but would discourage their use by limiting their noise output to 25 decibels, equivalent to the volume of a purring cat.

This is so awesome! It even includes my factual research! I only recently met Representative Bozzio and already I'm helping to introduce legislation!

August 11

Coyote called me on the phone from EarthSage (which was weirdly shocking because he hates electronic devices).

It's official!

Very soon I will start building...

a strawbale home!

After I calmed down, I said we must discuss project specifications because the scope of the project has evolved. He asked what in heck I was trying to say, and I told him that I was inspired by Representative Bozzio to live in the home, so I decided to have electricity.

Coyote said that would cost another $1,000 for an electrical contractor. He also reminded me that using it for an actual home would make it in violation of building codes. I said that I basically had congressional approval, even though it's from only 1/535 of Congress.

I wonder if Coyote likes me? It's so hard to tell with him, he's so mysterious. Not that it matters to me, I was just wondering.

I was just thinking about what Doug Normalson the developer said: "The meaning of life is to leave the world better than when you found it." If that's really true, then why did I never hear of it before? Shouldn't it be on the news or something?

I was curious about the organization "People for Economic Common Sense" so I did some research and I was SHOCKED. The name makes it sounds like a bunch of regular people. But I found that it's an organization to represent THE BIGGEST AND MOST POWERFUL CORPORATIONS IN THE WORLD. So OF COURSE a book published by such an organization is going to say that the solution to all our problems is more money for THE BIGGEST AND MOST POWERFUL CORPORATIONS IN THE WORLD.

This economic stuff keeps coming up. Whenever there's an idea that is sustainable and good for saving the earth, the argument AGAINST it is always "we can't afford it."

So it looks like my intellectual journey to discover the roots of ecological destruction needs to travel into the world of economics.

I'm NOT thrilled about this. I really do NOT understand economics stuff which seems to be VERY complicated.

But the solution of "more money" just doesn't seem right. I'm always hearing that we're "the richest nation on earth." If that's right, then why can't we afford to be sustainable?

August 12

I decided today to ask Tiffany about "the meaning of life." I wanted to see if she agrees with Doug Normalson that it's "to leave the world better than we found it." She said, "Oh, of course! Our purpose in life is to evolve humanity." I thought that sounded really good, but then realized I had no idea what it means.

Then I asked Katherine. She said the "leaving the world better than we found it" idea is pretty universal, and that many deep thinkers have arrived at the same answer. She said she learned this in college but sort of stopped thinking about it. I was kind of amazed. I mean how could you learn the meaning of life and then sort of stop thinking about it?

I talked to Katherine about my idea of a big presentation on the theme of "Out of Sight; Out of Mind." But unfortunately as a result of it not being very clear in my mind, it was not clear coming out of my mouth. She told me to let her know when my idea was "more organized."

August 13

MORE WEIRDNESS! I was at my desk and opened the latest issue of HomeEarth magazine, and this note fell out:

IMPORTANT – Do not discard, this is not a joke. I have information that you want. You have expressed your desire to discover the roots of ecological destruction. You are very close to the answer, but also very far from the answer. Forces more powerful than you can imagine do not want the answer revealed.

I want to help you, but must do so anonymously. I am taking a tremendous risk but I feel it must be done to save humanity and all life on earth.

I am contacting you because I believe you are the only person in a position to turn things around before it's too late. I hope for the sake of the earth that you believe me and are ready to hear what I have to say.

If you wish to meet with me, put a "save the earth" flag in the flowerpot next to your office window before 9:00am on the day you wish to meet. We shall meet at 3:00pm at Laurelhurst Park by the duck pond. I shall be heavily disguised as an elderly homeless man. If you feel safe, initiate contact by lecturing me on how it's bad to feed breadcrumbs to the ducks.

Please do not share this letter with anyone or tell anyone about our meeting. This is for your safety as well as my own.

Sincerely,
Deep Ecology

Is this real, or is it some kind of joke? Is "Deep Ecology" a weird psycho pervert? I have this weird feeling in my stomach. I feel like I have to decide all by myself what to do. Because if what the message says is TRUE, then sharing it with somebody would put them in danger. But if it turns out to be FALSE, then I'll be all alone with someone who is maybe a weird psycho pervert. But if it turns out to be TRUE, then I might discover the answer to saving the earth.

What should I do???

August 14

The totally nice neighbor Carol came over, all cheerful as usual. I was very excited to show her my "household ecology project." She agrees that blueberries are the most delicious thing ever, and promised she'd bring Grandma's recipe for blueberry pie.

But I was really surprised when I showed her the clothesline and her smile went away. I'd never seen that happen and it scared me a little for some reason.

She said, "Isn't a clothesline for poor people?" and felt bad that our dryer must be broken. I said I put up the clothesline ON PURPOSE to demonstrate ecological values. I explained that it saves energy and also saves money. But that didn't convince her. She just said it seemed like "a step backward."

August 15

Katherine said I can put "fun" stuff in my blog, not just environmental policy stuff. I asked her what about some of my nature writing? She said that would be great. Yay! So I think I'll put in a short one that's one of my favorites that I wrote last year for school.

CYCLES WITHIN CYCLES

By Amy Johnson-Martinez

I recall a day in June on the north shore of Lake Superior. As I sat on the beach a frigid wind blew in over water of the deepest blue. The beach was nestled in an old glacial valley. On each side were granite headlands with signs of glacial scouring, from the last ice age that ended 10,000 years ago.

The beach was scattered with driftwood logs, scrubbed smooth and clean by crashing storm waves and bleached white by the sun. I realized they were like skeletons of past forests, as future forests rise from the thin carpet of soil.

Everything seemed to consist of cycles within cycles. I pondered that this place was here long before I was born, and would be here long after I died. The driftwood skeletons would still be here, but from trees that don't yet exist.

This scene was prepared over millions of years in a process of volcanoes and tilting plates of earth and the scouring flow of glaciers a mile thick. Such an immense scale of time and energy makes us seem tiny and transitory.

And you know what? We are! But I was sure glad to be part of the scene. Because even though we aren't here very long in the "big picture," that scene sure is beautiful!

I reminded Katherine about my presentation idea "Out of Sight; Out of Mind" and gave her a non-confusing description. She said she'll talk to the board about funding for a test version!

I've decided to meet with Deep Ecology tomorrow. I don't think this is a trick for somebody to murder me, because if somebody was going to murder me then why go through all this? Why not just murder me?

So I really don't expect that to happen, but in case it does I want you to know, dear diary, that I've really enjoyed writing in you. Make sure to tell Dad I love him, although I'm not sure how you would do that. I guess he would have to find you and turn to this page.

August 16

Well, obviously I wasn't murdered at all, since here I am writing again. WHAT A WIERD MEETING! Once again, I think that my life can't possibly get any weirder and then it does.

Right away was the problem that there were three homeless men feeding breadcrumbs to the ducks. So I went to the first one and said, "Excuse me, but ducks are not evolved to eat bread and it gives them a stomach ache." He sort of yelled at me, "Then why do they keep eating it?" and he threw a breadcrumb at me. I decided that this whole approach was stupid, because if the idea was to not attract attention then it was NOT WORKING.

So I just announced to the other ones, "Hey is one of you guys Deep Ecology?" One of them growled at me and fell over, and the other one got up and said (in a pretend old man voice), "Perhaps you are in need of certain information?"

I said, "Wow your disguise is INCREDIBLE!" and he sort of panicked and said, "Shhhh!" and motioned that we go to a bench with no homeless men or ducks.

It took forever because he was pretending to be about 200 years old. I felt safe because there were people close enough to hear me scream plus I had my hand on my cell phone all the time.

I asked if he was some sort of government official or top scientist or something like that. He said (still using the pretend old man voice), "That's not important. You want to know the roots of environmental destruction, am I right?" and I said of course because otherwise I wouldn't spend such a nice day coming here to get a breadcrumb thrown at me.

Then he said, "Follow the money."

I said, "What do you mean? Where?"

He said (very mysteriously), "I can't tell you that. You need to find out on your own. I'll keep you going in the right direction if I can, but that's all I can do."

Then he asked me, "Does it make sense to you that money is connected with the roots of environmental destruction? Tell me what you know."

I said that I was pretty sure there was a connection because environmental protection always seems to be opposed because "we can't afford it" and "it will hurt the economy." But I said that even though I knew all that stuff, I was stuck at getting any farther. It was like I had these "pieces" but didn't know what the "puzzle" was to fit them all together.

He said, "Excellent. You've made good progress. But you have made a fundamental error in your approach." I thought he was just pausing and was going to finish the sentence, but I guess he was waiting for me to say something and I noticed that some hipsters were playing Frisbee on the other side of the pond.

Finally he said, "Okay I'll tell you. You have been following the money, but you have been following it in the wrong direction. You need to follow it to its source."

I asked what he meant. He took out a dollar bill and asked me, "What is this?"

I thought that was silly and said it's a dollar bill. But he got all serious and said, "No, that's only what it's called. But WHAT IS IT?"

How could I respond to that? I mean, showing me a dollar bill and telling me it's not a dollar bill???

He said there are two levels to the answer I'm looking for, and if I succeed in the first level then he will guide me to the second level.

I thought this was all pretty ridiculous. I asked him why can't he just tell me? He said, "I just can't, and I can't tell you why I can't."

Then he said, "However, I am able to give you a clue to the first level." He said to remember three words very carefully: "internalize the externalities."

I was like, "Huh? Can't you give me easier words?" He said NO, it was "extremely important" to get the words exactly right.

He made me repeat the words to make sure I remembered, then he said he must leave and don't try to follow him or it will put us both in danger. He said that when I have discovered the meaning of the first level, then contact him again the same way as before.

I started to walk away, and just a few seconds later I turned around he had totally vanished. I couldn't see him anywhere. It didn't seem possible, but he was gone.

WHAT AM I SUPPOSED TO DO? How can it be that this adult person can't use this information, but a 14-year-old girl can? Why can't he just send it to the media, or write a book about it, or post it on the internet? Very strange! But at least I will research "internalize the externalities" and see if it leads to anything.

August 17

Dear diary, guess who is featured in the current issue of People magazine? It's somebody you know VERY well - somebody you know better than anyone else in the world. You have no idea? I'll give you a hint: She has dark hair and likes to work in her garden, and according to People magazine she is "saving the earth one wetland at a time."

Even though I'm looking at it RIGHT NOW I can't believe it. Dad of course is SUPER excited, I can't ever remember seeing him so excited. After he smiled and laughed and hugged me he left the house to buy a bunch of copies. To celebrate he's buying me ice cream!!! He said any flavor I want so I said Ben & Jerry's Chubby Hubby because it's organic and it's SO GOOD!!!

I can't wait to show Katherine!!! There's a picture of us at work that looks like we're having a serious discussion but we were actually talking about where to go for lunch. The caption says, "Amy often discusses environmental policy with Katherine Bliss, president of HomeEarth." If the caption was real it would have been, "Amy and Katherine discuss whether to have Thai or Mexican." Haha!

The strawbale workshop starts in only a few days! Coyote is coming to Portland tomorrow to prepare. I wonder how much he knows about economic stuff? Maybe I'll ask him if he knows what money is.

Oh - somehow I forgot to write this before. How could I forget something so important? The article is also in "People en Español." This made Dad SUPER PROUD. In addition to buying tons of the English version, he bought even MORE of the Spanish version. He said they're for the guys at work, many of whom don't read English too well. Also lots of copies to send to his family back in Mexico.

I'm very glad because the Hispanic community is not very represented in the environmental movement. I am incredibly honored that the article compared me with Caesar Chavez. That's a little funny because he was famous a long time ago, but I guess there aren't too many Hispanic activists that people know about. Of course his activism was more about worker rights. But that included being exposed to toxic agricultural chemicals, which of course is also an environmental issue.

But I have to be honest, dear diary, that I feel a little "funny" about "People en Español." Not about the article, which is GREAT. But about the rest of the magazine.

I don't know how to write this without sounding like I'm judging, but I really could not identify with the rest of the magazine at all. The women were all super made-up and wearing very tight clothes and it seems like all that mattered was to look sexy. I think half the ads were for make-up, which is weird because the women in the magazine didn't need any more make-up. And the men did not look very smart at all, and it didn't look like they even wanted to look smart. (Actually, the women didn't look very smart either.)

It seemed like romance was hugely important. A bunch of the photos were of a man and woman kissing. I felt bad for the guys because they were kissing make-up. I mean, there was a woman's face there, but it was underneath a layer of cosmetic products and I don't think any of them were organic. That means they were kissing chemicals! Yuck!

I didn't see a single thing in the magazine (besides the article about me) that said anything about environmental values or even anything positive about nature.

I guess I can understand in a way. For one thing, Hispanics might not care a lot about nature because of their history of being used for farm work. So maybe when

Hispanics hear about "getting back to nature" they think about "getting back to hard work in terrible working conditions for hardly any money."

Hispanics are very familiar with being poor. Maybe "natural" seems like "poor," so in getting away from being "poor" they also want to get away from being "natural"?

So I'm sort of wondering why they wanted to do an article about me. I mean, my message doesn't really "fit" with the rest of the magazine. I hope it's not just the novelty of being a 14-year-old activist that happens to be Hispanic, like I'm the "token teenage Hispanic environmentalist" or something like that.

On the bright side, maybe I'll inspire other Hispanics by showing them that it's important to save the earth. Maybe some teenage girls will see my example and realize that it's okay to look "natural" and not be super made-up and try to look sexy to impress boys that are trying to look stupid.

It's okay to be smart! We're all going to have to be very smart to figure out how to save the earth!

Katherine says there is budget approval for a test version of my presentation "Out of Sight; Out of Mind"! She said my non-confusing description was clear enough for the board to understand, and now it will be sent to a local production company. It's the same company that does the "dancing banana" commercials!

August 18

Coyote is here! A few days from now I'll have my very own strawbale eco-home! The workshop will be three days and will go like this:

- Day 1 - Stack the straw bales and secure them together using long bamboo stakes.

- Day 2 - Construct the roof and attach it to the top of the walls. Then put in the door and windows.
- Day 3 - Cover all the straw with wire mesh and apply a coat of stucco. Coyote says this will part will be the most work.

Coyote was only here for a few minutes, but then he had to leave to get a bunch of hardware stuff. I think he said there will be six people taking the workshop, building an eco-home in only three days! And for only 2,000 dollars! Which to me seems like a LOT of money, but I know there are homes in the neighborhood (much fancier of course) that cost a hundred times more than that. I think people will be so excited to see there's an alternative that costs way less and is also ecological!

Coyote came back and dropped off all the hardware stuff, and then right away he left again. I asked when we'll have a chance to talk, and he said, "You mean about the workshop?" I said maybe we could talk about other stuff too. He just made a weird expression, and then drove off. He didn't say a word, he just drove off. Frustrating!

Some neighbors have expressed concern to Dad about the clothesline. Several people said they were sorry we've fallen on hard times, and some people even tried to give him envelopes with money inside. This made Dad non-happy because he's very proud that even though we aren't "rich" we can take care of ourselves just fine.

I asked, "Are you forbidding me from having a clothesline?" He said he didn't want to go that far, but asked if I would please move it to a place that's not "where the whole town can see it." He was exaggerating, of course.

August 19

I just got back from a lunch meeting with Coyote. I insisted on paying for us both, which made me feel very mature.

After talking about the workshop, I told him that I was in the mood for an intellectual conversation about deep subjects. I said, "You're a very intelligent person so maybe you know the answer to the question: What is money?"

He laughed and said, "Well, the Bible says it's the root of all evil." But I wanted to be serious so I showed him he's not the only intelligent person.

"Actually," I said, "the Bible says the LOVE of money is the root of all evil."

I think he was surprised that a 14-year old girl knew something he didn't! He said, "Really? That's what it says?" And I said therefore money isn't the problem, it's GREED. He thought about that for a while, then he said that was a very good analysis and that I was very intelligent. I decided not to tell him that actually this was my mom's analysis.

He said this is agrees with his theory that the root of ecological destruction is human greed, which I do NOT agree with.

Coyote told me something very interesting: He said that money is a matter of faith. A dollar bill isn't worth anything unless everybody agrees that it does. It's just a piece of paper!

I thought this made sense. For example, if you gave a bird a dollar bill it would think it's useful only to rip up to use for a nest. A bird definitely wouldn't try to sell you anything in exchange for the dollar, although I can't think of anything I would want to buy from a bird. Maybe it would whistle a song for me for the dollar? No, it would just rip it up for a nest. If it happened to whistle, that would be just a coincidence.

Coyote said more, which honestly I couldn't follow because I didn't understand the words he was using, things like "microeconomics" and "macroeconomics" that sound to me like the same thing. Why can't economics be in a language that people can understand?

He got to a point where he just sort of "stopped" and looked bored. He said, "Why bother? It doesn't really matter."

Then he saw something out the window that got him excited. He said, "Oh, this is a good one!" It was a motorhome that just parked across the street. It was towing a jeep. And the jeep was towing a motorboat. Also there were four motorcycles sort of hanging everywhere. Then the family got out of the motorhome and came inside, and they all ordered bacon cheeseburgers. Also, fries and large Cokes, except for one Dr. Pepper which I guess doesn't make a lot of difference.

Coyote said that if you counted the two motors on the boat and the generator inside the motorhome, the family was travelling with nine gas engines. Not even close to a new record, he said, but a good try. Judging by their "dietary preferences" (he laughed when he said this) he put them in the upper one-percent of unsustainable food choices. He said this was "a family of winners." (He was making himself crack up now.)

Then he said something that honestly got me MAD. He said, "Oh, I should be careful about what I say so I don't dampen your youthful idealism."

Oh, so I'm JUST a youthful idealist? I'm an intelligent young woman, and I should let you know that intelligence is not measured by how cynical a person is. And if you're so "intelligent," then why are you using your intelligence to calculate things such as how many calories of bacon a family eats? Wouldn't it be more intelligent to use your intelligence to do something useful?

I didn't say any of this out loud; I just thought it to myself. But I thought it very loud. It's like I was yelling inside my brain.

I decided to NOT act out of anger. I asked him, very calmly, "Did you come here to help me build a strawbale home? Or did you come here to show me how smart you are by making fun of stupid people?"

That shut him up fast!

August 20

I just met all the people that are here for the strawbale home workshop!

- Krystal - dreadlocks, kind of "spacey," says that "art is not creating things; it's a way of experiencing the world."
- Daniel - has a beard which means he is a serious person. He said that he is "engaged in political discussions" then looked to see if we were impressed.
- Melinda & Greg (married) - they call themselves "urban homesteaders" and are trying to adapt permaculture principles to city life. Greg said he hates rural areas because they're full of rednecks. Melinda likes the idea of "building community." Greg made a funny face when she said that.
- Urban Survivor (that's what he calls himself, I don't know his real name) - kind of "grungy" looking. Teaches classes in "apocalypse training" which he says makes him lots of money for stockpiling beer. He asked, "After civilization collapses where are you going to find beer?" Nobody answered.
- Phil - from the suburbs in Beaverton. He seemed a little "uncomfortable," like he didn't fit in with the rest of us. He's interested in the workshop to build a strawbale playhouse for his kids. He showed us a picture and asked, "Aren't they the cutest kids you've ever seen?" Everybody said yes.

End of Day 1! We finished the walls for my beautiful strawbale home! What's amazing is how it went up FAST. So we had lots of time to get to know each other.

Krystal showed us a painting she did, called "The Balance of Nature." She said it's possibly her "masterpiece." It has a lot of very colorful animals getting along in peace and harmony.

I don't know if it's a "masterpiece" artistically, but scientifically it's not accurate at all. In real life, all those animals would not get along so well. All those animals have to eat something, and in real life mostly they eat each other. The dragonfly would eat the butterfly, and the frog would eat the dragonfly, and the eagle would swoop down to eat the frog. Unless the snake got the frog first, then the eagle would eat the snake.

Everybody really liked the painting, and nobody mentioned the non-scientific things. Maybe art isn't supposed to be judged scientifically?

Time for bed. I'm tired, and there are still two days to go.

August 21

End of Day 2! We used special saws and cut out the places for the doors and windows, but the hardest part was making the roof. Coyote said that a good roof that doesn't leak is VERY important. The only really "bad" thing that can happen to strawbale home is if the strawbales got wet, because they would decompose (rot).

We made the roof separately on the lawn. Then all of us working together moved it on top and attached it with cables that go down to bolts in the concrete. Then we tightened the cables to sort of "press down" the straw bales and make the walls very solid. There are no hurricanes or tornadoes in Portland, but even if there were they wouldn't blow my home away.

There was a very interesting conversation about sustainability that started when Daniel asked the question: "How unsustainable are we?"

Because of my research I was able to say that humanity is 1.5 times unsustainable. Coyote said, "That's the average for the whole world, but this country is way above average." He said that the United States is approximately 10 times unsustainable."

Then Urban Survivor said something REALLY interesting. He said that it would be possible to have our current lifestyle and we could still be sustainable. He said all we have to do is reduce the population by 90%.

He said: "It's simple math. If we want to be sustainable, we have 2 choices: We can reduce our consumption by 90%, or we can keep our current lifestyle and reduce our population by 90%. 300 million people can't keep living this way, but 30 million people can."

This started an argument.

Phil said that we were exaggerating, but he was arguing with the WRONG people, because everybody starting talking about scientific studies of facts that can't be denied. Actually, they can be denied because Phil was doing it. He just said, "I don't believe any of it." In other words, he didn't believe the work of thousands of scientists that are much smarter than Phil. It's weird that one person can do that.

This has me a little worried. I'm counting on using facts in my mission to save the earth, but what if people don't accept facts? I'm hoping that people like Phil are just a tiny minority. And maybe people like Phil can be reached in other ways, such as emotionally. A good example would be the pictures of sick babies after the GloboChem spill.

I wonder if there's a way to show that the earth is sick? I'm not sure, since it's not obvious like it is with babies because of their crying.

Phil said he would not make either choice and neither would anybody else. Urban Survivor just smiled and said, "That's why my apocalypse training classes are doing so well."

Later on I sort of "overheard" Coyote talking with Urban Survivor. They were by the EarthSage truck, away from everybody else. Okay, maybe I was "eavesdropping" which isn't ethical, but it started by accident and then I just sort of didn't stop.

But now I know about the mysterious "supplies" that Coyote picked up. It was all kinds of stuff for EarthSage for their long-term survival. I didn't hear all of it, but some of the things were solar electric panels, lots of wire, and plastic pipe. Coyote said, "The top priority is for things impossible to make ourselves and difficult to obtain post-collapse."

Then what they were saying got a little scary. Urban Survivor asked, "How are you going to keep desperate people away from your valuable stuff?" And Coyote answered very quiet, I could barely hear him. He said, "By any means necessary." Then he said, "Hopefully it won't come down to that, but..." (I couldn't hear the rest.)

Urban Survivor said it was important that the surviving humans be the ones with the right ideas about how to start over. "Yeah," said Coyote, "not the morons like Phil."

They both laughed! I thought it was very mean to say that about Phil who has two cute children. I snuck away then because I was afraid I was going to start arguing and they would know I was eavesdropping.

What's weird is it's like Coyote is a different person around me than he is around somebody like Urban Survivor. It's like Urban Survivor brings out more of the pessimistic side, versus with me Coyote is more thoughtful. I feel like I know the "real" Coyote. Maybe for some reason he lets himself be his "real" self around me?

It's very late – almost midnight. But I MUST write about what happened tonight after the workshop. I was helping Coyote clean up and prepare things for tomorrow. He said something (I can't remember what it was now) that was very pessimistic. Then something happened to my emotions that was weird and out of my control. It was ANGER that came up and exploded into words that I yelled at Coyote.

I yelled: "It's easy for YOU to abandon the human race because you can afford to. I also think you secretly WANT society to collapse to prove that you're right!"

Then suddenly I was done and then I felt really weird for yelling and I didn't feel very good about myself.

Coyote didn't get mad back; he just looked off into the distance in that way he does for a long time.

Finally he turned to me and said, "I wanted to argue with you but I couldn't. There might be something to what you said. I'll need to think about this."

Then he said something that got me feeling really strange. He said, "I don't know how you do it, Amy. You seem to be able to point out truths to me that nobody else does. Maybe it's because nobody else has the guts to get angry with me."

This seemed like the perfect time to ask him if he'd help me with my intellectual journey. I told him that I felt "stuck." I told him I was discouraged because I want to get to the roots of ecological destruction. But it isn't coming from one place; it's coming from millions of places.

I asked Coyote if there could be a law that everything has to be sustainable. He said he didn't think so because that law would be super complicated. It would affect pretty much everything, and people wouldn't like that because they hate laws and think there are way too many already. And it would take away our freedom of choice, which is the foundation of this country.

For example, could you say it's against the law to drive a car when you could have walked? Could you have a law against "unnecessary driving"? But how would could you say what is "unnecessary"?

He said that when people make their choices they don't choose what's most sustainable; they choose what's most cheap and easy. Then he said, "It's like I've been saying all along, it all comes back to..."

He stopped himself, but I knew what he was going to say. So I yelled out, "Human Greed!" He said he stopped himself from saying it because he felt it was his pessimism coming out and he caught it.

It was late and Coyote had to leave. After he left, I suddenly I got a strange idea. It's weird that I'm a little scared to write it down, since it's only an idea. I thought: What if I was a few years older. Or in other words, about the same age as Coyote. Could I possibly think of him as a potential "boyfriend" or something?

August 22

Day 3, lunch break. Coyote was right, today is the HARD work. The wire mesh had to go on very carefully to cover all the straw. That wasn't too bad. But then we had to mix the stucco and start applying it over all the mesh. That part is HARD WORK. Wet stucco weighs a TON. My arms were getting so tired I kept dropping the spreader tool thing.

While we were working I got an idea. Coyote is always so "serious" so I thought I would try to get him to have fun. It would be a test of my idea that I'm a "good influence" on him. While we were working, I told Coyote - in front of everybody and very loud - "Coyote, I think you smell very 'earthy.'"

(It was hard to not laugh when I said this!)

He got all pretentious and said, "I am of the earth. What else should I smell like?"

I said, "Well, roses are also of the earth, but they smell nice!"

Everybody CRACKED UP! Eventually Coyote even laughed.

My theory of being a "good influence" has been totally proven! I'm starting to feel like I know the mysterious Coyote better than anyone. Maybe I even know him better than he knows himself. That sounds impossible but I know it can be true, because Mom often said the one person in the world we least understand is ourselves. That's amazing to believe, because you'd think we would understand ourselves best because we're around ourselves most of the time.

Another break. I'm TOTALLY EXHAUSTED. The first coat of stucco is almost done, so you can't even tell it's made of straw bales now. It looks more like an adobe home. But alas it is hard for me to appreciate because I'm going through emotional turmoil.

It all started when Krystal started flirting with Coyote. She was smiling at him a lot and saying "Oh really?" every time he said something. And she was making her eyes look all "romantic." And she was touching him a lot and trying to make it look accidental. Accidental on purpose!

But what happened is that I felt totally angry at her - for no reason! She didn't do anything bad to me. It makes no sense. And then Coyote started smiling back at her! And then I started getting angry at Coyote, which makes NO SENSE AT ALL.

I HATE emotions, they're so confusing and illogical. How can I be mad at Coyote because some woman is flirting with him? The only reason I could think would be jealousy, which makes no sense because it's not like he's my boyfriend. Although when that idea occurred to me yesterday it wasn't repelling.

So I kept telling my emotions, "Anger does NOT make sense in this situation. Coyote can flirt with anybody he wants it makes no difference to me." But the more I told my emotions, "Don't be angry," the more angry they got!

Then this violent scene started to happen in my mind. I had super-strength and I knocked Krystal down and kicked her! This was VERY shocking to me since I am committed to non-violence, but to be honest kicking her felt good. What happened next was REALLY weird and I feel weird even writing about it, but in my imagination I started hitting Coyote! I just kept hitting and hitting and he did not hit back or defend himself. What were my emotions trying to tell me???

I think I figured out the answer. I think my emotions are telling my mind to get rid of any silly idea that Coyote could ever be a "boyfriend" or anything. It's very simple: My emotions were mad at such a silly and wrong idea being in my mind. Maybe emotions aren't as stupid as I thought?

The workshop is over. I'm so tired I can hardly move. Right after I help Coyote do some final clean-up things, I 'm going to take a loooong hot bath that will feel SO GOOD. Next weekend Coyote will be back here to check that everything is okay. The main thing to check is that the stucco could crack after it dries, which means we have to do fix the cracks. Then when that's finished I can paint it!

COYOTE GOT HURT! He's mostly OK now. But it was SCARY!!! At first I thought he cut his hand off, there was so much blood! He slipped and fell, and his hand landed in a box of tools and got cut really bad.

My body forgot that it was exhausted and I jumped into action. I said, "I'll get the first aid kit from the house!" He was trying to be all "joking" about it, and said, "Looks like we'll have to amputate, get a saw and a bottle of whiskey." When I came back, he said (in a cowboy accent) "It's just a flesh wound, ma'am. Wrap it up and help me find my horse." But he was pale and not smiling very much.

Why do guys have this thing where they have to pretend they're not hurt?

I ignored the joking and went right to work very professionally because I know it's possible to bleed to death. Or if the wound isn't cleaned right away, there can be an infection that can cause death of the brain. Good thing that because of the GreenKids program I had to take first-aid training!

I wrapped his wrist to slow down the bleeding (but not enough to stop circulation) and put a LOT of antiseptic on the wound. It stung a lot, which had the effect of making Coyote stop joking around like he was a cowboy looking for his horse.

I applied a bandage to the wounded hand, and took Coyote's other hand and put it over the bandage and told him he had to apply firm pressure for 10 minutes. He started to complain in his stupid cowboy voice but I was FIRM and said "10 MINUTES!"

Then he was quiet and looked at me with a shocked look. He probably thought it was weird to have a 14-year-old girl telling him what to do!

OK this is where it gets really hard to write. After the emergency wore off and I was cleaning up his hand, I realized that I'd been touching him a lot. My heart started beating so hard I thought Coyote was going to hear. I actually told my heart "Shut up!" I thought this was just in my mind, but then Coyote said, "But I wasn't saying anything."

It's VERY hard to describe what I was feeling. It was like the air between us was "vibrating" and I didn't feel solid - like my body didn't have any bones. And I felt like I was floating like a balloon even though I checked and I was still on the ground.

I think if this was happening in a movie it would be the part where the people start kissing. And for the first time in my life, the idea of kissing somebody sounded OK and possibly even good. I guess after a while you get used to the idea of having somebody else's spit getting on your face.

But of course this was not a movie and there was no kissing. For one thing, I'm way too young for Coyote. I'm 14 now, and I guess when you're 18 you're considered to be an adult and nobody is in charge of you. When I'm 18, will Coyote still like me? Actually, does he even like me now?

I cannot know, and I cannot afford to think about it too much. The costs are too high. I have a very important destiny to save the earth. That is far more important than kissing. There will be time for that later, after the earth has been saved, and after I get used to the idea of kissing.

Of course I can't tell any of this to anybody (except of course for you, dear diary). Nobody would understand. They would think it's just a silly teenage crush, not something genuine and deep and real.

So this will be my deepest secret. Even though Coyote inspires emotions in my heart and ideas in my mind, I must not let him know what's in either of those places. I must allow him the freedom to flirt with women like Krystal, even if they have poor knowledge of ecology. I must keep my tragic secret to myself. Actually my secret isn't too tragic since nobody is dying or anything like that. But it feels like my secret is at least partly tragic.

August 23

I guess Tiffany meant well, but after the exhausting weekend I really needed to have a quiet day at work. But there were huge posters of the People magazine article all over the place, including People en Español in what she announced was the "HomeEarth Hispanic Division" (my office) which was full of piñatas. She said the piñatas were organic, but I think maybe she was kidding because she also said the balloons were full of organic helium.

Then a guy Philippe showed up with a traditional Mexican-style band. I wasn't sure if Philippe was Tiffany's friend or boyfriend. I asked her, and she said he's a "friend with benefits" which I guess means he works at a company with a good medical plan.

They tried to get me to dance a traditional dance which normally might have been fun, but I tried to explain that I could barely move.

Finally Katherine "saved" me by taking me into her office. Katherine said she is very pleased with the article. She said membership applications are way up. As a result of People en Español, there are a lot of Hispanic memberships. Apparently that's "very significant" since environmental organizations have had a hard time trying to "crack the Hispanic market."

She asked if it would be possible for me to "act a little more Hispanic sometimes," and to maybe mix in some Mexican words "for flavor" when doing public speaking. I think she could tell I was uncomfortable with that idea.

When I got home tonight I discovered that the totally nice neighbor Carol left me a bag of cherry tomatoes and a note:

> *Hi Amy, here are a few cherry tomatoes from my garden. Hey, that was a very "interesting" group of folks that helped you build your shed. A few of us neighbors couldn't figure out why you went through so much trouble to build a shed when you can buy one pre-made from Home Depot. Any-who, enjoy the tomatoes – more to come soon! ~Carol*

This note made me a little ANGRY. (Okay maybe more than "a little.")

A SHED?

It's not a "shed"! It's a demonstration project that's an important part of my mission to save the earth. I need a plan to make people realize how important it is.

Okay, here's my plan:

- Phase 1: Write about it in my blog, including pictures of how it was made.
- Phase 2: Contact newspapers to get them to write articles about it.
- Phase 3: Make it "homey" looking so neighbors don't think it's a shed. I'd like to paint it a nice color because stucco sort of looks like mud.

My muscles are still too tired to start on phase 3 of my plan, but tomorrow I can start on phase 1 & 2.

I'm too tired to even harvest a garden salad to go with Carol's delicious cherry tomatoes.

Online research is about the only thing my poor worn-out body is good for. So I'm finally going to start my research into "internalize the externalities" and see if Deep Ecology is a practical joker.

So... what in heck are "externalities"?

Interesting. I'm finding LOTS of stuff on that topic. Even though I never heard of "externalities," apparently they're a big deal for economists.

Here's a definition: "An externality is a cost of economic activity that is not paid by the individual or organization that profits by the activity." Here are some examples of what that means:

- Coal companies that don't pay all the costs to clean up the toxic waste and the health costs for people who get sick. The health costs from burning coal are $100 billion PER YEAR! And the coal companies pay approximately $0 of that cost.

- Huge corporate farms that don't pay for the cost of eroding soil, or polluting the water with agricultural chemicals, or the health costs of farm workers who get sick from those chemicals.
- Oil companies that don't pay for the costs of acid rain and global warming. Plus the cost of all the wars to protect our oil supply. One study estimated that those externalities cost about $8 per gallon - which is way more than what the gas costs!

In these examples (and a lot more) the companies "externalize" the cost. In other words, they don't pay for it themselves: The cost is "external" to the companies. But somebody has to pay the costs. And that "somebody" is us.

This reminds me of many previous realizations throughout my intellectual journey, all the times when it's not fair to be ecological. For example, my friends John and Linda at Laughing Ladybug farm who have to charge more for organic food that doesn't poison the soil. And this seems to be true for anything recycled or natural, which always seems to be more expensive. Is "externalities" the reason?

Okay... now my BRAIN is tired in addition to my muscles. I'll get back to this later.

August 24

I just read something that seems very related to what I was thinking about last night. It has to do with the cost of destroying the earth.

People don't think that nature has economic value. They think there's no cost for destroying the pattern of life. BUT THAT'S NOT TRUE AT ALL! Nature (the pattern of life) provides all kinds of benefits that we don't even think about because we don't have to pay for them.

But if you think about it (or read the article I just read) it's very clear that the benefits are totally important.

By "benefits" I mean things like: making clean drinkable water, creating fertile soil capable of growing healthy plants, and converting carbon dioxide to oxygen.

But here's what's really interesting: According to the article, some economists figured out the value of those benefits by calculating what it would cost us to create those things artificially. The cost would be 33 TRILLION DOLLARS! So anytime somebody tries to say, "Nature has no value," I can say: "WRONG!"

August 25

I just published an article about my strawbale home on my blog! I sent the link to the Portland Tribune, to the editor of the "Green Living" section.

Katherine wants to make very sure that I don't "burn out," so it's important to limit my appearances to only the most important audiences. I'll be doing the usual HomeEarth presentations, but to bigger audiences. I told Katherine I was fine with that, since they're pretty easy. But I'm excited (and a little nervous) about these two:

- A TV interview on the talk show "The Raul Rodriguez Show." He wants to discuss the question "Should Hispanics Be Green?" This one is coming up very soon. The show is filmed in San Francisco, so this will be my first business trip! Tiffany will go with me as my "assistant."
- I got an invitation to go to the City Club of Portland's "Friday Forum." It's going to be a panel discussion on the question, "Does it pay to be Green?" I'll just be on the panel (I don't have to give a speech). I hope that my intellectual journey (the economic part) has some ideas to share by then.

I heard back from the Tribune editor! She's really excited about publishing an article about my strawbale home! She wants to interview me tomorrow! She wants to do it quick because she thinks it will be a great article, and also they didn't have anything for the "Green Living" section and they're desperate.

I told her my home is not painted yet, but she says that's okay they'll have the graphic artist do Photoshop to add a color that's not like mud. Unfortunately, that means I won't have time to make the inside "homey" in time for the article.

I have to start figuring out how I'm going to furnish my brand-new home. Maybe when Coyote comes to do the final work on the house he'll be okay with using his truck to pick up some stuff with me? (It will also be kind of a "test" to see if he likes spending time with me.)

Stuff I'll need to make my new home homey:

- Candles (lots!). Beeswax, of course, not paraffin because they are petroleum-based. I think there's a place I can get candles made out of organic beeswax. I think they're also made by free-range bees.
- Writing desk, made of actual solid wood - not plywood which is full of awful chemical glues that contribute to bad health effects.
- A big rug, hopefully with a nature design - maybe a big design of the earth. No animal designs out of respect for animals that I wouldn't want to step on. I guess the earth would be okay to step on since I step on it naturally.
- Fabric for curtains. Something pretty but not too fancy. Something earthy as long as it's not too hippie-looking.

August 26

I got interviewed today for the Tribune! It was really fun! The article will be out the day after tomorrow!!!

August 27

I was thinking about what "internalize the externalities" could mean. Here's an idea: Whoever makes money from something that creates an "externality" has to "internalize" it. Or in other words, pay for it themself. Does that make sense?

I've gotten several positive comments on my nature essay blog! One woman said my essay was "perceptive and sensitive." There was a comment from a woman in Washington saying that she's been to Lake Superior, and my essay "captured the essence of the spirit of the lake."

Sometimes I'm not sure how to reply to people. A guy said I must visit Costa Rica. He just flew down there to stay at an eco-resort, and he told me about all the great eco features. But the problem is: Flying to Costa Rica uses up the same amount of gas as driving a car for a year. I mean, it's great that the resort in Costa Rica recycles and uses low-flow water fixtures, but I'm not sure it all balances out to be "ecological."

August 28

The Tribune interview just came out! The interviewer was very good because she made me think of things in a new way, such as how building a strawbale home is important for reasons of freedom and individual liberty (I need to do research to see what "Libertarian" means).

Why did you decide to build such an unusual home?

It's an important part of my mission to save the earth.

How does a home built out of straw help save the earth?

Well, a regular house creates a huge amount of waste and uses lots of energy for heating and air-conditioning. A regular house causes 18 tons of greenhouse gasses every year! My strawbale home uses hardly any resources and it's super-insulated, so it will use hardly any energy.

Are you worried about the Big Bad Wolf huffing and puffing and blowing your house down?

Haha! Not at all, because my eco house is very strong. There are steel cables through the roof right into the ground, so not even a hurricane could blow it away.

What about fire? Aren't you afraid it will burn down?

Everybody asks me that! But the straw is completely sealed by the stucco coating. And even if the coating broke off somehow, straw is almost impossible to light on fire.

That's very surprising!

I want to say how a strawbale home is not just better for the earth, but also better for people.

How so?

Because it's so inexpensive. A regular house costs about $200,000 or a lot more. And my home only cost $2,000. That's 100 times cheaper! I'm only 14 and I have my home paid for. I think it's sad that people have to pay a huge amount of money for 30 years just to afford a home.

Do you think people would want to live in a home like this? A lot of people might think it's like going back to the Stone Age.

That's funny. It's not a stone house; it's a straw house!

I was thinking more about how your home doesn't have a kitchen or bathroom.

My strawbale home could have a small kitchen or bathroom, but it would still be way cheaper than a regular house.

Also, your home is much smaller than what most people would want.

It's possible to make a strawbale home that's bigger, but it's not allowed because of the law.

Do you mean the building codes?

The small size is so that it doesn't have to meet the building codes. If it was any bigger, it would be against the law. Also, I can't officially use it for a home, only for an office.

What you're saying is unbelievable. You're saying that it's actually against the law to build a home that's inexpensive and sustainable.

I think the building codes need to change so people can build any kind of house they want!

It sounds like the building codes are unconstitutional.

If this is a free country then why can't we build our homes any way we want? Why can't we build a home that doesn't cost $200,000?

Amy, do you consider yourself to be a Libertarian?

I guess. I mean, I'm all for liberty.

What do you think the homebuilding industry would think of this idea?

Well, I personally know one homebuilder who likes the idea of inexpensive sustainable homes!

The most fun thing was sitting down with the graphic artist who used Photoshop to help me choose what color to make my home. I decided on a shade of light green. Now I can take the photo to a paint store and say, "Mix me a color exactly like THIS!"

August 29

I found out some very disturbing facts about pesticides and herbicides. It's not just a problem with big farms. It turns out that homeowners use a lot of them on their lawns. Each year, it adds up to 70 MILLION POUNDS!

I think I'm going to turn this into a post on my blog. I bet a lot of people have NO idea they're poisoning the earth when they apply poisons to the earth.

I don't believe it! Anthony Iron quit his job as spokesperson for GloboChem! He left an EVIL company to work for an EVIL lobbying group!

New Face for Economic Group

Boston, Mass. – Earlier today, the lobbying group Citizens for Economic Common Sense announced their new spokesperson. They have hired legendary spokesperson Anthony Iron, until recently the spokesperson for agricultural giant GloboChem.

Anthony Iron has created an extremely lucrative career by representing the most hated and despised corporations in America.

He is pleased to be representing a lobbying group for the first time in his career. "They offered me more money than you could possibly imagine," says Mr. Iron.

The eco home article only came out yesterday but already there are lots of online comments! People really agreed with how a regular home is WAY too expensive, and could NOT believe it's against the law to build an inexpensive home.

One guy asked, "Could I still have my big-screen TV?" I replied, "Of course you could, but why would you want to?"

I just remembered to look up what the word "Libertarian" means. That's not what I am at all! A lot of the Libertarian philosophy sounds like, "I can do anything I want and I don't care about anybody else."

If someone asks me, "Amy, what is your political philosophy?" I don't know what I would say. From what I've seen of politics, the 2 sides mostly argue about how big the government should be. But I haven't heard either side say ANYTHING about our relationship to the process of life that sustains everything on earth including us. Don't they think that's important?

August 30

OK, back to the economic aspect of my intellectual journey.

What if a company that made something had to "internalize the externality"? How would that work?

Let's say it was a huge wasteful industrial farm that was causing pollution and destroying soil fertility. So to "internalize" those costs would mean that the company would be "charged" for them? Such as sending them a bill that says something like, "Please pay $100,000 (I'm just guessing) to clean up the pollution and restore the soil."

How would the cost of the bill be figured out? How could you figure out the cost of the pollution and lost soil fertility? That sounds practically impossible. And a bill would have to be sent to every single farm, which sounds way too complicated.

I don't know if "charging" a company would work. But how else could a company "internalize" the cost?

Could the cost be "internalized" some other way? How about by the people who buy the stuff from the farm? They would have to pay extra somehow. How could that be possible?

What about adding to the price of what the company charges? I guess that would be sort of like a sales tax. But instead of a sales tax it would be a "sustainability tax" (Or something like that). Would that make things sustainable?

Let's say a bag of industrial farm carrots cost $3. But let's say we figured out that the "externalities" come to $1 per bag. So the bag of carrots includes an added "sustainability tax" of $1. So now the carrots cost $4 a bag.

Let's say a bag of carrots from Laughing Ladybug costs $4. Since their carrots are sustainable and organic, they have no "externalities." Therefore their carrots have no "sustainability tax" - so their carrots are still $4.

Now the price is the same. So when people are comparing the carrots in the store, they have two choices:

For $4 they can buy evil carrots from a huge industrial farm that hates the earth and is destroying the environment, or for $4 they can buy good carrots from a friendly local farm that loves the earth.

So people would buy more carrots from Laughing Ladybug and local organic farms like them. The big industrial farms would have to change to be more sustainable. Or else they would go out of business very fast!

This is kind of an interesting idea. It could apply to everything grown on farms. Actually, it could apply to other kinds of things.

Such as my diary. My beautiful diary is made out of the most sustainable paper in the world. It sure cost a lot though. But I couldn't imagine writing in a diary made with paper from a forest cut unsustainably and made in a polluting paper mill like the one I saw in Canada. How could I write about my love of nature on paper that was made by hating nature?

But the sustainable paper is expensive because other kinds of paper don't pay the cost of unsustainable forestry and paper mill pollution.

But if that kind of paper had a "sustainability tax" to pay for all that, then it would cost more and NOBODY would buy that kind of paper. Unless they were really stupid or crazy and had lots of money to waste.

In my research about externalities, I found out that burning coal in old power plants to make $1 in electricity results in $1.20 in health cost. So if the old coal-burning plants had to "internalize the externalities," there would be a "sustainability tax" of $1.20, so now the electricity would cost $2.20.

That means green energy options such as wind and solar would actually be cheaper! So naturally people would want to pay less AND save the earth.

Could this idea be used for EVERYTHING?

I just thought of another example. It seems like practically everything is made out of plastic – which of course is bad because plastic is made out of oil. But it's possible to make plastic out of natural ingredients, such as soybeans. But we don't because it's much cheaper from oil. But it's only cheaper because oil probably has more externalities than anything on earth.

But what if there was a "sustainability tax" on things made from oil-based plastic? The price would go way up, and it would become cheaper to make things of plastic made from soybeans.

This idea seems really great. Who could possibly be against it?

Actually, I'm thinking that the unsustainable companies would be against it. For example, the big industrial farm would probably say something like, "It's not fair that our product gets taxed more!" But this isn't true at all. It's the big industrial farm that hasn't been playing fair. They've been cheating by NOT paying to clean up the damage they cause.

And besides, big companies aren't the boss of us; we're the boss of them. I learned this in school. Even though some companies are big and powerful, we're a democracy which means the people are the boss.

I wonder if my idea makes any sense. Would it work?

Coyote will be here tomorrow, so I'll see what he thinks about it. He's very intelligent, and will probably know reasons that it won't work. But that's good, because then I won't be embarrassed by sharing it with other people. When I tell him I'll act all casual, like it's not a huge big deal or anything.

I definitely want to give Doug Normalson a tour of my eco home. He'll probably want to be in disguise, though. I'm going to send him an email with links to my blog and the Tribune article.

August 31

Coyote agreed to take me shopping. But he wasn't crazy about the idea, and didn't have fun shopping with me. He also had to do some shopping, and going shopping with him led me to the discovery that the feeling is mutual.

I used to think that Coyote was different than other guys, BUT HE IS JUST LIKE EVERY OTHER MAN. Not that I've known a lot of "men" but he's like Dad for sure. He hates shopping, unless it's for HIS stuff. For example, he took practically half an hour to decide on what kind of saw blade to buy, but when I was trying to decide on curtain fabric he got restless after only 3 hours. A saw blade is just a piece of metal that cuts wood. But a curtain is a vital part of my home décor that will affect my mood every day of my life. How can I love my home if I hate my curtains?

So the day hasn't been totally pleasant but at least we both got our shopping done. And I'm mature enough to realize that all couples don't get along 100% perfectly all the time, and even though Coyote and I aren't exactly a "couple" we did spend the day shopping together.

One place he had to go was Andy & Bax, the military surplus store. I didn't want to go inside because I'm anti-war. He said that he's anti-war too, but military gear is extremely tough and long-lasting which will be very important in post-collapse society.

He's still stuck on all these "social collapse" ideas. Wait until I tell him my idea that will save the earth, and then his ideas will sound silly. Unless my idea won't work.

I decided to stay here in the truck and catch up with my diary while Coyote is buying whatever it is he's buying. All he would tell me is it has something to do with "defending the perimeter."

Very late, just a quick note before bed. After all the shopping, we had to fix a few small cracks in the stucco. Then we painted it the beautiful light green color. I can't sleep in my new home tonight because the paint needs to dry. I'm off to the last night in my old room, and Coyote is off to his "temporary lair." I convinced him to come by for breakfast tomorrow because I had something important to tell him. He said, "As long as we don't have to do any more shopping." I hope he wasn't implying that I'm not fun to go shopping with, because I would say HE is not exactly outstanding in that department.

September 1

Coyote just left to go back to EarthSage and I want to write everything right away before I forget. What an AMAZING conversation. I think it was maybe a life-changing conversation.

I started off trying to be very casual, so I said, "Oh, by the way I have an idea that maybe gets to the root of environmental destruction by making the economy save the earth."

Then he gave me that look of his (which still makes me a little nervous) and said, "Are you kidding around? Because you would be bursting with enthusiasm if you were serious." I said, "OK, you got me! I've been going crazy not telling you, so ready or not here's my idea!"

I told him all the stuff I learned about externalities, and about my idea of how to internalize them with a "sustainability tax." The only problem was I had lots of enthusiasm about the idea, but not much organization of it. But since Coyote is very intelligent he was able to figure it out. I guess I was starting to repeat things, which is when he stopped me. He said, "I've got it. Give me a minute to think about it."

Then he was quiet for a long time but I could tell by his expression that he was thinking very hard. It seemed as if a lot of intelligence was happening in his mind.

Finally he asked me, "Amy, are you aware that economists have been wrestling with the problem of externalities for hundreds of years?"

I said, "Of course! Isn't everybody aware of that?" which I admit was kind of a "show off" thing to say since I didn't know it until two days ago. Then he got quiet again and went back to thinking.

I said, "Are you trying to think of a way to tell me that it won't work?" He said no, he had been trying to think of a reason it wouldn't work but he couldn't find any. He said he was "dumbfounded" that a 14-year-old girl could figure out something that had stumped the world's leading economists.

He said the best thing about the idea is how it targeted exactly the source of the problem in the one place that could change everything. He said that a basic design principle is to "make the smallest change for the maximum effect," and this was exactly what my idea does.

He said that asking people to pay more for sustainable options doesn't work very well. Anything that counts on people saving the earth "voluntarily" doesn't work, because most people will say, "I can't afford it" (even when they actually can but they just don't want to).

This made me think of all the presentations where I told people they should use re-usable coffee cozies. But even though that's a pretty small change, only some of the people used them.

And he said that trying to regulate companies with laws doesn't work very well. The laws have to be super-complicated, and it's hard to enforce them. A lot of companies just break the law. And even if you catch them, their lawyers will tie everything up in court forever. They'll say, "You can't prove it's our mess." So the government has to spend tons of money trying to prove it, and maybe the government finally proves it, but the company just goes bankrupt and says, "Ha ha, you can't sue us now!" (But they would probably say it in legal terms.)

Coyote said he likes that we wouldn't be telling companies they HAVE to be sustainable. But if they CHOOSE to be more sustainable, then their prices will be less. And that means people will choose their product. That means companies will WANT to be sustainable. They might even compete to be more sustainable!

Coyote said that the way it is now, companies can't afford to be sustainable. It's not the companies fault, because they're punished for being sustainable and rewarded for being unsustainable.

It's like I thought before, how everything was "backwards." But this idea would fix that. Companies would be rewarded for doing the right thing.

Then Coyote said, "I think the basic plan might work, but there would be a lot of details to work out."

He said that figuring out the sustainability tax would be very complicated. For example, a lot of companies put pollution into the atmosphere and it all gets mixed together and goes all over the place. So how could you sort out which company was responsible for what damage?

But he said a bigger problem was that some costs that would be impossible to figure out. For example, how could you figure the cost of losing biodiversity? How could you figure out the cost of losing medicinal plants that go extinct before we're able to discover them?

I said, "Oh no, my plan won't work!" But he said don't be discouraged, all new ideas need time to figure out.

So he sat there and thought for a long time. Finally, he said that the name "sustainability tax" gave him an idea. He said if the goal is sustainability, then set the price for that. He said it this would be easier, and also more effective and practical. I said it sounded great, but what did it mean?

He said that it would be something like the example I told him about a bag of carrots. He said that rather than try to figure out all the external costs of the non-organic carrots, just compare the cost to a bag of organic local carrots farmed sustainably. Then make the tax so the non-sustainable carrots are a little more. "That gets right to the point," he said.

And do the same not just with carrots, but with everything. Make the cost of the sustainable option a little less with every single thing.

That reminded me of another good thing about this idea. People wouldn't have to "sacrifice" by paying more for what saves the earth, because the sustainable choice would cost less. I thought of this because Katherine is always saying to NOT using the word "sacrifice."

Coyote said that wasn't exactly right. He said, "It doesn't mean the price of sustainable options would go down. It means the price of unsustainable options would go up."

I said, "Won't we save money in other ways? For example, we won't have to pay for the externalities such as health costs or cleaning up pollution. Won't everything sort of balance out?"

Coyote wasn't sure if it would totally balance out. He thought it would be pretty complicated to figure out.

Then he said thought of another problem: What about people that have very little money? A lot of people make barely enough money to survive, and what if suddenly the price of everything went up?

This was something I hadn't thought about at all. But he was right: It wouldn't be fair for poor people to sacrifice the most.

Coyote asked me, "Where would the money made by the sustainability tax go?" I had no idea. It was something else I didn't think about.

I said, "Couldn't it go to the poorest people?" And he said, "Of course. There could be a tax deduction. Or better, a monthly dividend."

I told Coyote I wished there was a way people didn't need so much money. It shouldn't be that saving the earth feels like a "sacrifice" - economically speaking. That's something I will put 100% of my brainpower to work on. Or maybe 90% of my brainpower, because I also need my brain for other things!

Then Coyote had to leave to get back to EarthSage. I said, "If my idea works, that means you won't need to prepare for social collapse and defend the perimeter." He said, "Do you think there's any chance this could actually be put into effect? It would be a huge political undertaking." I said, "Well you could run for president and make it happen."

After he stopped laughing, he said, "Can you imagine a picture of me on a campaign poster?" I imagined Coyote wearing a loincloth, and decided he had a good point. Plus I couldn't imagine people voting for somebody named after an animal.

He said maybe I should run for president! But of course I'm way too young. But I told him that I have some "political connections" with a United States congressperson!

September 4

Katherine wants me to edit my blog post about lawn chemicals. She thought I put too much blame on the people who apply the poisons. She thinks I should write about how the chemical companies fool us with deceptive labels, and how the government regulations need to be stronger, and how the banks encourage us to use chemicals that kill dandelions because they bring down property values.

I kind of see her point, except I'm not sure about the connection between banks and dandelions.

But still, it seems to me that nobody is "forcing" people to buy the chemicals and put them on their lawn. And even though the products are called things like "Happy Grow," if you look at the ingredients it's very obvious that they're poison.

Doug Normalson said he's VERY interested about my eco home and would LOVE a tour! I asked him what kind of disguise he'll be wearing. He said he's been working on his "courage issues" and is willing to look at an eco-home without a disguise.

In the last email I said I was working on a simple change to the economy that will save the earth. I guess he was curious, so he asked me what it was. Since he's a successful businessperson, I wonder what he'll think of a sustainability tax.

Tomorrow is my interview on "The Raul Rodriguez Show"! That really snuck up on me. Weird that I could almost forget about appearing on a TV show. I don't feel very prepared, but for some reason I don't feel very nervous. Tiffany said it's because I have "accepted my destiny."

Tonight I'll be sleeping in my brand new STRAWBALE HOME!

September 5

Very late. We (me and Dad) just watched "The Raul Rodriguez Show." They recorded the show earlier today - around lunchtime. It's funny that they "pretend" it's nighttime with the fake background outside of a window, like it's the city at night when really it's sunny outside.

Tiffany and I had to be to the airport very early. Since we had an expense account, Tiffany had many drinks in a variety of colors in the airport bar. And also on the airplane. And also when we got off the airplane. The funny thing is that she was supposed to be my assistant, but actually it was more like I was assisting HER with getting cabs and being on time.

Then right after the show it was back to the airport and back to Portland to watch the show. I don't know any other way to describe the experience except it was

REALLY

REALLY

WEIRD!!!

I guess the show went OK. The audience laughed a lot, which I guess is what they want. I'm starting to realize that on TV talk shows they don't want you to be very "thoughtful" or "serious." That's frustrating, because I have a message that requires people to be both of those things.

After the introduction about my activism successes and appearing in People en Español, the audience cheered and I felt like they really liked me! But then the host (Raul Rodriguez) said, "We're here today to talk to Ms. Johnson-Martinez about why Hispanics should be ecological." But when he asked me he made it into a joke. He said, "So Amy, do you think brown people should be green?" (Which made the audience laugh a little.)

I started saying something about how it doesn't matter what color our skin is, because we all need fresh air and clean water and healthy food. But the audience stopped laughing and looked bored. This made Raul Rodriguez very nervous, so he made another joke.

I had some ideas of things to talk about because of what I wrote in my diary when the article in People en Español came out.

I said that I kind of understood why Hispanics might sort of "resist" nature because of their history of being used for agricultural work. I said that makes me very sad, because I hardly ever see Hispanic people going camping or hiking.

Then I turned to the audience and said, "This planet is very beautiful and it's totally worth saving!" and the audience clapped.

But I guess it had been too long between funny things, so Raul Rodriguez made a joke about maybe he'll go camping as long as he can move his townhouse to the campground.

Then he can look at nature while sitting in his hot tub drinking Sangria. (The audience laughed a little more this time.)

The best part of the show was during the audience questions, because there was a conversation that included thoughtfulness.

A guy said, "I don't think it's cool to be environmental."

I said to him, "Oh really? Who is telling you that?"

This sort of stopped him, because obviously he hadn't thought about it. I think he didn't expect me to engage his mind.

So he just said something about on TV shows the "cool Hispanics" were never environmental. I pointed out that these shows are paid for by commercials made by huge multinational companies that don't care about the environment. They want to make money from Hispanics, so of course they want Hispanics to think it's "cool" to buy more things and destroy the earth just like everybody else.

Then it seemed like he "got it" because he said, "So you're saying that being environmental is like giving the finger to the man." And I said, "Exactly!" And he said, "Well just 'cause 'the man' shows me some product on TV doesn't mean I have to support 'the man' by buying it."

I don't think Raul Rodriguez was super-excited about this conversation. At this point he said, "We'll be right back after a commercial break," and he didn't look very happy.

Dad very patiently let me finish writing in my journal about the show, and then he said, "I want you to know I'm very proud of you." He said that he was sorry for not always being supportive and for being so busy all the time.

He said his little girl was growing up so fast and would soon be a woman and someday another man would take me away from him. And of course I told him that NOBODY will EVER take me away from him. I said that I have no desire to live anyplace else. I said that now I'm a homeowner,

I've set down roots! That made him laugh and he give me a big hug.

It is VERY LATE. I'm getting settled in bed for the 2nd night in my new home! (I'm writing by the light of organic beeswax candles!) My first night's sleep was very peaceful and comforting. I felt like a bird sleeping in a nest. That's probably because my home is made of straw, like birds makes nests out of.

If my home was made of paper, would I feel like a paper wasp?

September 6

I'm starting to have questions about the value of my activism. I was thinking about the "proper tire inflation" thing. Yes, we could save 1.25 billion gallons of gas per year, which sounds like a lot. But I found out that every year we use 142 billion gallons of gas. Even if everybody drove with proper tire pressure, we would be saving only 1 percent.

Same thing with the re-usable coffee cozies. I know for sure they're saving paper. But it's hardly anything compared to how much is being wasted.

But any savings is good, right? Shouldn't I be happy at any good news, even if it seems tiny? Am I greedy for wanting more? But if those are the only things we do, then how can the earth have a chance against being destroyed?

It's funny: I feel like I've "evolved" so much in my intellectual journey. I still see the value of things like re-usable coffee cozies, but another part of me is realizing that the changes need to be much deeper.

It feels like I have two "selves": The HomeEarth spokesperson, and the radical thinker. I wonder if the two "selves" will somehow merge together? I think maybe they'll have to, somehow, to succeed in my mission to save the earth.

Doug Normalson came by and he was only slightly paranoid. I was so excited to show him my eco home, especially now that it's all pretty with beautiful curtains and a vase of flowers picked from my very own garden.

But he seemed very "distracted," so I said, "Don't you like my eco home?"

He said, "We must discuss economics, because if you're right then building eco homes would be profitable and I can end the pain of living a lie."

I suppose that's important, but I felt a little sad that he wasn't more excited about my eco home.

All he wanted to talk about was the idea of a sustainability tax. He said he is "uniquely qualified" to comment on the idea, because he's a businessperson who is also an environmentalist (but still in the closet).

He said he knows a few other people in the building industry similar to him, but it's kind of a "secret club." He said the first rule of the club is that there is no club. But at a meeting of this club that doesn't exist, he shared the ideas and everybody was really excited about them. They think maybe it gets to the roots of environmental destruction.

Of course this makes me VERY EXCITED because that's EXACTLY what I wanted to do!!!

I asked if he thought businesspeople would like the idea. He said, "Oh at first they'll whine and complain." He said that they're kind of like grown-up crybabies, and that real babies are actually much better at adapting to change.

He said that businesspeople will probably react by saying "WE CAN'T AFFORD IT!" He said that happens in his business every time there's a new regulation, such as when they had to follow laws for the ADA (Americans with Disabilities Act). It meant more cost because public buildings had to be handicap-accessible. But now builders aren't mad about it, they just accept the extra cost as "part of doing business." Since everybody has to do absorb the same cost, it's a "level playing field."

He also said that businesspeople will go along with anything as long as it isn't socialism. He said if the choice comes down to "socialism versus anything," they'll always choose "anything."

He said it would be very important for businesspeople to realize that this preserves the free-enterprise system. He said it actually makes it MORE free, because there would be less need for laws and regulations.

I told him, "Because you're a businessperson you could help convince other businesspeople!" He got excited and said, "You really think so?" and I said, "Of course!" All you have to do come out as an environmentalist."

Then suddenly he got very UN-excited.

He said such an idea would never work without political support. So I asked, "If there was political support, would you be willing to help promote the idea? Because I happen to know a United States congressperson who wants to solve the roots of environmental destruction and save the earth."

He said, "Really?" and I said, "Really!"

He got a very worried look on his face. He said he has to think about his wife and family, and also the workers who depend on him. He said he would need to see that there was some chance of success before he would be willing to "go public."

So my next step is to contact Representative Bozzio to share these ideas.

September 7

Representative Bozzio is very interested in my economic ideas! We had a long "lunch conference" at a Mexican restaurant that's famous for its organic burritos.

His intern Montia was here to take notes. We were talking like CRAZY and he told Montia to write down everything. Later she'll organize it so it made sense, so he can present my ideas to Congress. I don't believe it!

He wants to present...

my ideas...

to Congress!!!

I have to admit, dear diary, that there were times when Representative Bozzio acted kind of "unusual." One time he stopped talking and looked at his hands and moved his fingers like he was amazed at how his mind could make his fingers move. I guess that's kind of amazing, but I thought it would be better to be amazed at another time since we were having an important discussion about how to save the earth.

But then I remembered Katherine told me that he's a part-time genius, when he's not acting crazy. But when you see the crazy part, it's hard to believe that a genius part can also be in there.

He said the idea of a sustainability tax solves problems that were driving him crazy. He said that it makes sense to tax "bad" things and not "good" things, but we've been doing the opposite. He said that in many cases we're taxing "good" things and subsidizing "bad" things. He said one example is that the U.S. Government pays $500 billion per year (!!!) to subsidize fossil fuels.

He said there are LOTS of subsidies for all kinds of bad (unsustainable) things such as industrial agriculture and big drug companies and over-harvesting the forest. He said the public is not aware of how much money we could save if we stopped giving tax breaks for companies doing things that make messes that we also have to pay to clean up.

He said that taxes are BACKWARDS because we put the most tax on things we should want to encourage (such as income) and put the least tax (or even NO tax) on things we should want to discourage (such as waste and pollution).

He said the idea of a sustainability tax puts government and business in the roles that they are the best for. I said I didn't understand, so he explained that free-enterprise (business) is the best at setting prices. He said the Soviet Union's attempt at communism is the perfect example that the government is not suited for that (because it collapsed). So it's best for the government to let business figure that out.

BUT he said that government can't forget its role to make sure the market is a positive force for good, and not a negative force destroying people's lives.

"And destroying the earth!" I added.

He told Montia, "Write that sucker down!"

He said a sustainability tax not only makes the economy sustainable, but also makes it more fair and honest. In fact, he wasn't sure if "sustainability tax" was the best thing to call it. He said calling it the right thing is very important for "marketing" because you have to "sell" the idea to voters. He thought maybe it should be called the "internalizing the externalities to make the economy fair and honest and create a sustainable society and save the earth tax."

I told him that was kind of long and maybe hard to remember. Then I asked, "Do you mean that it makes the economy more truthful?"

Representative Bozzio shouted out, "YES!" and fell over. But while he was down there (on the floor) he kept talking. He said, "It's about getting the market to tell the truth!"

He said that economists think of externalities as "market failures." He said that's because the free market doesn't work right without accurate information, and externalities are a form of "mis-information." He said a sustainability tax corrects the most important mis-information about the market, which is that destroying the environment has no costs.

I asked Montia if we should help him off the floor, and she said, "Never stop Representative Bozzio when he's on a roll."

"Actually," he said, "the Republicans - the so-called 'conservatives' - should be the most supportive of this."

He was quiet then, so Montia asked him (with a bored expression) "Why is that, sir?" and he answered (very excited and very loud) "Because they claim the free-market is the answer to everything! So they should do everything they can to eliminate failures in the free-market."

While he was still down there the waiter came by and said, "Would you like anything, sir?" and Representative Bozzio yelled out, "Unemployment!" That made the waiter confused, and he said, "I don't believe that's on the menu."

Montia told me, "He does this when he's on a roll. His mind jumps 10 steps ahead." Then she said to him, "Sir, can you go into a little more detail about what led you to that conclusion?"

Then suddenly he jumped up, which scared me a little and made a waitress drop a plate of drinks.

He said, "This is huge!"

I said, "Are you talking about the burrito?"

(Because our burritos had just arrived and they were very large).

He said, "No, I realized that this plan might solve the unemployment problem. But you're right that they don't skimp on the size of the burritos here."

Then he said, "Burritos are the ideal food!" and held his burrito up in the air to demonstrate. Then he started saying something about how in Portland you can't get a "real" burrito, not like you can in Baja, He said he likes to visit Baja, and had an especially amazing trip there last year, and started telling us all about it.

But then Montia seemed to be getting frustrated. She said (actually, yelled) "WHAT ABOUT UNEMPLOYMENT?"

Representative Bozzio said, "I'm against it." Then for some reason Montia's pen broke in half.

I said to him, "I think what Montia means is: What's the connection between the sustainability tax and unemployment?"

Then he put down his burrito (he was still holding it in the air) and explained that he read a study about how environmental businesses create a lot more jobs than un-environmental businesses.

He said a perfect example was the logging industry. He said logging companies do clearcutting because it's the cheapest way to do it. But the sustainability tax would encourage selective harvesting which creates a lot more jobs.

He said this was true in every kind of business. I said, "Just like with farming! Local organic farming takes a lot more workers than huge industrial farms!" Before Representative Bozzio could say anything to Montia, she said, "Got it."

He said that businesspeople oppose his environmental legislation because they say it will "cost jobs." But if they said that about the sustainability tax, he could say, "Oh yeah?" But more professionally, of course.

Then he picked up the burrito again and said (to the burrito) "If everybody was organic and sustainable like you, it would end unemployment!"

Maybe this was possibly kind of strange looking, but people didn't really care. It's good that Portland has the motto of "Keep Portland Weird" because all kind of behavior is acceptable here that in other places would keep you from getting elected as a representative in the U.S. Congress.

I asked Representative Bozzio if he was going to eat his burrito. I was concerned because he'd been making extravagant gestures, and the burrito was starting to spill some fillings. I was afraid the whole thing would sort of "explode" all over the place.

Then Montia said, "Hey wait a minute, won't an 'unsustainability tax' mean that prices will go up?" I shared all the stuff that I figured out with Coyote, about how there will be money saved by avoiding externalities and how over time prices will sort of "equalize." I also shared our idea that money raised by the tax would go back to poor people.

Representative Bozzio said, "That's so brilliant I might explode!" (But I was more worried about his burrito exploding.)

Then he announced, "WE NEED TO DEFINE THE PLAN!"

This is when his burrito exploded. It was a MESS. But he didn't even notice, and Montia and I were too busy helping define the plan. Poor Montia was writing like crazy trying to keep up.

Representative Bozzio got very "serious" and finally I was starting to see the genius side of him.

He said the key change would be a radical change to the Internal Revenue Service. It was so radical that we would need to change the name to indicate a totally new philosophy. He asked what we thought of calling it the "Sustainable Revenue Service."

I said, "That's brilliant!"

He said the main role of the IRS was charging income tax, but that would change because at first the sustainability tax would bring in so much money that we could eliminate income tax. No more income tax!

I said, "That will sure help the plan be marketable!"

"Yes," he said, "But we have to consider the long-term." He was being totally serious now. I couldn't believe this was the same person who was recently talking to a burrito.

He said that at first there would be lots of money from the sustainability tax, but as businesses became sustainable that money would go down. So we need to figure out other ways that the plan would reduce costs. This is what we figured out:

- Corporate subsidies - ELIMINATED
- Unemployment Insurance - Cut WAY down since the plan would result in lots of jobs
- Medicare & Medicaid - Will STEADILY REDUCE over time because the plan will reduce environmental-related illness and lead to healthier lifestyles
- Military - REDUCED BY 90%

We had an interesting discussion about that last one. He said the huge reduction was because most of our wars are over oil. But this plan will encourage sustainable energy and eliminate our need to import foreign oil.

Finally he stopped talking and Montia stopped writing. It was very quiet and this is when it felt like a historic moment.

Representative Bozzio said, "Montia, please organize all that into a bill I can present in Congress," then he sort of went "back to normal" (which means "not normal").

He got a confused expression on his face and said, "What happened to my burrito?" Montia sort of gestured around at what was left of it. He said, "Oh, that's why I'm still hungry. I better order another one." Then Montia said, "There's no time, we have to be at the airport in less than an hour." He said, "We do?" And then suddenly they were gone.

He wants to introduce the bill into Congress NEXT WEEK. I said, "So soon? Shouldn't we think about it more to make sure everything is right?" He said if we have ideas later we can just add them to the bill as an amendment. He said he does that all the time.

What a strange feeling I'm feeling right now! I know all of this happened, but it doesn't seem real.

September 8

I just got a letter from an editor at HarperCollins! They saw my essay "Cycles Within Cycles" on my blog. They want to do a book of my essays! They think it would be a "beautiful and inspirational book" and would be "highly marketable."

The letter said that if I would be interested in discussing such a project, please contact them at my earliest convenience. My earliest convenience was that exact moment, so I emailed the editor and said, "After careful consideration, my reply is YES OF COURSE!" I can't wait to tell Dad when he gets home from work tonight!

Dad can't believe that I'll be publishing a book so young. He said that he's very proud of me. But it got awkward when he asked me how much money I would get.

Oops! (I always forget about the money part of things.) He said I need to contact the publisher ASAP and get an offer in writing that he can look at. He said he doesn't know anything about publishing, but a co-worker friend has a wife who writes children's books and he'll have her look it over.

I met a family of "Northies" today. The dad asked if I could spare a full time job with benefits. I said I didn't have any, but I DID have a bag of organic fruit I just got from the farmers market. I said, "Here environmental refugees, have these delicious organic locally-grown strawberries and blueberries." They said they preferred "real" food, which means it comes in a box. They asked if I could spare some money to replace the son's electronic game that broke when he hit his sister with it. After I told them I didn't have any money left after shopping, they took the strawberries and blueberries. While I was walking away I heard the mom say, "Maybe we could sell this stuff?"

I felt very sad for this family. I don't think they have any idea they are environmental refugees, or that the solution to their problems is to create a sustainable society.

I'm working on my first project in my new eco home: Going through all my old writings to find the best ones to submit for my book. (MY book, I can't believe I just wrote that!)

September 9

I want to sort of "test" what people would think of the economic ideas I created with Representative Bozzio. So I'm going to write a sort of "preview" in my blog:

> Dear Blog Readers, I have a question for you: If whenever you bought something the sustainable option was always cheaper than the unsustainable option, would that be a good thing? Would you support congressional legislation to make it be that way? Would you think the representative that introduced legislation like that was a genius or crazy?

Wow, the response to my blog post was amazing! A lot of people said things like, "Is that really possible?" I replied back, "Keep your eyes open for some big news very soon!"

Katherine said she needed to have a discussion with me about my blog. I guess I sort of forgot to have her approve it. So I explained to her that I was creating legislation with Representative Bozzio to be introduced next week that will go to the roots of environmental destruction and save the earth. She seemed surprised.

She told me she's "concerned" that I'm going "off-topic" into economics. I couldn't believe it!

She said, "If the plan turns out to be wrong it could seriously damage HomeEarth's reputation." I said back,

"If the plan turns out to be RIGHT it could save the earth!" Then she said, "OK then, tell me about this amazing plan."

After I explained, she said it sounded interesting, but she wasn't qualified to know if it would work. I argued, "But Representative Bozzio helped create the plan!"

Katherine asked me, "Which part of him, the genius or the crazy person?" I said that I wasn't sure, but maybe some of both. But definitely more of the genius part.

Then I said Coyote helped create the plan, and he couldn't figure out a reason it wouldn't work. That really got her attention.

She said as soon as she sees the legislation she'll submit it to the HomeEarth board to examine. Until she receives board approval I can NOT comment on the plan as a representative of HomeEarth. I can only be involved as private citizen Amy Johnson-Martinez.

And she told me to contact Coyote immediately and tell him that she wants to meet him ASAP to discuss the plan. She said that she trusts his intelligence.

I warned her that Coyote recently left and he probably doesn't want to visit again so soon. She said that it's important to her, "not just as an employee of HomeEarth, but also as a person." She said it will make a big difference whether HomeEarth supports the plan. She asked me, "You want HomeEarth to support the plan, right?"

Ugh. I just wrote a letter to Coyote and I can just imagine his expression when he reads it. He wants to be a simple Coyote roaming the open spaces of the high desert, but this silly 14-year-old girl keeps saying, "Come back to the crowded noisy city." I explained how it was VERY important to Katherine and I promised it would be the last time I would ask him to visit. I promised NO shopping trips, but a good chance of homemade chocolate chip cookies.

I mailed the letter special next-day delivery. It's so FRUSTRATING that he refuses to have email. But I guess I respect how he's made choices to make his life less crazy even if it drives other people a little crazy sometimes. For example, making them have to pay several dollars to deliver a letter that will take a day, instead of sending an email instantly for no money.

I included what Katherine said about his visit was important to her "as a person," even though I don't understand what she means.

September 10

I just saw the initial "test" version of my presentation "Out of Sight; Out of Mind." It was mostly all computer animation. It showed people doing normal consumer lifestyle stuff, then expanded to the entire earth to show the effects of all these actions added together. It went through the last 200 years to show the effects of industrialism speeded-up, to show how much nature has been lost and how the destruction is happening faster.

It was really amazing how they could show all this. But it was also very emotionally hard to watch because of what it showed.

There were different colors to represent forests and lakes and wetlands and aquifers and glaciers and even soil fertility (the brown color faded to represent declining soil fertility). It used symbols of fish to show declining fish populations. It used black to show the spread of pollution.

It made it very obvious that we are destroying the earth. You could SEE the forests going away, and the wetlands and aquifers shrinking, and the pollution growing, and the deserts expanding. You could also see fossil fuels such as oil and coal (dark brown) depleting, right up to now when it's almost gone.

It felt like it was all leading to an "explosion" or something.

There was even a way to show how species are going extinct. Each time a species disappeared, an image would come up along with words that said, for example, "Passenger Pigeon, gone forever." Then there was a sort of "pop" sound (which honestly I wasn't crazy about). Over time the images came up faster and faster. Katherine said they couldn't use all the animals that have gone extinct because it would have been constant popping.

Katherine said the presentation was shown to a "test audience" to give reviews. Everybody filled out a card, and one of the questions was: "What emotion are you feeling?" The most common boxes checked were the ones for "total despair" and "I want to shoot myself." According to Katherine, those emotions translate to: "Why bother donating to HomeEarth?"

So the presentation is going back with instructions to change it to be less devastating.

September 11

The "Save the Earth Act" was introduced today!!!

FOR IMMEDIATE RELEASE:

Bozzio Introduces Bill to Save Earth

Washington, DC – Rep. Lester Bozzio (D-OR) has introduced the Save the Earth Act which, if passed, would save the earth.

The bill would resolve the roots of environmental destruction by removing the economic incentives that have historically rewarded it. The bill would reverse this by rewarding increased sustainability, thus converting the entire economy from an immense life-killing force to a power for life-enhancing sustainability.

Products and services would be subject to a special sales tax called the "sustainability tax" to the degree they contribute to the destruction of the earth's ecological productivity.

Since this will create a built-in incentive for companies to be sustainable, the government would no longer need to impose costly laws and regulations.

> The tax would have the effect of forcing companies to internalize the external costs (or "externalities") that have previously been paid for by society. Because of this, the "sustainability tax" will be offset by a substantial reduction in Federal income tax.
>
> In addition, citizens will receive a monthly tax rebate check funded by revenue from the tax. The rebate will be calculated on a progressive basis to assist low-income citizens most affected by the tax.
>
> The bill would radically transform the Internal Revenue Service (IRS) into a new role, re-naming it the Sustainable Revenue Service (SRS) to match its new purpose.
>
> Rep. Bozzio credits environmental activist Amy Johnson-Martinez for her critical role in developing this ground-breaking (and earth-saving) legislation. "Thanks, Amy!" says Bozzio.

I can't believe that the ideas we just figured out are actually being considered in the U.S. Congress! It was only last week that we were figuring everything out while Representative Bozzio was spilling his burrito all over. I still feel bad for the waiter who had to clean up the mess.

I hate spending lots of time online, but I'm excited to see the reaction to the press release.

7:25pm - nothing yet.

8:15pm - nothing yet.

WHAT'S GOING ON? THERE WAS JUST A PRESS RELEASE WITH A PLAN TO SAVE THE EARTH, SO WHY ISN'T ANYBODY SAYING ANYTHING ABOUT IT?

9:40pm - nothing yet.

Oh no! I found an article and it's extremely non-positive.

I suppose I should NOT be surprised, since it's from FOX NEWS which basically hates everything that's good.

World-Class Flake Does it Again

By Gregarious J. Profit

The question that comes to mind when considering Oregon Democrat Lester Bozzio is: "How did such a world-class flake get elected to Congress?"

Oh, that's right; it's basic math: Oregon + Democrat = Flake.

What other state would elect a representative who once introduced a bill that would extend rights to animals? As I asked at the time, would that forbid me from using mosquito repellent, since it would interfere with their right to suck my blood?

This was a very appropriate question, since Democrats are always trying to suck our economic life-blood with their job-killing taxes.

And speaking of those job-killing taxes… Bozzio's latest travesty is the "Save the Earth Act." Bozzio wants to take away our freedom and tax us to death to fund his elitist ideas. Of course, this is typical behavior for liberals who won't be satisfied until nobody has any freedom to do anything.

The only environment that matters is the economic environment. Because if we don't sustain a healthy business environment, we'll all be huddled around campfires eating mosquitos. Oh wait: We can't do that because it would be denying their rights!

There's no chance that this ridiculous bill will actually pass. But just to be sure, let's hope and pray to whatever diety we worship, as long as it's the Christian God, that Bozzio's latest bill crashes into the same burning failure pile as most of his previous bills.

This makes me SO ANGRY! I agree with freedom of speech, but does that include the freedom to print LIES?

September 12

I spent the morning online, looking for more responses. I found only a few, and they were not very encouraging.

But all of them were on business websites. It's exactly what Doug Normalson was telling me, that business people are whiners and crybabies.

They care more about business than the earth! The worst thing is that they're getting the facts wrong. Somebody has to tell people the truth! But who?

Why aren't any non-business publications writing about it? Why isn't Representative Bozzio promoting it more? And no environmental group said ANYTHING about it! WEIRD! I wonder if they're all waiting to see what HomeEarth says? Coyote needs to get here SOON to convince Katherine to support it!

I just had an "uh-oh" feeling. I wrote before that somebody has to tell people the truth. But I don't know anybody that is motivated to do that. Except me.

But how ? I can't post about it on my blog, because it's the HomeEarth website. What else could I do?

- Post comments on web articles
- Write editorials and "letters to the editor"
- Write a little booklet and print millions of copies and have them dropped out of airplanes all over the country. Would that be considered to be polluting?
- Ride around on my bike with a sign that says, "Ask me about the Save the Earth Act!"

I just remembered that the Portland City Club economic discussion is coming up very soon! That will be the PERFECT opportunity to publicize the Save the Earth Act!

September 13

My poor garden is getting so neglected! The weeds are going crazy. I'm sorry garden for neglecting you, but I PROMISE I'll take better care of you after the Save the Earth Act is passed.

September 14

The Oregonian published my editorial!!!

Hey Everybody, Let's Save the Earth!

By Amy Johnson-Martinez

Hi everybody! I hope you are well and are enjoying your time on this lovely planet earth. You may know me as the 14-year-old girl who saved Oaks Bottom wetland from destruction.
I met Juvie Starr!

I worked with Representative Lester Bozzio to create a bill called the "Save the Earth Act" which was recently introduced in Congress. You should totally support it! I mean, if you enjoy breathing air and drinking water and eating food. Do you know who provides these services? The earth does! Also it's very beautiful, in the places where it hasn't been destroyed yet.

But I am very sad to say that some people are spreading a lot of non-truths. Such as it will "tax us to death" (It won't!) and it will "kill jobs" (It will actually create jobs!) and it will "bring us back to the Stone Age" (That's ridiculous!).

Basically what the act will do is change the economy so companies make more money by making things that are sustainable and less money by making things that are unsustainable. So making things that are sustainable will do better and make more money and the earth will be saved.

Remember: Saving the earth is very important because if the earth is destroyed you will die. Have a great day and let's save the earth!

There are lots of online comments. None of them are super-positive, but a lot of them at least say the idea is "worth considering." One person wrote, "Is it a good idea to let a teenager set economic policy?" I couldn't resist commenting back, "My age doesn't matter, just look at if the idea makes sense, which it totally does." Someone wrote, "I was in the audience at a presentation you did, and you said all we had to do to save the earth was to buy re-usable coffee cozies." I commented back, "That's one way to save the earth, but another way is to completely change our economic system."

This is great progress, but I could really use some help.

Juvie Starr!!! How could I forget that she said to call her anytime if I needed help??? Well, if I ever needed help in my life it's NOW so I'm calling her right away!

No answer. She's probably on a movie set giving a great performance in another strong female role. So I left a message for her to call me back to help save the earth when she has a few minutes.

I JUST GOT OFF THE PHONE WITH JUVIE STARR!!! She said OF COURSE she remembers me from saving the wetland and how am I doing and I said you would NOT believe how crazy my life is and I saved another wetland and was in People magazine maybe she saw it and I built a home out of straw bales and helped write legislation that will save the earth and that's why I'm calling because I need help and she said to call if I need help and she asked me how my garden was doing and I said there are lots of tomatoes which are very delicious and the sweet corn is almost ready and if she's coming to Portland I'll save her some and the legislation is super important but not being publicized very well and if she publicly supported the bill it would be very helpful and she said it sounds worthwhile but she's very busy because she's in the middle of making a movie but as soon as she's done then she'll get back to me.

JUVIE STARR IS GOING TO GET BACK TO ME!

September 15

I just got a phone call from the Washington Post! They want permission to reprint my editorial from the Oregonian. Of course I said OF COURSE!

Finally a POSITIVE article about the Save the Earth Act! I found it on Huffington Post.

Bozzio Plan will Save Earth

By Mary Berry

Progressive champion Lester Bozzio, the maverick "eccentric genius" of Congress, has introduced his most far-reaching and deeply progressive legislation yet. It promises to do nothing less than resolve the roots of environmental destruction and create a healthy and sustainable world.

The bill, just introduced into Congress, is entitled the "Save the Earth Act." It gets to the roots of environmental destruction by eliminating the age-old problem of "externalities." At present, companies "externalize" the costs of environmental degradation, and therefore are rewarded by increased profit.

Bozzio's bill will make everything vice-versa.

Unsustainable products will be charged an extra "sustainability tax" – a type of "sales tax." Saving the earth will be more profitable for companies, less expensive for consumers, and better for the planet. It's a win-win-win!

The cost of the tax will be compensated by drastic reductions in environmental clean-up costs. It will also lead to the elimination of Federal income taxes.

We need to pass this bill for the sake of our children, so they don't end up living in a polluted environmental wasteland like in the movie "Soylent Green" where dead people are made into food. Sorry for the spoiler if you haven't seen it.

I agree totally 100% completely with everything, except I'm not sure if income tax will be totally eliminated but it will for sure be reduced be a lot. Also, it's not exactly that sustainable things will be "less expensive," they'll actually be the same; it's just the UN-sustainable things will be MORE expensive. I don't know where the reporter got that information - not from me!

STILL waiting for a reply from Coyote! I'm always hearing that guys are going crazy waiting for their girlfriends, but Coyote is WAY worse. Of course, I'm not exactly "officially" his girlfriend.

A reporter called me from the Chicago Tribune! He wanted to know if I would give a comment about the Save the Earth Act, and I said OF COURSE. I asked what part of the bill he would like a comment about, if it was the employment aspect or about taxation or about how the bill gets to the roots of the problem in a way that other approaches don't.

I think he was shocked at the amount of my knowledge and how intelligent it was. He wanted to confirm I was really only 14 because he thought maybe it was a mistake. I asked, "Are you surprised that a 14-year-old girl is intelligent?"

We talked for a long time about the different aspects, including how the Save the Earth Act will reduce market failure. He couldn't believe that I understood what market failure is!

He said that Republicans should be for the act, because it was the Republicans who had the idea for a "carbon tax." He said the Republicans created it as a free-market solution to pollution and global warming. He said that the Save the Earth Act was basically applying that idea to everything.

I said, "I totally agree!" (Later on I'll research "carbon tax" to see what he was talking about.)

I looked at the clock and saw that two hours had gone by! I said, "Hey didn't you call me for a comment?" He said, "I have enough information here for a whole article!"

September 16

More web commenting. I've been web commenting for approximately the last 17 million hours. I am getting VERY TIRED of web commenting.

There is definitely growing support, or at least people thinking, "It's maybe worth discussing."

Three more newspapers want to reprint my editorial!

STILL no reply from Coyote!!! What is he doing that's so important he can't even write back? I even included a return envelope with a stamp on it in case he didn't have any. (The stamp is an image of the earth and underneath I wrote, "Please help me save this planet!")

September 17

The Chicago Tribune article came out! The title is "Not as Crazy as it Sounds" and it gave a very accurate description of the bill. He made me sound so intelligent I didn't believe it was really me that said all those things! It was weird that the article barely mentioned Representative Bozzio.

He wrote, "It might be tempting to automatically reject anything coming from Bozzio, a politician whom some see as 'crazy' yet others see as 'insane.' Yet forget the source of the bill and focus on the content, and you might be surprised to find that the more you think about it, the better it sounds."

He ended the article with, "Could it somehow be possible that a 14-year-old girl created a plan that could save the earth?"

FINALLY a letter from Coyote! He said he had doubts about Katherine's motivation to see him, and wasn't sure if it was REALLY about discussing economic ideas. I don't understand. What else would she be interested in?

But the good news is that he WILL come to Portland (reluctantly) but this will be the FINAL final visit.

He said he wasn't doing it for Katherine; he was doing it for ME! Which is a clear sign that he DOES like me, at least a little, although he doesn't show it or say it. But this is because he's not good at expressing feelings. (Tiffany said it's because, "He's not in touch with his emotional core.")

Katherine requested a meeting, which always makes me nervous. She said she knows I've been spending work time on the Save the Earth Act. I thought I was in trouble, but she said, "It's not a problem. Do you have any idea how much time Tiffany spends on dating websites?" I said I had no idea but I hope she uses the website "EnviroSingles" where people find other people that have environmental values and it wouldn't work to date somebody who doesn't recycle.

She told me she has doubts about the Save the Earth Act because it was introduced by Representative Bozzio. She questions whether he has "a full set of tools in the shed" (I think she means he's crazy). I remembered she told me before that he's part-genius and part-crazy which I thought meant half-and-half. But she said it might be more like 10% and 90%.

She said this is why she hasn't been more encouraging. But the Chicago Tribune article made her think the bill is "legitimate."

But she still needs Coyote's "seal of approval" before she can convince the HomeEarth board to officially endorse it.

September 18

I heard back from the HarperCollins book editor, he said my essays were "completely adequate." He probably meant to say they were "awesome," but editors have to be very professional in their use of words.

Doug Normalson came out of the environmental closet! He did an interview on the TV show "Good Morning Portland" and talked about how he found the courage to end the horrible secret that was tearing apart his soul. He's no longer afraid of other developers pointing at him and calling him the "E" word.

He said, "I must relinquish my hold of the past so I can be a pioneer in the new age of sustainability." I was surprised because he never used to talk like that. I guess there was a poet that was living in the closet along with the environmentalist.

He said the Save the Earth Act gave him hope, which helped give him the courage to come out. He said, "I want to give special thanks to Amy Johnson-Martinez who helped create the act and is working to gain acceptance for ecological homes."

The interviewer was SHOCKED that he thanked me after my activism stopped his development. But he said the loss of that project was a "blessing in disguise." He said it was "the straw that broke the camel's back."

(I must mention that I do NOT like that metaphor because it involves animal cruelty.)

He's going to become an activist! His plan is to start an organization with other environmental developers called "Homes for People and Planet." They're going to work on changing building codes so it's legal to build homes that are in harmony with nature and are affordable.

The interviewer asked him if this change will mean he will make less money. He said, "Oh yes, I'll make much less money, but I'll have the satisfaction of knowing that I have left the world better than when I found it."

He said his wife has begun divorce proceedings. Also he's not sure what his kids think of all this because they won't speak to him.

September 19

TIME magazine did a major story about the Save the Earth Act! Unfortunately I can't print a copy because the printer jammed really bad. Why doesn't it like recycled paper? So I'll just write down some things I thought were VERY interesting:

- At first, most people rejected the act as "just another one of Bozzio's idealistic pipe dreams." But a growing number of influential people are realizing that the ideas "actually make a good amount of sense."
- It helped a LOT that Doug Normalson "broke the ice" by expressing support for the bill, which led a lot of business people to take it seriously.
- A Republican senator expressed "tentative support "for the act, which shocked the Republican Party. He said, "I studied it carefully, and it is not an anti-business bill. It's time for the Republican Party to realize that destroying the environment is not good for business."

The article is really great, except for one part that has me very confused. They interviewed two Democratic politicians who were NOT excited about the act. I thought that was weird. I thought the Democrats were pretty much automatically "for" environmental protection. One of them said, "We're concerned that the loss of tax revenue will threaten a variety of government programs." I don't understand this concern AT ALL! I mean, isn't the idea to make people not need government programs? The Save the Earth Act will help make that happen!

WHERE IN HECK IS COYOTE???

I just realized that the big economic panel discussion at the City Club is TOMORROW! I haven't even started to prepare! I also need to weed the garden. I can't even see where the carrots are anymore!

OH NO!!! I just got a message with details about the panel discussion, including who's going to be on the panel, and one of the panelists will be ANTHONY IRON!!!

Of all the people in the world, why him? Yes, once I was feeling courageous and said I wanted to debate him. But now I would not describe how I'm feeling as "courageous" at all. But he'll be easy on me, right? I mean, I'm just a 14-year-old girl. He wouldn't destroy a 14-year-old girl, would he?

September 20

Is it possible that a life can be over at the young age of 14? Can one continue living after one's dreams have been crushed? Perhaps it is easier to have never had dreams? Or at least to have them at a later age so as to not live so many years with crushed dreams?

Nature has always been my solace during rough times, but I fear that now nature may not be enough. I watched the sunset tonight. But while others probably saw a display of vibrant colorfulness, for me the world holds only the grayness of despair and sadness. "She had such potential" is maybe what people will say of me, if they remember me.

They probably won't though - not after today. Perhaps there will be a vague memory of "that crazy girl who camped in the wetland and had the idea that she could save the earth or something." And then they'll go see a movie and laugh and have fun and have the kind of normal life which is now denied to me forever.

I suppose it was crazy to think a 14-year-old girl could save the earth. It even sounds kind of funny to me now that I think about it, even though I am currently not capable of laughing.

I just remembered the talk with Tiffany, about how she said saving the earth was my "destiny." I guess I just wanted to feel "important" so I let myself believe it.

But don't get TOO down on yourself, Amy. It's important for me to remember that I DID make a difference. I helped to save a wetland. I can still make a difference; I just have to be more realistic. Maybe another word for "realistic" is "mature"? I definitely feel more mature - like I've aged 10 years in one day.

Dad could tell something was wrong. He asked me why I'm so sad tonight because I'm usually never sad. I said I can't really talk right now but there's an article that explains what happened. I gave it to him and said I need to be alone for a while. He said he understands because he's like that, too. Sometimes we don't agree on everything, but when it really comes down to underneath it all, he totally supports me. Thanks Dad, I love you!

Dad gave the article back to me and said very quietly, "Let me know when you're ready to talk."

Thanks for Trying, Amy

The Washington Post

By Paul Zientek

Being a reporter on the DC beat for over 20 years tends to make a person cynical. That's putting it mildly. Reporters generally begin their careers as idealists. But how often can you watch idealism murdered before it starts dying within yourself?

They say that if you scratch a cynic you'll discover a jaded idealist. The idealistic young reporter is still there, underneath the tired and bloodshot eyes caused by too many late nights of gin and bourbon, by too many visits to a seedy whorehouse in doomed attempts at real human connection.

Occasionally, the cynicism melts away, despite everything, by a voice so fresh and pure that it nearly breaks your heart.

For this battered old war-horse, that fresh and pure voice belonged to Amy Johnson-Martinez, a shooting star in the world of environmental activism. The light burned bright and early in this young woman. Only 14 years old, an impulse arose within her, an impulse the rest of us have learned to ignore: "Something isn't right, so I must change it."

For young Amy Johnson-Martinez, that impulse led to her famous "wetland camp" which saved an important wildlife refuge. This led to being hired as the Communications Manager for HomeEarth – becoming the youngest spokesperson in the nation's history.

Amy went on to co-write the Save the Earth Act. The bill was initially ridiculed, mostly due to the bill's introduction by Representative Lester Bozzio (D-OR). I still have vivid memories of Mr. Bozzio subjecting the House to grisly photographs of slaughterhouses in at unsuccessful attempt to make Congress vegetarian.

Yet word spread that the act might actually work. Much of this was due to the efforts of Amy herself, who worked diligently to correct misperceptions.

Which leads us to yesterday's eagerly-anticipated economic discussion at the City Club of Portland's Friday Forum. Amy was on the panel, as was the infamous Anthony Iron – currently the spokesperson for the powerful corporate lobbying group People for Economic Common Sense.

Mr. Iron played softball with Amy. He is experienced enough to know that you don't play hardball with a 14-year-old girl. Especially after she displayed a bowl of tomatoes and said to the audience, "I grew these in my garden and they're delicious! I wish I had enough to share with all of you."

His first question was a misfire, an attempt at mocking humor that fell flat. With his trademark smirk, he said, "I have a question about the sustainability tax. How much would you add to the cost of lumber if the logger bothered a deer?"

The audience didn't laugh, and the question merely allowed Amy an opportunity to give a clear explanation of how the tax would work.

Of course, with someone like Anthony Iron it's impossible to know whether this was a misfire or part of a clever strategy.

His subsequent attempts to mock the act were easily answered, being the type of arguments she has been rebutting for weeks. When he claimed, "You must really hate free-enterprise," she was able to explain how the act would actually improve free-enterprise.

After she had countered all his arguments, he said, "Well Amy, it looks like your plan will help sustain the environment. But will it sustain economic growth? Because all good things come from economic growth."

Amy answered, “That’s only according to that book published by your organization, the one that says economic growth is the solution to all our problems.”

“Ah yes, „Money Fixes Everything.’ I’m so glad you’ve read it.”

“I don’t agree with it at all!” she said.

He replied, “Amy, let’s be honest. It doesn’t really matter whether anything in that book is true or not.”

Rumblings in the auditorium.

“It doesn’t?” answered Amy. “Won’t you get in trouble for saying that?”

“It doesn’t matter whether economic growth solves all our problems,” he said, “because of a simple yet profound truth. We have to have economic growth. If we don’t, the economy will collapse.”

More rumblings in the auditorium. Mild panic from Amy who apparently had not considered this question.

At this point, this reporter got a sinking feeling. The idealist felt a small tremor. The cynic began to wake up.

He asked, “This plan will reduce consumption, is that correct?”

“Yes, but we have to reduce consumption because it’s not sustainable.”

“Well, of course you’re aware of what a reduction in consumption will do to economic growth.”

At this point, Mr. Iron briefly explained economic throughput and the relationship between consumption and economic growth. He explained that a minor reduction in growth causes a recession, and a major reduction in growth causes a depression. And if growth were to stop completely, it would result in a total economic collapse.

It seemed Amy was either having trouble following the logic, or having trouble believing it. She turned to her fellow panelists for support, but all they could do was confirm Mr. Iron’s analysis.

One of the panelists came to Amy’s defense, and put forth the idea that we are now living in an information economy, which is not tied to physical resources. Therefore, growth can continue infinitely without destroying the earth.

Mr. Iron replied, “I’m not enjoying bursting your bubbles tonight, but consider that the information economy is dependent on the resource economy to support it. The information economy didn’t replace the resource economy, it just added another level. Surely you're aware that as the information economy has grown, so has overall consumption."

The panelist turned to Amy and said, "Sorry, I tried to help," then sunk back in his seat.

Then Mr. Iron said to Amy, "That was a nice little idea you had, but since it would lead to economic collapse it probably won't work too well. Nice try, though. Hey, can I try one of those tomatoes? They look delicious."

Amy remained in her chair, in a state of numbed resignation, as other panelists engaged each other with esoteric economic concepts and a battle of PowerPoint presentations.

As for this reporter, the idealist slinked back into hiding as the cynic sneered and said, "I knew it all along." This was a tough loss for the idealist. It was not easy coaxing him out of hiding. After this, I wonder if we'll ever see him again.

But before he is quite gone, he has a message. He wants to say something to Amy Johnson-Martinez, wherever she is. He wants to tell her, "Thanks for trying, Amy."

Dad means well, I guess. He said, "You gave it a good shot. I'm proud of how far you got." I guess Katherine means well, too. She sent me a message that said, "There's still a lot of meaningful work to do at HomeEarth where we're saving the earth in less radical ways."

Am I really defeated? Everybody is thinking I'm defeated and I'm giving up, but I haven't agreed to it yet. It's like they're making up my mind for me, then agreeing with it.

Would Mom want me to give up? But if what they said about economic growth is right, then I have no choice.

I'm going to go by myself to Oaks Bottom and sit in my special place and see if I can figure things out.

I just remembered something. Anthony Iron told me before he didn't want to debate me because he would win, and "if he wins against me he will lose." I didn't think that made sense, and I definitely don't think it does now. I mean, he won and I definitely feel like I'm the one that lost. I guess he lied to me. He said he "never lies" but I guess that was a lie.

I feel so much better. I had an AMAZING experience in the wetland. I was sitting there feeling pretty defeated, like why should I even bother doing anything anymore.

And then suddenly the voice of Mom spoke to me. It was WEIRD. It was so powerful that at first I didn't think it was out of my imagination, I thought she was actually there. But I found if I closed my eyes it seemed real. And we had a sort of "conversation" in my mind.

She said, "Why are you feeling so defeated?" and I said, "Well everybody seems to think I'm defeated." Then she said, "Remember what I told you that one time? 'Nobody can make you feel defeated without your permission.'" I asked, "What about that stuff about economic growth that makes it so my plan won't work?"

Then she went into kind of a speech: "Amy, you are an intelligent young woman and have been through a lot in your young life. In the long run, you'll see that everything you go through is necessary to fulfill your destiny. And you have to go through a lot because saving the earth is a pretty big destiny. Remember: Life never gives us more than we can handle."

Maybe I wasn't defeated. Maybe I just missed something. Maybe the debate just brought out a problem I need to fix before the plan will REALLY save the earth.

But I know one thing for sure: I am NOT giving up!

I VOW TO FIGURE OUT HOW TO SOLVE THE PROBLEM AND FIX THE SAVE THE EARTH ACT. All I have to do is get past the problem of nobody else thinks it can be solved and I have no idea how to solve it.

WHERE IS COYOTE? I could REALLY use his help right now.

September 21

Back to work. Everybody is sort of leaving me alone today. Tiffany got me a big bouquet of flowers, and I don't even care that they're not organic. Katherine told me to take it easy and don't work too hard.

I DON'T BELIEVE IT! I opened the latest issue of HomeEarth magazine and a note fell out. It's another note from Deep Ecology!

> **WHY DIDN'T YOU CONTACT ME AGAIN? I TOLD YOU TO CONTACT ME AGAIN WHEN YOU WERE READY FOR THE SECOND LEVEL OF THE ANSWER.**
>
> **Because you formulated your economic plan without the full answer, it was doomed to fail. Your task was to follow the money to its source. You have not done this because that would have answered the question about economic growth. Your economic plan is valid, but it is missing the final piece that will allow it to save the earth.**
>
> **I can guide you to the answer. However, the answer to this question is extremely powerful and very dangerous. We must take extraordinary precautions.**
>
> **As before, put a "save the earth" flag in the flowerpot next to your office window before 9:00am of the day you wish to meet. We shall meet at 3:00pm by the Willamette River next to the Salmon Street Springs fountain. I shall be disguised as a Scottish bagpiper riding a unicycle. If you feel safe, initiate contact by asking me, "How's the weather up there?"**
>
> **Sincerely,**
> **Deep Ecology**

Oops! I guess I sort of forgot about the "second level," probably because I've been so CRAZY BUSY. I'll meet him tomorrow. He'll be a Scottish bagpiper on a unicycle? Well at least there shouldn't be the problem with his last disguise of figuring out which one he is!

September 22

I can't believe it! There were THREE Scottish bagpipers on unicycles! No other city except Portland would have THREE Scottish bagpipers on unicycles.

When I showed up, the one that was Deep Ecology stopped playing his bagpipes and pedaled over to me (I guess to save me the embarrassment of asking all of them "How's the weather up there?"). He said (in a Scottish accent) "Sorry about that. Who would have thought?" Then he motioned over to the benches by the river where it was less crowded and the bagpipes weren't so loud.

Just like he did last time, he took out a dollar bill and showed it to me. He said, "You still haven't figured out what this is. Your instructions were to follow money to its source."

I said, "Oh, that's obvious. The government prints it."

He laughed! I couldn't believe he laughed at me!

We had to stop then because this weird little kid came up and stared at the bagpipes and said, "Is that an animal?" Then the mother came up and said, "I've never visited Scotland, what's it like?" so to get rid of her Deep Ecology talked in an accent so thick it was impossible to understand. But she kept listening with an expression like she was concentrating REALLY hard. She wouldn't go away, so he started playing the bagpipes and the little kid started crying and finally they left.

Then he continued and said, "Sorry for laughing, but that's a common misperception that's almost totally wrong."

I asked, "So it's a little bit right?"

He said it's complicated, but for one thing printed money is just a TINY amount of the money in the world. He asked me if that made sense. I thought about it, and realized he's right. Most of it is just numbers. For example, you get paid with numbers on a paycheck, and then you bring it to a bank and exchange it for numbers in a checking account. Then you buy things with those numbers.

He said, "Excellent. So then the question is: Where do those numbers come from?"

This is where I got stuck. But I guessed that maybe since the government prints money, maybe they also create the numbers.

He said the government has a limited ability to create "electronic credits" by buying government bonds. He said it's a "tool" that the government can use that's mostly only for economic emergencies.

Economic stuff is very complicated, and I didn't understand a lot of what he said about "liquidity traps" and "quantitative easing." But he said creating money this way is only a temporary solution. And it's risky because it can cause inflation. It also increases government debt. And the debt can only be paid back with more economic growth. He said that's the important question, how the entire economy can grow.

He said that when this country started, the economy was only a few million dollars. Now it's many trillions of dollars. He asked me, "How did that growth happen?" I said, "I don't know," and he said, "Well, you need to find out." I said, "How? I don't even know where to start."

He said he could give me an important clue. He said, "You need to find the answer to the question: How is money introduced?"

Then he said something very mysterious. He said, "If you answer that question, you will also know the answer to the question of how money can grow. Those two questions have the same answer."

I said I didn't understand, but he said he couldn't tell me more. I said I was getting tired of this and it was getting ridiculous. Why couldn't he just tell me?

Then he looked over at the big lawn where people were playing volleyball and said, "How did an antelope get here?" I was shocked, because there shouldn't be any antelopes in Portland. But I looked and couldn't see it, and when I turned around he was GONE! It was just like the last time. It didn't seem possible, but he had totally vanished.

Coyote FINALLY got here! He called me from the Bagdad Pub on Hawthorne and said if I want I can meet him there. He knows it's kind of far to ride my bike (about 5 miles) but it's the only place he knows that serves good microbrew beer and also allows "minors" (ugh).

I won't hurry because I don't want to give him the satisfaction of thinking I would hurry just for him.

(Late, back at home) I hurried over to the Bagdad and I'm pretty sure that Coyote was a little "tipsy" (I think that's the right word). He was staring at a big glass of very dark beer. It looked like a glass of oil. As I was walking over, I saw him say to the beer, "I'm going to miss you." I said, "What are you talking about?"

He didn't even say "Hi Amy" or "I'm glad to see you." He just said, "People take things like a pint of beer for granted, but after the collapse they'll realize what a luxury it really is."

I accused him of talking crazy because of being DRUNK! He just laughed, which might prove he was drunk but might not (I'm obviously not an expert in this area).

Whenever I become a girlfriend I really don't want to become a "nagging" girlfriend. But I thought I had a right to know why Coyote came straight to a bar, and why talking to a glass of beer was apparently more important than talking to me.

Finally he asked me how I was doing. I said to never mind about that because something HUGE came up and it's an emergency situation because a huge problem was discovered with the Save the Earth Act that if don't solve will be the end of the Save the Earth Act and I REALLY NEED his intelligent mind to help me solve it.

I gave him the Washington Post article and said READ THIS. I started talking about how the experience was so horrible and then Coyote told me to stop talking so he could read the article.

I watched his eyes carefully as he was reading. I was looking for signs of emotion, and with Coyote that's very difficult. When he stopped I urged him to please help me figure out a solution or else the earth is DOOMED and so is humanity because our plan to get to the roots of environmental destruction missed something and needs to be fixed so it REALLY get to the roots. But Coyote said he wasn't done reading he was just thinking, so I had to be quiet again.

He was taking FOREVER which was making me crazy, but then my food arrived. I chose tater tots which was kind of weird because normally I eat very healthy. But they were SO GOOD. I asked the waitress if they were organic tater tots, and she just gave me a funny look.

FINALLY he said, "Okay, you can start talking again." So I told him we HAVE to solve this final problem about economic growth, about how the economy has to grow or else it will collapse. I told him I have one clue to the solution, which has to do with the answer to the question: How is money introduced?

He looked at me funny and asked, "How do you know that?"

Of course I couldn't say the real answer so I decided to be mysterious just like he can be. I said, "Let's just say that I have my sources." Then I stared into the distance like he does sometimes, except I couldn't see very far because the view only goes to across the street.

I asked would he please help me, for the sake of the earth. At first he didn't say anything, he just ordered another beer. (Does he have a "drinking problem"?)

Finally he said, "This is getting interesting."

I couldn't believe it! I said, "Are you crazy? The future of the earth is at stake and that's all you can say?"

He said, "This whole process has forced the questions deeper, and it's fascinating to see how far down the rabbit hole it goes." Then he laughed.

I asked what was so funny, and he said the beer he was drinking is called Black Rabbit Porter. He thought that was hilarious. I thought it was just a meaningless coincidence, and not funny at all. It seems that beer does weird things to the part of the brain that decides what's humorous.

I asked him what he knew about how money gets introduced. I said, "Of course, I'm not talking about 'electronic credits,' which everybody knows is just a temporary government measure that's only a tiny part of money creation."

He asked, "How in heck do you know this stuff?" But I just went back to staring across the street.

He said it was too late to start thinking about that. But he had an idea. He said we should meet tomorrow at the coffeeshop at Powell's Books - the main one downtown. He proposed a major brainstorming session. He said we can take over a big table and get "jazzed on coffee."

It was getting late so I said I had to bike home. I asked if he would be going to his "temporary lair" as usual. He said no, he was too drunk to drive and would just sleep in the truck.

As I wrote before, I don't want to end up as a "nagging" girlfriend, but I sure wouldn't let my boyfriend drink beer very often and no more than one beer and if I found any beer in the house I would pour it down the sink.

September 23

We're at the coffeeshop at Powell's Books, trying to answer the question HOW IS MONEY INTRODUCED? Which will supposedly also answer the question HOW DOES THE ECONOMY GROW? There's a huge pile of books spread out on our table.

We're drinking a kind of coffee called Stumptown Coffee which Coyote says is "excellent" and "world-famous," which I wouldn't know about. I've hardly ever drunk coffee. It's very bitter, so I had to add a bunch of cream and sugar (organic turbinado sugar made from natural cane).

We're sort of "stuck" right now. The table is full of economic books, but we STILL haven't even answered the question of how money is introduced. It doesn't make sense. That question is very basic, but none of the books mention it - not even books such as "Basic Economics."

How does money get introduced? Why is it such a secret? But it has to get introduced somehow, and it has to grow somehow, since it DOES get introduced, and since it DOES grow.

I've been looking at tons of books, but hardly anything makes sense. Everything is so abstract and weird, and it doesn't have anything to do with anything real. How did our entire culture get based on something that doesn't make sense?

I don't want to blame my confusion on the excuse of "I'm only 14" because this would be to use ageism on myself. Coyote is just as frustrated as me, which makes me feel good in a weird way. I mean, if someone like Coyote is confused, then I feel better about being confused myself.

It's 1:50pm, and still no progress. Since we can't find any answers in books about current economics, we're going to try looking at books about the history of economics. Coyote said we should focus on someone named John Maynard Keynes, who was from England and invented the basic economic ideas we still use.

I found something interesting that John Maynard Keynes wrote in 1933. It's the first thing I found that talks about economic growth. Basically, he thinks it's important to have the economy grow, but when everybody is doing OK then growth should stop:

> Suppose that a hundred years hence we are eight times better off than today. The economic problem may be solved. The economic problem is not the permanent problem of the human race.
>
> The economic problem, the struggle for subsistence, always has been the primary, most pressing problem of the human race. Thus for the first time since his creation man will be faced with his real, his permanent problem - how to use his freedom from pressing economic cares, how to live wisely and agreeably and well.
>
> When the accumulation of wealth is no longer of high social importance, there will be great changes in the code of morals. The love of money will be recognized for what it is, a somewhat disgusting morbidity, one of those semi-criminal, semi-pathological propensities which one hands over with a shudder to the specialists in mental disease.
>
> I see us free, therefore, to return to some of the most sure and certain principles of religion and traditional virtue - that avarice is a vice, that the exaction of usury is a misdemeanor, and the love of money is detestable.

But the prediction that economic growth would end poverty hasn't happened. In fact, even with all the economic growth that's happened since then, poverty is getting worse. Obviously, the idea that economic growth will end poverty isn't right.

I had to ask Coyote what "avarice" means, and he said it means "greed." I also had to ask what "usury" means. It means to charge interest on loaning money. It's a religious word and at one time all religions were against it as unethical.

Even though the quote was interesting, it didn't answer our question about how money can grow. So we'll have to go back even farther. Coyote said the ideas of John Maynard Keynes were influenced by another guy - John Law.

It looks like John Law didn't write any books, but he's definitely mentioned in a lot of other people's books. What a weird person! According to one book, in addition to being a banker and economist he was "a gambler, swindler, rake, and adventurer forced to flee the British Isles after killing an opponent in a duel." This kind of person helped invent our economic system???

I asked Coyote was a "rake" is, and he looked at me with a weird expression. He said, "You mean the thing you use to rake up leaves?" That made me crack up. Coyote made an even weirder expression, which made me crack up MORE.

I think coffee is doing weird things to my mind. I feel sort of "nervous" and my sense of humor is acting strange and my emotions are going up and down like crazy.

I just found something in a book about John Law that seemed important: "Law made clear the distinction between a passive treasury, where money just accumulated, and an active bank, where money was created."

That doesn't make sense that banks create money.

I thought they just kept money and loaned some of it out. I'm going to show it to Coyote and see what he thinks.

He said that also sounds weird to him.

I noticed Coyote looking super-confused. I asked him why he was confused and he said he found something that might be the answer, or very close to the answer, but it didn't make any sense.

He said it had to do with the "fractional reserve system" which started in the 1700s. Coyote said it used to be that money was sort of a "receipt" for gold. I think he said the receipt was called a "banknote," which was printed by the bank. But then some bankers figured out they could print more "receipts" than the gold they had, therefore they only had a "fraction" of the gold compared to the "receipts" (money).

Of course, money isn't a receipt for gold anymore. But Coyote said banks still use the fractional reserve system.

Coyote said that explained how it came to be that banks could create money, but it didn't explain how money could "grow" - since banks were only allowed to print a certain percentage extra.

As for when money started to "grow," that seemed to have something to do with this next part. Coyote said that some bankers figured out a way to become more wealthy with this "extra money" they could print themselves. What they did is to give out the money in the form of a loan. Since they charged interest on the loan, they would get back more than they gave out. But Coyote said he was totally confused about how this could possibly work.

I told Coyote I didn't understand, so he gave me an example. He said, let's say the bank gives somebody a one-year loan of $100 and charges 10% interest. Eventually the person pays back $110.

Coyote said, "I just can't figure it out?" and I was confused as to why he was confused. He asked, "Where did that extra $10 come from?"

I started to answer but I realized I didn't know.

I thought maybe the person just got it from other people? Coyote said that wouldn't explain it, because where do THOSE people get the money? Where is the money coming from to pay back the interest on the loans?

He said, "The bank can print extra money, but people can't. So how did the person get that extra $10? Where did it come from?"

Okay Amy, THINK! Coyote said the effects of coffee wear out so you have to drink more to keep thinking, but it just feels like my thinking is going faster but not going anywhere. I think my brain is losing its mind.

It's almost 6:00pm and I haven't eaten since breakfast! No WONDER I'm going crazy! I NEED FOOD! Fortunately the coffee shop sells vegetarian sandwiches. They look really delicious.

So... Money is created when a bank makes a loan. But the loan has to be paid back with more money. Can the money just come from another bank?

I asked Coyote and he said no, because then the other bank would run out of money. So that can't be the answer. I said, "Well if you have a better answer, then let me know, I'll be right here with my delicious veggie sandwich, eating and thinking very hard." Then I said, "I mean, I'll just be THINKING very hard, not EATING very hard!" I thought this was very funny. Yes, the coffee is doing weird things to my sense of humor.

I had a funny idea. "I've got it!" I told Coyote. "If you need money to pay off the first loan, get a loan from the other bank!" Coyote made an expression that looked like he drank grapefruit juice. He agreed that my sense of humor was getting very weird.

Then he said, "Wait a second, I think you might actually be on to something." He pulled out a notebook and started drawing a bunch of circles. I added a smiley face to one of the circles but he frowned, so on another circle I added a frowny face. He told me to get serious. I told him the coffee is making my mind weird.

He said my idea might make sense if you don't think of just a couple banks, but think of the entire banking system. I told him it really wasn't an "idea," I was sort of making a joke. But he said maybe it's not a joke.

He said people get loans, but what's more important for the economy is business loans - loans to start or expand a business. Of course all the loans have interest, which means paying back more money. But we've already figured out that money is "created" by banks issuing loans. So to pay off the past loans, somewhere else in the economy there has to be new loans which create more money. But then THOSE loans have to be paid off with money, which means MORE loans.

I said, "Loans to pay off the loans?"

He said yes, it's very complicated (and pointed to his circles). But it always comes back to the banks making more loans to pay off the existing loans. This has been going on for hundreds of years, which is how the economy "grows."

He said, "Economic growth needs more money, but more money needs more economic growth, which needs more money. And it doesn't stop. It can't stop."

He said that's not only how the economy grows, but why it HAS to grow. He said everybody is right that the economy has to "grow or collapse," but now he understands why. He said we can never get to a point where growth is "enough."

Then he got a very worried look and said, "Do you realize what that means? This is addiction: We're addicted to economic growth."

I said that I thought addiction was only to things like alcohol and drugs. He said those were just the obvious ones, but it's possible to be addicted to all kinds of things.

He said this has all the classic signs of addiction: It's out of control, and we're dependent on it, and we keep doing it even when it's not working any more. This is why even when it's obvious that economic growth isn't solving unemployment or ending poverty or doing any of the other stuff it says it can do, we keep trying it anyway. It's because we have no choice! It's why even though we have more money than ever before in history, we still need more. Since we don't understand what's happening, we keep defending it even though it's obviously not working.

He said this explains a lot of what's happening that he didn't understand. Eventually all addictions "bottom out" and that's what will happen to our economy when earth's resources run out. He said maybe it's already starting to happen, and that's why the economy keeps getting worse.

Coyote is off looking for something written by Thomas Jefferson. I think I need more coffee, even though it's making the inside of my mouth feel weird and I have to go to the bathroom all the time.

Coyote found the Thomas Jefferson thing. Jefferson wrote it during the time when the United States was just starting out. As part of being independent, the colonists wanted to create their own money. But only two years after the Constitution was signed, there was something called the First National Bank Act. It allowed European banks to make interest-based money the official U.S. money. Jefferson did NOT like this! He wrote:

> I believe that banking institutions are more dangerous to our liberties than standing armies. Already they have raised up a money aristocracy that has set the Government at defiance. The issuing power should be taken from the banks and restored to the Government to whom it properly belongs.

Coyote said this shows that America was starting to get dependent on banks from the very beginning, even when this country was supposed to be about freedom and independence. Why didn't I learn any of this in school?

Coyote found something else in the same book, about how Abraham Lincoln was ALSO worried about the power of the banks. Lincoln tried to fix the problem by having the government print a kind of money called "greenbacks" - $450 million of interest-free money. But the banks did NOT like this because they wanted to create all the money themselves! So they bought up all the "greenbacks" and forced the government to buy it back in exchange for gold.

Coyote was staring out the window for a long time, looking very thoughtful. Then he said, "What's so amazing about the dynamic is that it's a huge problem that affects every single aspect of society, but the solution is actually very simple. As a design problem it's very interesting, because changing one thing would change the entire dynamic."

I said, "WHAT IS IT???" He said, "You haven't figured it out yet?" I said "TELL ME!!!" and he said, "It's simple: Just stop the introduction of money as interest-bearing loans." He said Lincoln had the right idea, but he didn't go far enough. We have to eliminate debt on ALL money.

I said I needed him to be more specific so I can have the solution added to the Save the Earth Act. He wrote it down on scrap paper and gave it to me. Here is exactly what he wrote, put into all capital letters because it's VERY IMPORTANT:

> STOP THE ADDICTION TO ECONOMIC GROWTH BY ENDING THE INTRODUCTION OF MONEY AS INTEREST-BEARING LOANS. PUT AN END TO FRACTIONAL RESERVE BANKING AND DON'T ALLOW BANKS TO CREATE MONEY. PUT THE FEDERAL RESERVE SYSTEM UNDER THE CONTROL OF THE U.S. TREASURY WITH THE EXCLUSIVE RIGHT TO ISSUE U.S. CURRENCY FREE OF DEBT.

I said, "Is that all?" which he thought was funny. "Oh yeah," he said, "just that one little change. Piece of cake!" Then he started packing up his

OH NO! It's almost 9:00pm and the coffee shop is closing! I'll have to finish writing at home.

It's past midnight, but I want to write everything while I still remember it. Also, I think all that coffee will not let me go to sleep anyway. Also, my stomach doesn't feel very good.

Where was I? Coyote started packing up his things and said, "Well this has been very interesting but I have a long drive back to EarthSage."

I grew very bold and said, "No! You still need to meet with Katherine! You need to tell her that we figured out how to fix the Save the Earth Act!"

Finally Coyote said he would talk to Katherine tomorrow. He'd been obviously resistant to the idea of talking to Katherine for some reason, so I asked him why.

He said, "I have this feeling like Katherine wants to discuss more than just economic theory." That's when my throat got dry and my stomach got this weird feeling like it was sinking.

He said, "It was years ago. Katherine and I have some history." I had trouble talking but I asked him, "Do you mean she was your girlfriend?"

He said, "Well, I wouldn't put it like that, it was more of a physical thing. Young people do foolish things."

Even though I was still "recovering" from the shocking news, I wanted to appear very grown-up and mature. So I said, "Sometimes older people do foolish things, too," even though I didn't know what I meant by that.

Oh no - what if Katherine wins him back? No, that's crazy! They're too different, there's no chance. Is there?

September 24

I tried to call Representative Bozzio but I couldn't reach him. So I called Montia and said THIS IS AN EMERGENCY because we need to add an amendment to the Save the Earth Act to stop our addiction to economic growth which started back in the 1700s and money is really debt because of how money is introduced as loans and if we don't stop it will destroy the earth. She told me slow down and asked if I was drinking coffee, and I told her that I'm quitting coffee for the rest of my life after the experience I had yesterday.

She told me to send her an email with EXACTLY what the amendment should say. I said I had that ready, because Coyote helped me figure it out. Montia said, "An animal helped you figure it out?" because she didn't realize Coyote is a human being. I guess technically human beings are animals, but I'm pretty sure that's not what she meant.

The email took me THREE HOURS. The amendment part was easy. I made sure to copy the words EXACTLY from my diary. But Montia also wanted an explanation of the reasons for the amendment. In other words, the stuff I was telling her on the phone but in a way that made sense. That part was HARD. But it's very important to give a good explanation, because people will maybe be curious about why we need to change our entire economic system.

I just had an idea. I'm going to make a copy of the explanation I wrote in the email, and turn it into an article. I'm not sure who will publish it, but I'm sure somebody will.

This is AMAZING! I just got a call from Doug Normalson. As part of his building code activism, he said it's very important to add an amendment to the Save the Earth Act. He said to call him ASAP. He said the Save the Earth Act MUST include changing building codes. It's not only important for sustainability reasons, but also to make the Save the Earth Act work, economically-speaking.

He explained it like this: Housing is the biggest expense for most people, and the Save the Earth Act would make the prices go up - right when people have less money to spend. So we have to give people the freedom to build homes that are ecological AND affordable. "Just like your strawbale home," he said.

I told him to send me an email with the EXACT WORDING of what the amendment should say, so I can send it to Montia.

OK, this is his EXACT WORDING:

> To make housing sustainable as well as more affordable, the International Building Code (IBC) shall be radically overhauled to remove minimum size restrictions and other standards that have thwarted regional differences and made housing so freaking expensive. The IBC shall return to its original goal of setting standards for public safety and will remove other restrictions in order to allow wide latitude in construction materials appropriate to the region,

> such as Amy's strawbale home. It will also allow construction techniques that encourage individual creativity so we can be free like the Constitution says we're supposed to be.

I wrote back and asked if he's sure we want to use a word like 'freaking'? And also does he really want the amendment to refer to my strawbale home? He said don't worry, they'll change the wording into "official Congress-type language."

I called Montia and said THIS IS AN EMERGENCY because we need to add another amendment to the Save the Earth Act. She said, "Another amendment?" and I said, "Yes, it's very important that sustainable and affordable housing is part of the act!"

She told me to send her another email with EXACTLY what the amendment should say. I told her that Doug Normalson the developer helped me figure it out. Montia said, "Wasn't he the developer that was trying to destroy the wetland that you saved?" and I explained yes it was him but it's OK because he came out of the closet.

It has been practically a whole day and Representative Bozzio has STILL not contacted me about the amendments. I tried calling Montia but she didn't answer. Maybe she accidentally dropped her cell phone in a swimming pool?

I called Montia back and left a message asking what's going on with the amendments. I told her it's very important, so please call me back as soon as her phone dries off.

I waited practically a whole hour and didn't hear from Montia, so I left a message for Representative Bozzio. I said I was sorry for bothering him because I know he's super busy, but this is very important and since Montia's phone fell into a swimming pool I want to make sure he knows about the amendments.

FINALLY I heard back from Representative Bozzio! He sent me a text message: "liked your ideas for the save earth act montia will amend tomorrow watch for press release."

September 25

The press release just came out!

FOR IMMEDIATE RELEASE:

Bozzio Amends the Save the Earth Act

Washington, DC – Rep. Lester Bozzio (D-OR) has added two amendments to the Save the Earth Act. The first amendment is something about housing. The other amendment is something about economic reforms that will allow us to save the earth without causing total economic collapse.

AMENDMENT A:

To make housing sustainable as well as more affordable, the International Building Code (IBC) shall be radically overhauled to remove minimum size restrictions and other standards that have thwarted regional differences and made housing so freaking expensive. The IBC shall return to its original goal of only setting standards for public safety and will remove other restrictions in order to allow wide latitude in construction materials appropriate to the region such as Amy's strawbale home. It will also allow construction techniques that encourage individual creativity so we can be free like the Constitution says we're supposed to be.

AMENDMENT B:

STOP THE ADDICTION TO ECONOMIC GROWTH BY ENDING THE INTRODUCTION OF MONEY AS INTEREST-BEARING LOANS. PUT AN END TO FRACTIONAL RESERVE BANKING AND DON'T ALLOW BANKS TO CREATE MONEY. PUT THE FEDERAL RESERVE SYSTEM UNDER THE CONTROL OF THE U.S. TREASURY WITH THE EXCLUSIVE RIGHT TO ISSUE U.S. CURRENCY FREE OF DEBT.

> As with the original Save the Earth Act, Rep. Bozzio credits environmental activist Amy Johnson-Martinez for her critical role in developing these amendments. "Thanks again, Amy!" said Bozzio.

Montia just copied my amendments straight from my emails! She must have felt rushed. I hope it wasn't because of me trying to call her every 15 minutes. But what's important is that now the Save the Earth Act is officially amended. There's no way that anybody could possibly be against the act, unless it was a crazy person.

I got a message from Montia. She wanted to know what I meant about her phone drying off. I didn't call her back, since if she called me then obviously the phone was already dry and there was no need to explain.

A reporter from Newsweek called me! Her name is Diane. She saw the press release and wants to do a story about how the Save the Earth Act came back to life "like a phoenix rising from the ashes."

I told her I was working on an article about the 1700s and John Law and why our economy is addicted to growth. She said maybe she could use it as a "sidebar" (which she explained is sort of a mini-article that goes on the side of the main article).

She asked if I would be willing to do an interview. I said, "Aren't we doing it already?" She said no, we're just chatting right now. So we scheduled a "real" interview for tomorrow at 2:00pm.

September 26

The phone interview went GREAT! Diane said she's going to work very hard to get the article published this week. She said my economic article was "very clear and extremely helpful" in understanding the economic stuff, which she said was "mind-boggling."

Doug Normalson was just interviewed on TV! He announced his plan to totally transform his building company to make homes that are 100% sustainable!

He can't actually start a "total transformation" until the Save the Earth Act passes and building codes get changed. But for now he found a "loophole" in the building codes. I guess the building codes don't apply to "mobile housing" - such as mobile homes.

So he got an idea, which is to make something like a mobile home park for progressive ecological people. He said he would reinvent the mobile home park to be a model of sustainability. The homes would be built on trailer frames in all kinds of unique and awesome styles, but all of them would be very affordable and built from local natural materials. Cars would be restricted to a parking lot on one end, so there wouldn't be cars driving through all the time. And in the center there would be a community area with a big garden and a playground for kids.

Sorry, diary, but I'm putting some more "bad news" articles into you. The only good thing about these articles is it means there's no way people can deny things are getting much worse.

Michigan Tapwater Concerns Residents

Grand Rapids, Mich. – "I don't know why people are complaining," said state toxologist Nancy Willakers, "it's like they've never seen brown water that smells like death." This response did not completely satisfy residents of Grand Rapids concerned about their tapwater. Willakers hypothesizes that the color and odor are due to an unforeseen reaction of industrial chemicals that have leaked into the city's aquifer and combined in unknown ways.

The chemicals include organophosphate insecticides, organochlorines, dinitro-ortho-cresol, the organophosphate chemicals propetamphos, parathion, disulfoton, thiometon, etrimphos and fenitrothion, as well as metoxuron, benzene, barium, cadmium, and thallium, and also benzelhydrinate, chloriximalia, ardinatilhyriphorax, and other chemicals with names that are even longer.

When asked whether this "soup" of toxic chemicals poses a health risk, Willakers stated that citizens don't need to worry. "We have no test results that show that this specific combination of chemicals poses a problem," stated Willakers, "because the Michigan Department of Toxicology doesn't have enough money in the budget to conduct any tests."

African Elephants Not Extinct

New York, N.Y. – The United Nations reported today that three African elephants still exist in the wilds of Kenya. Those three elephants are surrounded by a heavily-fortified concrete barricade and are guarded around-the-clock by a division of the Kenya armed forces to protect against poachers.

"The animals are safe and happy and living their lives somewhat naturally considering the circumstances," stated United Nations spokesperson Jessica Taffy.

Taffy hopes to reassure people that are concerned about the survival of these majestic animals. "Three elephants are adequate for a viable population," stated Taffy, "although it definitely would have been better for long-term viability if one of the elephants was a female."

Challenges in Nebraska

Lincoln, Neb. – The drought that has decimated neighboring South Dakota has spread south to the state of Nebraska.

Compounding the lack of rain, the underlying Oglalla Aquifer – until recently the source of 30 percent of the nation's groundwater used for agricultural irrigation – is nearly empty. It has been drained to the point where what little liquid that can be forced out of the ground resembles a chocolate milkshake, although not tasty like a chocolate milkshake.

The collapse of the agricultural sector has proven to be problematic in a state whose economy depends totally upon the agricultural sector. "We have no other sector," said Governor Nelson Gopher.

Attempts to develop tourism based on the state's massive dust storms have been unsuccessful. The problem, according to

Governer Gopher, is that very few people are interested in watching a dust storm. As a result, construction of the destination resort and amusement park "Dust World" has been cancelled.

Mutant Guinea Pig Hybrid Threatens Forests

Cincinnati, Ohio – The Ohio governor confirmed today that forests in the state of Ohio are threatened by a bizarre creature that had nothing to do with human interference with nature.

A hybridized guinea pig, developed for warfare and cosmetics testing, somehow escaped a lab enclosure despite the "Do Not Leave Door Open" signs on all the doors. According to a genetic study made by the University of Cincinnati, the hybrid guinea pigs interbred with sewer rats and have become "super-rats" immune to every known human poison. The study describes them as "indestructible creatures that can be stopped by nothing."

Although the creatures can utilize anything as food, they have a strong preference for tree bark. This results in stripping the bark along the base of a tree, which is fatal for trees. Although currently limited to forests in Ohio, if the creatures cannot be stopped they are expected to spread throughout the country, and then the world. If left unchecked, they will destroy every forest on earth.

The University of Cincinnati study downplays the seriousness of this by asserting that the creatures are a threat only to trees made of wood.

Fire + Explosion = Oops!

New Orleans, La. – A fire led to an explosion at chemical manufacturer HappyChem, Inc., which resulted in the entire contents of the facility flowing into the Mississippi River.

Company CEO Joe Felt reported he felt very bad about the accident because, "Those chemicals are worth a lot of money."

The chemicals killed all life in the river and also the entire Mississippi River Delta and possibly the Gulf of Mexico. Although this means the death of what was formerly the richest estuary and river fishery in the country, residents were struck by the beauty of the chemical-filled river. "The water was a bunch of pretty colors," according to local third-grader Ralphie.

September 27

The Newsweek article just came out. And it's INCREDIBLE! It's called "New Life for the Save the Earth Act." In my entire career as an activist, I would say that Diane is the best reporter I've ever worked with.

My economic article WAS published as a sidebar. It's called, "Amy Explains How We're Addicted to Economic Growth."

Our interview turned out really great. It made me think of my ideas in some new ways (such as how an economic system can support the meaning of life).

Ms. Johnson-Martinez, a lot of people are surprised that your plan to save the environment is focused primarily on economics.

Please, just call me Amy! As for the focus on economics, my intellectual journey to go to the roots of environmental destruction just led me there. Every time I proposed saving the environment or changing to a sustainable option, the response was always, "We can't afford it." And that led me to ask, "Why is it that the most destruction option is always cheaper than the sustainable option?" That's when I learned all about what economics calls "externalities."

Which you figured out how to solve with a "sustainability tax." How much will prices go up to make everything sustainable?

The costs would have to be figured out by experts at the IRS – which would be turned into the SRS, or Sustainable Revenue Service. I can't give an exact number, such as prices would be 10 percent more or whatever.

I would say that 10 percent more is worth it to save the earth!

Oh, that was just a guess. But isn't any price worth it to save the earth?

Also, the plan would help compensate for the higher prices Is that correct?

It will lead to federal taxes going way down. And for the poorest people, the money generated by the sustainability tax will be sent as a rebate.

The economic aspects of the plan essentially change the entire focus of the economy.

The problem is that the economy didn't have a focus before, except for growing bigger. It didn't care if it was making people happier or more secure, or if the earth was being destroyed.

The economy had no meaning?

That's a good way to put it. At one time I was very interested in discovering the meaning of life. Everybody said the meaning of life is to leave the world better than we found it.

And our economy does the opposite?

Yes! Because it counts destruction as profit. And because it can't stop growing.

This brings us to what is perhaps the most radical aspect of your plan, the need to stop – as you put it – "our addiction to economic growth."

That also wasn't part of the original plan, but we had to add it. I said before how whenever you try to do something to save the earth somebody says, "We can't afford it." Well, the other thing you hear is, "It will hurt economic growth." Basically, if we stop destroying the earth it will make the economy collapse.

But it's possible to change that?

The amendment to the Save the Earth Act will stop the addiction.

It's very interesting how you were led to that amendment by a dramatic event where it looked like the Save the Earth Act was doomed to fail.

Anthony Iron thought he killed the plan. But I refused to believe that the economy can survive only by destroying the earth. So instead of giving up I looked harder until I found the answer.

So in a strange way, Anthony Iron actually helped you.

I'm pretty sure that's not what he meant to do! He thought he was killing the plan, but actually he pointed out a problem that had to be solved to make it work.

Well Amy, your plan is very interesting. I'm sure there will be widespread debate and discussion about it. Anything else you would like to say?

The earth is a lovely planet and it would be a shame to destroy it. So let's save it instead!

September 28

This is VERY INTERESTING! The New York Times contacted Anthony Iron for his reaction to the article. Somebody from People for Economic Common Sense responded that he resigned his job "to spend more time with his family."

I'm thinking about what this means and I can't believe it. Did I actually "beat" Anthony Iron? I think I did.

I BEAT ANTHONY IRON!

Mom always told me, "Truth will win over lies in the long run, but you might wear out a few pairs of running shoes."
I guess that means it takes a long time?

I wish it didn't have to be that some people have to "lose" so others can "win." Why can't we work it out so everybody can win? But sometimes people don't give you that choice.

I just realized something. They said he's resigning "to spend more time with his family"? But he doesn't HAVE a family! Tiffany told me (after she shamelessly flirted with him) that he was "single and available." At least she wasn't flirting with a married man.

September 29

I'm going CRAZY with all the requests for comments. But I only have to go crazy for another few weeks, until Congress votes on the Save the Earth Act. Then I can curl up in my cozy strawbale home and sleep for 14 days.

Juvie Starr called me back! She said she was sorry it took so long to finish the movie, and I said that's no problem because I realize she's always busy on worthwhile projects, and I explained about how the Save the Earth Act was going well and then not so well but now it's going VERY well, but we still need to do promotion for it and if she would be willing to make a statement or mention it on talk shows I would appreciate it VERY much. She asked if I could send her some information about the Save the Earth Act and I said, "OF COURSE, Juvie Starr!"

I watched Representative Bozzio on an interview show on TV. I can't watch him do any more interviews because I get SO NERVOUS. He'll be talking very intelligently, but then his "crazy side" starts coming out. I don't know why his mind is stuck on that badger he saw in Eastern Oregon. The interviewer was asking him about how the sustainability tax would apply to energy use, and then Representative Bozzio said, "That badger was the strangest creature I've ever seen." The interviewer said, "What badger?" and they never got to talk about the energy question.

I spent all afternoon on my computer to see what people are saying about the Save the Earth Act. Here are some of the things I'm finding out:

- The idea that our economy is addicted to growth is pretty shocking to pretty much everybody. Half the people are trying to deny it and other half of the people are calling those people stupid.
- The economic experts are admitting it's true that our economy is addicted to growth. But they don't know what will happen if we end the addiction. One economist said, "We've always relied on sharing an economic pie that keeps growing."

- It seems like a lot of people don't take Representative Bozzio very seriously. Instead of Lester Bozzio they call him "Less Bozo" and make fun of him.
- A lot of people seem to think that passing the Save the Earth Act will mean we don't have to change anything, but magically the earth will be saved. That's not correct, but the problem is it's impossible to know exactly what the changes will be.

I need to do everything I can to convince people we have to try it, even though it's taking a chance. Because we know FOR SURE that the way we're going isn't working.

I just thought of a good way to put it: It's like we're on a road that we know is going over a cliff, and I'm asking people to change to a road that's curvy and a little rough and maybe has potholes and we can't exactly see where it's going. But at least it's not over a cliff.

Aimee from People magazine called! She said People en Español is very interested in doing another story about me. They see it as a really big deal because so far no Hispanics have saved the earth.

September 30

I just got an invitation to speak at a major conference! It's called "Creating a Sustainable Future for Our Children." Creating a sustainable future is so important for kids, because if we keep using up the earth there won't be any left for them!

It would be great to get parents on my side because parents are a large percentage of the population.

It's in only a few weeks and it's not far away, only down in Eugene. I can take the train there! The person I talked to said she's sorry she can't provide a lot of details on the conference right now, but as soon as she has more information she'll send it to me.

I'm seeing many articles and comments supportive of the Save the Earth Act because, "10 percent more to save the earth is worth it." I wish people would stop saying it will be only that much because maybe it will be more. I realize that in the interview I said 10 percent, but that was just an example. I said so very clearly.

I read a follow-up story about the Republican senator who expressed "tentative support" for the Save the Earth Act. (His name is Jefferson Bontrager, from Minnesota.) He said, "I'm convinced that the Republican Party needs to take the lead in passing the act."

He said that the majority of Republicans are expressing "increasing displeasure and dismay" at the direction the Republican Party is heading. He said the Republican Party has lost touch with many of its core conservative values, such as conserving.

He said, "We have two options. We can wait until environmental degradation increases to the point where the free market collapses. Or we can be leaders in promoting reforms to save the free market as well as the environment."

He has convinced many other Republican senators and representatives, and they've started a group called "Republicans for the Earth."

October 1

I got invited to speak at ANOTHER big conference! But I'm not too sure about going, since I knew so little about the subject. The conference is called "Environment and Religion" and is put on by a big Christian church right here in Portland. I think I'll talk with Tiffany about it. She knows a lot about religious stuff, although she's very insistent that she's "spiritual but not religious."

Katherine called me to see her in her office and said, "I have great news for you." She said that the HomeEarth board has decided to "fully endorse and support" the Save the Earth Act. I started to get all excited but the excitement stopped because of the way Katherine was NOT excited.

I asked if the board made their decision on account of Coyote saying that the plan would work. She said that she never even got to say that at the board meeting. One of the board members discovered that another environmental group called BlueSky has endorsed the plan. Then another board member said that several other groups were just about to announce they were endorsing it.

So the board decided that they sort of "have to" endorse it because it would look bad if they didn't, especially since it was co-written by the HomeEarth Communications Manager.

Katherine said the good news was that now it would be okay to promote the plan in my role as the HomeEarth Communications Manager, not just in my role of myself. She said, "You can blog about it to your heart's content." The editor of the HomeEarth magazine was at the meeting, and is planning a special issue devoted to the Save the Earth Act. Everything will have to be a super-rush to get the issue done before Congress votes on it.

My emotions are feeling really strange. I should be totally happy at this news, but I feel weird that HomeEarth's support is because they "have to" and not because they "want to."

I CAN'T BELIEVE IT! That hip-hop group that was at my wetland camp wrote another song about me! Somebody sent me a link to their video on YouTube. It's called "Amy's Song." This is my favorite part:

She saved Oaks Bottom back in June
But bigger changes comin' soon
She showed how wetlands got great worth
But now let's save the whole d*mn earth

I looked them up on amazon.com and they just came out with an album of ecological songs. I guess it's the first environmental rap album ever! There are rap songs about all kinds of great subjects, like bringing a cloth bag to the market and keeping the windows closed when the heater is on.

It's GREAT that there are rap songs about saving the earth. But I'm not comfortable with the profanity, and also the grammar is very bad.

I just got a joke text from Representative Bozzio! It says: "if run for prez will you be secretary of sustainability?" Haha! There's no such thing as a "Secretary of Sustainability"! I texted him back: "yeah sure whatever"!

October 2

I finally had a chance to talk to Tiffany about the "Environment and Religion" conference. I told her I wasn't sure about going, and she asked what I was worried about. I mentioned my experience in Lincoln City when saving the wetland was opposed by people from a church. I had the idea that religion was sort of "against" nature because I've heard a lot about nature-worshipping people labeled as "pagans" (in a non-complementary way). Also, I've heard religious statements saying the earth isn't that important because the goal is get the earth over with and get to heaven.

Tiffany said that's "old paradigm" religion, but most churches have gotten very progressive about ecology. She said many religions now recognize that since God created the earth then it must be sacred. She said a lot of religious people now realize that the Bible is full of all kinds of sayings about the beauty of nature and the importance of conservation.

She said the fact that THEY invited ME was a sign that they're receptive to my message. She also pointed out that there are a huge number of religious people. Therefore it's important to reach them because I'll need their support for the Save the Earth Act.

She said something else I hadn't thought of. She said that religion is one of the few areas where it's very common to talk about "deeply serious" subjects like values and meaning, and it's about the only place left where the subject of ethics is taken seriously. She reminded me that if you look at history, religions were very active in ending slavery and in the civil rights movements and ending apartheid in South Africa.

She said it would be a good audience to talk about the evils of greed - which is important because the Save the Earth Act is about stopping a greedy economic system. This made me remember about how religion is against "usury" - which is what our economic system is based on!

I wrote back and said I would be very pleased to speak at the "Environment and Religion" conference!

October 3

I found a VERY INTERESTING article in The Economist magazine by somebody that I guess is a major economist. He concluded that the Save the Earth Act would "drastically reduce unemployment," just the way we predicted. It would maybe even end unemployment.

He said something about our economy that's SHOCKING. He said that unless we end our addiction to economic growth, full employment is impossible. Full employment "creates an economic environment that's not conducive to growth." He said that the last time the unemployment rate got under 5 percent, economists were worried about "dangerously low levels of unemployment."

He said the reason for this is that when there's lots of unemployment, people are afraid of being fired so they'll work for less money. And that's important for businesses to create economic growth. But if we're not addicted to economic growth, then full employment isn't a problem.

This means that all the people who said economic growth is the only way to solve unemployment are totally wrong. Because economic growth DEPENDS on unemployment!

This is even MORE reason that people should support the Save the Earth Act - and it's a reason we didn't even know about!

October 4

NO!!! I CAN'T BELIEVE IT!!!

FOR IMMEDIATE RELEASE:

Bozzio Announces Candidacy for U.S. President

Washington, DC – Rep. Lester Bozzio (D-OR) has announced his intention to enter the race to become the next president of the United States of America. "I'm running because I best represent the direction that Americans want this country to go," stated Bozzio, "especially if they agree with me on what that is."

Although currently a Democrat, Bozzio plans to abandon his party affiliation. He says, however, that this does not mean he is running as an independent. "I am an ‚independent' only in the sense of being independent from old patterns and obsolete ideas. And one of those obsolete ideas is the whole idea of independence."

"This country was created with the Declaration of Independence," says Bozzio, "and now is the time to declare our *interdependence*, to declare that we are all interconnected forms of life sharing this beautiful planet earth."

Accordingly, Representative Bozzio will be running as an Interdependent.

Bozzio has not yet chosen a vice presidential running mate. However, he is proud to announce he has chosen Amy Johnson-Martinez to be his Secretary of Sustainability, a brand-new position he will create especially for his administration.

Montia just called me to say "Congratulations!" I told her, "I THOUGHT HE WAS JOKING!" She asked if I want to be at the press conference tomorrow. I said that I prefer not to on account of being in shock.

October 5

I got a letter from Coyote. I was disappointed that the letter was very short. But I shouldn't be surprised because Coyote is "a man of few words," which means he's not chatty.

Just thought you'd be interested in knowing that Katherine had zero romantic interest. I could tell that the news of our past "history" was upsetting to you, so I'm hoping this makes you feel better. She just wanted me to confirm that the economic ideas of the Save the Earth Act made sense. Mostly, she wanted to know what effect it would have on "the numbers." As I suspected, she's gone totally corporate.

I think it's very interesting that he wanted to tell me that Katherine had no "romantic intentions." I wonder if that's a "sign" that he's trying to tell me something, such as he's willing to wait for me to get a few years older?

I heard back from the book editor. He said that due to my "increasing popularity" my book has gone into rush production and they'll start printing in only a few weeks! I asked if he thinks the book will help promote the cause of saving the earth, and he said he thinks it will make a lot of money. It's strange that his answer was for a different question than what I asked.

I decided that I'm going to write a series of blog articles about the Save the Earth Act. Each article will be about one of the ways it's awesome. Maybe they can be turned into articles for the special issue of HomeEarth magazine that's coming out?

October 6

This is SO WEIRD! I GOT A POSTCARD FROM ANTHONY IRON! He doesn't seem to care at all that he's been defeated. He seems to be having a great time! The postcard is from Las Vegas, from a fancy hotel.

> *Hey Amy, hope you're having a great day because I sure am! That was a fun little ride we had, while it lasted. Don't worry your perky little self that you hurt my feelings by defeating me. Good luck on your saving the earth thing. Make sure you save Vegas while you're at it! It's important to preserve the "wild life"! ~Anthony Iron~*

October 7

I had a feeling things were going too well. Today was a sign that saving the earth won't be easy. The first big resistance to the Save the Earth Act came from big financial companies. That makes sense because the plan would stop the greedy economic growth system that they make their money from.

Financial Industry Opposes Save the Earth Act

The Wall Street Journal

By Jason L. Ortiz

In a joint press conference today, CEOs and presidents of the nation's major banks and Wall Street investment firms announced their strong opposition to the Save the Earth Act. "We are against the plan to the very depths of our souls," stated Goldman Sachs CEO Douglas McDougal.

"Despite what some people think, we actually do have souls," added Bryce Dunlap, president of Morgan Stanley. "Each of us has a mother that loves us, or did when we were small and cute."

"We're against the act because it will cause the entire banking and finance industry to collapse and take the entire U.S. economy with it," said McDougal. "There might even be cannibalism," added McDougal, "with your neighbor roasting your children on the barbeque."

The representatives concluded their presentation with a version of "rock-paper-scissors" in which the "rock" was a Barbie doll representing "tax-paying citizens," the "paper" was a dollar bill representing the economy, and a pair of scissors represented the Save the Earth Act. They demonstrated what would happen if the Save the Earth Act passed by having the scissor cut up the dollar bill and then stab the Barbie doll.

I'm thinking back to what Mom said, about if you have enemies that means you're getting somewhere. I wonder: If you have REALLY BIG enemies, does that mean you're REALLY getting somewhere?

AMY JOHNSON-MARTINEZ, GET READY FOR THE FIGHT OF YOUR LIFE!

I will be inspired by a couple of the sayings Mom used to say:

> "If the path you're on has no obstacles, then you took a wrong turn or missed an exit or something."

"There's always free cheese in the mouse trap, but the mouse in there probably didn't think it was a good price."

Actually I don't understand what that last one means.

I sent a message to Representative Bozzio. I asked him, "Is it a problem that the major financial institutions of the country are all in opposition against us?"

Representative Bozzio called me. He said don't worry, they're just using "scare tactics" because we're a danger to their huge wealth. They wouldn't dare collapse the economy because they're dependent on it just like all of us.

He said stopping economic growth would stop what he called "speculative income," which I didn't understand. He said it's making money based on doing nothing, just by investing in future growth. He said it's based on a wrong idea that you can make money for nothing, because there's always a price to be paid in the long run. It has to be paid by future generations who have to keep the economic growth addiction going. Which means that it also has to be paid for by the earth.

I told him the people are probably smart enough to realize this, but still it would be a good idea to let the public know so they don't fall for the scare tactics.

He said he'll work with Montia to write a powerful editorial response. He'll say that the financial CEOs are a bunch of jerks, and if they ever had souls they sold them a long time ago, and he doesn't believe they had mothers. I said it would probably be better to leave out the stuff about not having souls or mothers.

October 8

The editorial just came out and it's VERY POWERFUL!

Don't Listen to the Money Changers

By Representative Lester Bozzio

Long ago, Jesus threw the money changers out of the temple. He accused them of turning his home into a "den of thieves." This story is called "the cleansing of the temple."

My fellow Americans, the threat of the money changers is very much alive. However, today's money changers have turned their attention from religious temples to the temple of the earth. They are turning our entire earthly home into a "den of thieves." And it is time that the temple is once again cleansed of their thievery.

Today's money changers are the hedge-fund managers, the national and multinational bankers, the financial speculators of Wall Street, and others of their kind. They create money from nothing, from abstract mathematical constructions such as "derivatives" and other forms of legalized gambling.

They are false prophets who only care about their false profits. They do not care that their immense wealth is at the expense of the very real planet and its very real ability to sustain life. Their profits are being made from an economy addicted to infinite growth on a planet whose resources are not infinite. The earth is paying the price. And as a result, we are paying the price.

The Save the Earth Act will stop the addiction to growth that literally forces us to destroy the earth. As things stand now, we do not have a choice. Either we save the earth or save the economy. The addiction to growth will not let us save both.

The money changers have made immense profits from the addiction they have made us all dependent on. And it is time to put it to an end.

There is a very good reason that interest-based debt has been seen as morally wrong throughout history. The church has traditionally condemned it as "usury." Gandhi includes the concept of "wealth without work" as one of his "Seven Deadly Social Sins."

Now the money changers are frightened. Their scheme has been exposed. Like cornered animals, they are lashing out. They are lashing out with lies and with threats.

They are afraid because they know that if the Save the Earth Act passes they will have to do something they've never done before. They will have to find jobs in which they actually produce something. Or provide a service. In other words, they'll have to make money the same way as the rest of us: By working.

I urge you, fellow Americans, to stop the addiction. Let's force the money changers out of the temple and save the earth.

What a GREAT EDITORIAL! And people really agree with it! There are a TON of comments. I printed out some of my favorites:

You said it, Lester! Let's throw the bums out! First the Wall Street bums, then the politicians. Oh wait, you're a politician.

What a radical idea: A financial system NOT geared toward profit for financial speculators, but geared toward ecological sustainability and the public good. Sometimes you talk a little crazy, but maybe what we need is more of your kind of crazy.

Yeeaahhh! Thanks for being the only politician with the gonads to stand up to that filthy rich bloodsucking Wall Street scum!

This is SO GREAT! People are seeing through the lies to where the truth is!

I saw a poll and 73% of the people said they support the Save the Earth Act!!! I guess it's not super shocking that the rich financial people are afraid of it, but the regular people see the truth!

I didn't know what the word "gonads" means, so I looked it up. Oh no!

October 9

I met Doug Normalson downtown for lunch. He said to get ready for MORE resistance! He said that even though affordable housing is good for 98% of the people, it's bad for the rich developers like he used to be. He said he's very glad he's not going to be the kind of businessman who makes money from other people's unaffordability.

He said it's not just the developers. It's also the huge real estate business that makes trillions of dollars because houses are so big and expensive.

He told me, "Be prepared for heavy-duty resistance. And don't be shocked if they get personal."

I thought he was exaggerating. But he gave me an article about a recent "Friday Forum" given by the local Homebuilders Association.

HBA Presentation Affirms Anti-Nature Stance

By Jeff Lynne

The presentation, entitled "Save Nature or Save American Jobs: Our Choice for the Future," was given by John Wetton, spokesperson for the Oregon Chapter of the American Homebuilders Association.

Mr. Wetton began his presentation in a way that left no doubts about his position, saying that homebuilding supports "everything great about America" and that preserving nature is "dumb."

He claimed that environmentalists are "hypocrites." He said, "If environmentalists are against homebuilding, then what about the fact that they live in homes? Why don't they abandon their homes and live under a pile of leaves and poop on the ground like animals?"

He stated that if environmentalists really cared about nature they would support homebuilding, which is the main stimulant for the economy. He said that environmentalists require the economy to provide them with money for "organic bean sprouts," just as everyone else requires money for "real things."

Mr. Wetton then turned his attention to the recent environmental action that stopped the housing development in the Oaks Bottom wetland. He said it was responsible for the loss of "up to a million jobs, maybe more."

He stressed that Americans require money much more than they require the opportunity to see a frog. "If you give

> people a choice between food on the table and looking at a frog, which do you think they'll pick?"

Doug Normalson said you have to be very careful when you deal with the building industry, because it labels itself as "Pro-America, Pro-Family, Pro-Freedom, Pro-God, Pro-Life, and Pro-Children." I asked him, "So is being for nature supposed to be 'against' all that?" He just said, "Be very careful."

On a "personal note," I noticed that he was more relaxed than I ever saw him. He said that yes, he feels much less "inwardly conflicted" although his wife still wants a divorce. One of his kids started speaking to him again, which I thought was great. But he said that it was only to ask for a bunch of money before he "blows it all on his stupid ecological homebuilding idea."

October 10

I just published my first Save the Earth Act article in my blog! My first article focuses on unemployment which is very important, especially to people that are unemployed. But it's also very important to employed people, such as when your unemployed friend asks to stay at your house for a few days but they never leave.

I explained how the Save the Earth Act will lead to more jobs. For example, it will encourage local organic farms, so lots of people get to be farmers! They can have healthy work providing good food for humanity, and without using poisons that kill all the worms and other beneficial soil organisms.

I included the stuff from that article I found earlier, about how our addiction to economic growth also means being addiction to unemployment. I explained that the Save the Earth Act solves that problem, too!

Tiffany just sent me this REALLY BIZARRE editorial from USA Today. She said, "This is so twisted it's hilarious!"

The Meaning of Life

By Patrick M. Weiner, CFO MallWart, Inc.

It is deeply engrained in the human soul that today should be better than yesterday, and that tomorrow should be better than today. It is within the nature of human beings to grow and evolve, to invent and explore, and to seek better ways to live. Our goal is to leave the world better than when we found it.

In other words, to leave the world with more money.

Economic growth is what brought us out of the Stone Age where we ate mud and leaves. Economic growth is what created the wonderful cornucopia of modern civilization: Snickers bars, hair conditioner, big-screen television, Tupperware, shoelaces, cordless electric drills, sticky pads, and much more.

Unfortunately, there are some people who think progress means to turn back the clock, to toss all the comforts and luxuries of life into the landfill of history.

We should not be against sustainability. Yet we should not be against economic growth. So I propose a compromise. Let's put the word "sustainable" in front of "economic growth" to create "sustainable economic growth."

Because I have no desire to eat mud and leaves.

I told Tiffany that I agree that it's "twisted," but NOT "hilarious." The words "sustainable" and "growth" contradict each other! You can't just change that by putting the words together. Tiffany said, "Amy, you just have to accept that a lot of people are totally nuts." I said I hope it's not too many people, because we are a democracy which means everybody votes including people that are totally nuts.

October 11

I CAN'T BELIEVE IT!!!

Doug Normalson warned me, but I STILL can't believe it! There's a TV commercial playing all over, a political commercial by some organization called "All the Real Estate and Builder Associations Put Together."

It starts with a scene of a typical suburban home which is totally oversized (probably costs a fortune to heat in winter) and a fake family like from an old sitcom. Everybody is way too happy, like they're on drugs. Mom is making a drink in a blender (she's probably an alcoholic) and the daughter is on a huge riding lawn mower mowing the tiny lawn which is so perfectly green it must use tons of chemical fertilizers. Then dad pulls into the driveway in a huge SUV that gets probably 2 MPG.

Then a narrator says, "You worked for this. You deserve it." But then the voice of the narrator gets very sinister and says, "But some people want to take it away." Then the narrator stops talking, but there appear the words "SAVE THE EARTH ACT" in scary black letters which turn red and start dripping like blood. And the blood starts getting all over the fake sitcom family who start screaming. Then the mom drops her alcoholic drink and the daughter runs the lawnmower over the dad.

Then the narrator says, "Some people want you live like this," and the scene changes and it's HORRIBLE! It's a different family, and their "home" is pile of sticks and the family is wearing rags. They are sitting in the mud at breakfast, and the mom says, "Has everybody had enough grubs to eat?" Then the dad says, "Well, I'm off to work to hunt rats for dinner so our daughter doesn't starve to death." And the daughter turns around and says, "Thanks to the Save the Earth Act we're living sustainably."

But the WORST PART is that the daughter LOOKS EXACTLY LIKE ME! I'm sure it was TOTALLY ON PURPOSE! I wonder if I can sue them for desecration of character?

Dad saw the commercial and said, "Amy, that's not what you want to happen, is it?" And I said, "No, of course not!" Then he asked, "Well, why did you say it on TV?"

I CAN'T BELIEVE IT! HE THOUGHT THAT WAS ACTUALLY ME!

I put my anger to good use, to FINALLY weed the garden. I'm afraid it was a very violent weeding (sorry, garden!) but it helped me get over my anger. I'm glad that I got it done because the tomato plants were getting smothered by weeds. I would be a hypocrite if I'm telling people to save the earth and I don't even save my own tomato plants.

I just got an email from Montia. She said she had some "insider information" about what Congress is REALLY saying about the Save the Earth Act. She said that so far they've been "cautiously supportive" while they check out public opinion. But she's been hearing some "concerns," mostly about the "stop economic growth" part. These are the two biggest concerns I need to be prepared for:

- The government has always avoided the delicate problem of how to divide up the economic pie by just making it bigger. In other words, instead of figuring out how to share money, just make more.
- If the economy doesn't grow, how will we pay off the U.S. deficit, which is almost 2 trillion dollars?

I wrote Montia back and thanked her for the "insider information." I said that I don't exactly have answers at this time, but I'll put a note on my calendar for later this week to think very hard.

Why do people keep using the metaphor of the economy as a pie? Sharing a slice of pie gets very messy. For example, if I want to give somebody 10% of my slice that's almost impossible to do without it getting all mushed up. And how can you "grow" a pie? You would need to put it into a bigger pie plate and add more ingredients. But when you put it into the oven to bake the new ingredients, wouldn't the old pie get burnt?

I think it would be better to use the metaphor of a huge bowl filled with M&Ms candy. It's much easier to share M&Ms with other people. And if the economic bowl of M&Ms grows, it's much simpler to just add more M&Ms.

October 12

I must confess to you, dear diary, that I'm very confused by the comments to my blog article about full employment. Many of them were not exactly totally positive.

For some reason, many people seem to be anti-farming. One comment was: "Full employment by turning us into farmworkers? Are you trying to take us back to the 1800s?"

One person had the comment: "Are you telling me I'll have to pay more for food because it was grown in soil that's good for worms?"

That person understood it exactly right! That person obviously understood the connection between healthy food and healthy soil.

Unfortunately, many people didn't understand the connection. I was prepared that rich financial people would be resistant, but it's weird to get resistance from ordinary non-rich and non-financial people. It doesn't mean these people are dumb or stupid; it's just that they aren't very smart.

I thought it over very carefully. I decided it's my responsibility to comment on my blog article in order to reduce the lack of smartness.

Wow, what an interesting and amazing experience! We (me and my online community of fellow earth-savers) made an exciting new discovery about the Save the Earth Act. It's so amazing to have a community of thinkers thinking together. It proves the saying that "two heads are better than one." (Or more heads, as long as they're all good thinkers.)

Posted by naturedude
3:56PM
Prices will go UP??? I thought everything was supposed to "equalize"?

Posted by AmyJohnsonMartinez
3:59PM
Prices only go up for non-sustainable options.

Posted by mamadolphin
4:02PM
I think the higher prices will be equalized by other costs going down, such as income taxes. At least that's how I understand it.

Posted by AmyJohnsonMartinez
4:05PM
You have it totally right mamadolphin!

Posted by naturedude
4:08PM
I thought "equalize" meant prices for "green" things would be cheaper than the prices for destructive non-green things.

Posted by lubejob77
4:11PM
Prices will only go up about 10 percent.

Posted by AmyJohnsonMartinez
4:14PM
That "10 percent" rumor keeps going around. I've said many times that the exact amount of the sustainability tax would be very complicated and would need to be figured out by the economic experts at the Sustainable Revenue Service.

Posted by ramalamadingdong
4:17PM
I knew it! Prices will probably go up by a million dollars. I went to a "health food" store once and a tomato cost $5!!!!!! We'll have hardly any money left to buy cool stuff.

Posted by AmyJohnsonMartinez
4:21PM
Totally! In addition to all our purchases being sustainable, we'll be encouraged to consume less. Have you ever heard of "Voluntary Simplicity"? It's "a way of life that's outwardly simple and inwardly rich." And besides, all that "cool stuff" we buy is destroying the earth.

Posted by lubejob77
4:25PM
It will force us to consume less??? Nobody mentioned that before!!!

Posted by AmyJohnsonMartinez
4:28PM
It's our unsustainable level of consumption that's destroying the earth. Don't you want to be sustainable?

Posted by lubejob77
4:31PM
Of course I want to be sustainable! I just don't want to change my lifestyle.

Posted by AmyJohnsonMartinez
4:35PM
But our lifestyle is unsustainable! Our lifestyle is what's destroying the earth!

Posted by mamadolphin
4:38PM
I thought economic growth was destroying the earth?

Posted by AmyJohnsonMartinez
4:41PM
It's our addiction to economic growth that makes us HAVE TO destroy the earth to keep the economy going. The Save the Earth Act will STOP our addiction to economic growth. That's why all the big banks and financial companies are against it, because it will mean they can't get rich from

speculative income. If we stop the addiction to economic growth then we are free from being forced to over-consume.

Posted by mamadolphin
4:45PM
What do you mean "speculative income"?

Posted by AmyJohnsonMartinez
4:48PM
That's how the big banks and huge Wall Street financial companies make money out of nothing. The banks charge interest and create money that's based on debt, which is the source of the economic growth addiction. And the financial speculators get rich by doing nothing except investing on that addiction. It has to stop!

Posted by ramalamadingdong
4:51PM
Are you talking about the stock market?

Posted by naturedude
4:54PM
She must be. Wall Street is the stock market, basically.

Posted by lubejob77
4:57PM
Wait a sec... the Save the Earth Act would STOP money being made in the stock market??? FYI it's not just "huge Wall Street financial companies" that make money from the stock market. Everybody that owns stocks or mutual funds or a 401(k) retirement fund invests in the stock market. Are you saying we couldn't make money with these kinds of investments?

Posted by AmyJohnsonMartinez
4:59PM
That is a very interesting discovery! I don't think anybody else has figured that out. If we've been making money that way, then obviously we have to stop because it's destroying the earth and it's unethical. That money is based on debt-based interest which the church is against.

Posted by ramalamadingdong
5:02PM
Are you freaking SERIOUS??? There goes my retirement plan!

Posted by lubejob77
5:05PM
Why didn't anybody say before that to save the earth I have to sacrifice my retirement plan?

Posted by naturedude
5:07PM
Is it really necessary to take such drastic action to save the earth? Isn't it enough just to recycle more?

I'm so GLAD that we made that discovery! Because now that people will realize their investment money has been made in a way that destroys the earth. Therefore, their own ethics will make them realize, "I can't ethically live with making money from destroying the earth." This will make them SUPER motivated to support the Save the Earth Act.

October 13

That comment string turned out to be newsworthy. Somebody at the New York Times saw it, and mentioned it in an article.

Can We Afford the Save the Earth Act?

By Coralline Woodham

Recent revelations have cast some dark clouds over the sunny future forecasted by the Save the Earth Act. Some of those revelations came from the Earth Brain Institute, a non-partisan think tank specializing in environmental issues. The other revelations came from Amy Johnson-Martinez, co-writer of the controversial act, via a remarkable string of comments to an article published on her blog.

The economic experts from the Earth Brain Institute have published a preliminary report on the projected costs of the Save the Earth Act. They have confirmed that consumer prices would rise by more than ten percent. Much more.

The problem is that the products currently rated as "most sustainable" are not truly 100 percent sustainable, and making them fully sustainable would cause substantial price increases.

The report explored the example often used by Ms. Johnson-Martinez: A bag of carrots produced by industrial agriculture compared to a bag of carrots produced by a local organic farm. The report noted that such farms still use large supplies of fossil fuels and create other environmental impacts that are not currently internalized. Doing so, according to the report, would raise agricultural prices by approximately 80 percent.

In another example, the automobiles currently rated "most sustainable" are hybrid vehicles. Even though buyers pay a premium for these vehicles, they are far from fully sustainable. The report estimates that a fully sustainable vehicle – made totally from plant-based materials and recycled metal, and designed to run on bio-fuels – would cost upwards of $70,000. And according to the principles of the Save the Earth Act, this vehicle would be the least expensive option.

In the comment string on her blog, Ms. Johnson-Martinez admitted that consumer prices would likely be much higher than the ten-percent figure she had earlier claimed, although she refused to give an exact figure.

Yet the most shocking revelation was a previously-unknown effect of ending economic growth. The comment string revealed that the end of speculative income not only effects wealthy Wall Street financiers, but everybody who earns income derived from stocks, mutual funds, and market-based retirement plans. Of course that means – directly or indirectly – nearly all of us.

What this all adds up to is that the Save the Earth Act would impel us to change our lifestyles. It would not only "encourage" us to simplify our lives; it would essentially require it.

On a positive note, the institute report confirms that if the Save the Earth Act were implemented, it would indeed save the earth: It would halt ecological destruction, create a sustainable society, and end the addiction to economic growth without avoiding financial collapse. The question for us to answer is: Can we afford it?

I'm glad this article "set the record straight" about the Save the Earth Act. I'm going to write a letter to the reporter and thank her for her support.

Some people still aren't convinced, but soon I'll be getting the support of religion on the ethical aspects. Once religion supports the Save the Earth Act, people will HAVE to agree. Maybe people don't think they have to agree with a 14-year-old girl, but how can they argue with religion? I wonder if it would be possible to get the Pope to support the Save the Earth Act?

Same thing for the Sustainable Children conference. It's the kids that will inherit the earth, so parents will totally be supportive. Obviously, parents don't want to leave their children with a destroyed earth.

October 14

HUGE NEWS! THE OIL FROM THE ARCTIC NATIONAL WILDLIFE REFUGE HAS RUN OUT! That didn't take long at all! It's such a shame because we (the environmental community) told them it wouldn't last long.

Peak Oil Hits Home

Fairbanks, Alaska – Oil output from the Arctic National Wildlife Refuge dropped abruptly, signaling the impending end of the available supply. This marks the depletion of the last known major reserves in the world.

The six-month supply resulted in oil revenue of $80 billion, which is just enough to pay for the cost of extracting the oil. The recent economic boom triggered by the short-lived bonanza is over, according to most economic experts.

Unfortunately, the recent economic boom was triggered by loans based on the expectation that the oil supply would continue. Economic experts are predicting a plunge into a recession so dark that they don't want to think about it.

The era of cheap fossil fuel energy appears to be over. The problem is that civilization as we know it is totally dependent on cheap energy. Energy experts recommend that we don't panic, although they don't have any better ideas at this time.

I guess most people would think of this as bad news, but the "good" thing is that it should make people wake up and realize that we REALLY need to pass the Save the Earth Act.

Weird. I was watching a TV news show with a reporter interviewing random people in the street. NOBODY said that now we need to focus on conservation and alternative energy. Actually, one guy did but other people got mad at him and one person hit him in the head with a newspaper. Everyone else was saying things like, "There must be more oil, we have to look harder" and "Can't we make oil out of gasoline?

October 15

The media is going CRAZY. The Oregonian today is full of bad news, pretty much all the result of running out of oil in the Arctic National Wildlife Refuge. Here are some of the headlines:

GAS PRICES SKYROCKET

HIGHER ENERGY PRICES PREDICTED TO CAUSE SPIKE IN CONSUMER PRICES

MASS LAYOFFS STRAIN UNEMPLOYMENT BENEFITS AS BUSINESS PREPARES FOR BOTTOMLESS RECESSION

Oh no! In the Oregonian is a story called "CONSERVATION SUFFERS AS GOVERNOR FOCUSES ON THE ECONOMY." To raise revenue quickly, the governor is trying to get the legislature to end the logging ban on the very last of the old growth forests.

This is TERRIBLE! There's hardly any old growth left, and if they cut it down then all the old growth forest in Oregon will be gone FOREVER! Or at least for another 1,000 years, if the logging companies will leave the forest alone that long. I have a feeling they won't, though.

There's a quote from the governor: "I think I can speak for the fine people of Oregon when I say that if it comes down to a few trees versus avoiding economic collapse, we should choose to avoid economic collapse. Hardly anybody looks at those trees anyway."

Well Mr. Governor you don't speak for ME!

It's a fake choice! It doesn't have to be "nature or the economy"! What you should do, Mr. Governor, is support the Save the Earth Act so we can have BOTH! We can have old growth forests AND economic collapse. Oops, I mean AVOID economic collapse!

The governor also said: "We need to balance ecological integrity with economic realities. In other words, we need to liquidate our natural assets to balance out the economy's deficitness." That makes me SO MAD! That's not "balancing," that's sacrificing one thing to save another thing. I'm going to write a letter to the newspaper RIGHT NOW and let them know that. Once the truth is out in the open, they'll have to change their mind.

P.S. - I'm pretty sure "deficitness" is not a real word.

I just saw another poll result about the Save the Earth Act. Support has slipped a little, down to 61%. I'm not worried because I'm sure it's just a temporary slip due to people are panicking.

I just saw an OUTRAGEOUS article online. The head person at the Environmental Protection Agency announced they are "reducing restrictive standards" that are slowing down the economy. He used the analogy of the economy is like a boat trying to go really fast, and environmental standards are like throwing out the anchor.

He said taxpayers should be "delighted" by this news, since it will save taxpayer money that has been wasted to try to enforce these standards.

I saw some BAD news for GloboChem, which of course is GOOD news for everybody else and the earth.

Farmers are complaining that the GloboChem pesticides and herbicides aren't working any more. For a while it worked just to apply them more heavily, but now even if they apply them twice as much they're not effective. The reason is exactly what environmentalists warned would happen: Bugs and weeds have evolved to become resistant to even the strongest poisons. Basically, what GloboChem did was to create "superbugs" and "superweeds" that are taking over.

Farmers are mad at GloboChem for getting them in this mess, because GloboChem told them don't listen to environmentalists who want us to go back to the Stone Age. So a big group of farmers are organizing a huge lawsuit against GloboChem. One farmer said, "GloboChem got us addicted to their products; now they need to pay us to get free."

This is GREAT news because it means the end of GloboChem and their awful poisons. I can't wait to see how GloboChem reacts!

October 16

I can't believe how GloboChem reacted! Their press release came out so fast it's like they were prepared for this.

FOR IMMEDIATE RELEASE:

GloboChem to the Rescue

Recently GloboChem, Inc. has received some "less than fully satisfied" feedback on our agricultural products. We are pleased to respond to this feedback and offer what appears to be the only viable solution.

Apparently our GrowMagic™ agricultural helper has is becoming less effective over time, even by using heavier applications.

Some have claimed all along that this would happen, and that we have lied about it. That is true. But even though we lied once, that doesn't mean we're lying to you this time. Since we told the truth about our lying, that should make you trust us now.

But rather than engage in a useless discussion about "who said what when," we must forge ahead, like the courageous nation that we are. America has never turned its back on a challenge, and these tough economic times mean we must not turn our back like never before.

We recently announced our new HappyHuman™ product and sought to receive congressional approval to market it. But public reception was less-than-positive and the congressional bill stalled in committee.

We believe that now is the time to pass the bill and rush HappyHuman™ to the American public. Only by genetically engineering a human race able to withstand our products can we preserve our American way of life.

We must increase the "magic" within GrowMagic™ to a level high enough to kill every form of life that has not been genetically modified to resist it. There is no other option.

We have consulted with economic experts that we paid, and confirmed the following: Either we go forward with HappyHuman™, or food prices will increase by one thousand percent and the United States agricultural system will collapse and we will all die.

In other words, the only way to sustain human life is to modify ourselves to resist killing the rest of it.

More scare tactics! The good news is that the public is very environmentally aware and will see this is CRAZY.

October 17

I can't believe it! I just saw a poll of the public reaction to the GloboChem press release:

Strongly Oppose: 13%

Moderately Oppose: 26%

Need More Information: 61%

The "Need More Information" category included questions such as, "How much will 'HappyHuman' cost?" and "Will 'HappyHuman' work on my pet gerbil?"

The Portland Mayor just announced an emergency meeting of City Council to discuss building codes allowing affordable and sustainable housing!

I LOVE living in Portland because it's such a progressive city! Our leaders have decided that the bad economy is a sign not to go backwards but to be even MORE progressive. The meeting will include a public comment period, so definitely I'll be there to do some commenting!

I wasn't sure what to write about for part two of my blog article series about the Save the Earth Act, but the news about the oil shortage kind of decided for me. So I posted an article about how it will allow us to make the transition to alternative energy as smooth as possible.

October 18

Many comments were made to my blog article! One person wrote, "It sounds like a good idea but is there enough time?" Another person wrote, "To keep up our current energy use with alternative sources we'd basically have to cover the entire country with solar panels and windmills." I commented on that one and said, "Maybe we should think about conserving energy and using a lot less?" The person commented back, "You want us to sacrifice?"

With one person I sort of got into an "argument." He did not agree that we need to conserve. He thought there were all kinds of options besides fossil fuels. So I was forced to contradict his ideas with facts.

I explained how all energy on earth is SOLAR power which many people are still surprised to hear. Many (most?) people don't realize that oil (and coal) is made of solar energy that was built up in plants over millions of years.

He said that we could "grow" fuel using crops like soybeans or corn (ethanol). But I pointed out that this was very inefficient and we're already using pretty much all our productive land to grow food. There isn't enough productive land on the planet to grow enough fuel to meet our current energy use.

Then he said that's okay because we can turn our waste products into fuel, such as turning used cooking oil into biodiesel or turning organic wastes into methane. But I pointed out that even though we produce a LOT of waste, it's only enough to produce a tiny fraction of our energy needs.

Then he said that's okay because we can build more hydroelectric dams. But I pointed out that we've already put dams on pretty much all the rivers of the world, and actually we have to take some of them out because they screwed up the ecology and killed many fish runs. Also, dams have a limited lifetime because they fill up with silt, so therefore over time there will be LESS hydroelectric dams.

Then he posted a very short comment: "Nuclear?" And I said "Sure, if you want to live with growing piles of radioactive waste contaminating our land and water and air, and the cancer caused by accidents and radioactive leaks."

Then he said, kind of joking-like, "Well we can always go back to riding horses, right?" but I asked him where all the hay would be grown to feed the horses since the productive land is already being used to grow food.

Then his next comment (his last) was, "I think smart girls are really cute." Of course, that had NOTHING to do with energy use. I think he changed the subject because he didn't want to admit a girl was smarter than him.

Well, this article isn't TOO shocking. It was kind of unbelievable the Republican Party would turn into the "Ecological Earth-Saving Party."

Republican "Pro-Nature" Group Disbands

Washington, DC – In a press conference this afternoon, Senator Jefferson Bontrager (R-Minn.) announced that he is disbanding the "Republicans for the Earth" group.

"I don't know what I was thinking," said Senator Bontrager. "The only explanation I can come up with is that somebody put LSD in my coffee."

The senator said he suspects it was hippies from Oregon who tricked him into wanting to preserve nature. "I don't even like nature," said Senator Bontrager.

Now that the effects of the drug have worn off, the senator welcomes the chance to go back to familiar turf. "I can help the Republicans reaffirm our stance as the anti-environment party, just like before. This is especially important in these tough economic times when we need to do anything we can to stimulate the economy."

Well, at least this means the Democratic Party can go back to being the pro-environment party and not be wishy-washy like before.

This is weird. I checked the Democratic Party website and went to their "policy position" page. The part about the Save the Earth Act said: "The Democratic Party is currently forming committees and focus groups."

I guess it's a good thing that Representative Bozzio is running as an Interdependent instead of a Democrat.

I called Montia to see if she knows why the Democratic Party is being so weird about the Save the Earth Act. She said she had a pretty good idea, but what she said made NO sense at all. She said they reviewed the act very carefully and had a major problem with it. I said, "You mean they don't think it will work?" She said it's kind of the opposite: The problem is they think it WOULD work. I said that makes NO SENSE! She told me to think of it in the form of a question: How many people are going to vote for a political party that will require them to lower their standard of living?

Well at least tomorrow is the City Council meeting about changing the building codes!

October 19

The meeting was a DISASTER! I can't believe that the City Council meeting was not to ENCOURAGE affordable sustainable housing but to BAN it!

The mayor said the meeting was a response to "intense pressure" by the construction industry. The industry predicted "catastrophic loss of profit" if people were allowed to "cheat the system" by building sustainable homes for reasonable prices.

Therefore, the mayor wants to immediately adopt special Portland building codes that are even MORE strict than the IBC! He said the IBC currently makes a home expensive "indirectly" because of minimum size requirements and standards that can only be met by expensive materials.

He said, "Now is the time to get specific. The new codes abandon all the unnecessary details and simply spell out that a new home must cost a minimum of $400,000."

I do NOT understand! Is the purpose of homes for people to live in or to make money for companies?

He said it's not just about sustaining businesses, but about sustaining government. He explained that property taxes pay for lots of city services, such as schools. So if people started living in affordable housing, tax revenues would go way down and the children of Portland would become street hooligans.

He said the new codes would close the loophole that allows code variations on mobile homes. THIS MEANS DOUG NORMALSON CAN'T BUILD HIS AWESOME

ECOLOGICAL MOBILE HOME PARK! I wanted to yell that out, but it was not yet the public comment period which I assumed also meant no public yelling.

Then the mayor said the MOST CRAZY THING I'VE EVER HEARD. He said, "We have examined this issue very carefully, and have reached the conclusion that we can't afford affordable homes."

This is when I thought I was having a bad dream and I tried to wake myself up, but I confirmed that I was already awake.

Then the mayor said he wanted to assure us that this change did not affect Portland's desire to be a national leader in sustainability. He said the Portland Office of Sustainable Development is working with major banks and developers on a prototype "ultimate green home" to be revealed at this year's "Street of Green Dreams."

He started a PowerPoint show with pictures, and the "ultimate green home" looked to me EXACTLY like a regular big suburban home, except for the solar panels on the roof. Then he said, "This 'ultimate green home' is projected to sell for $950,000!" and then the people applauded like crazy.

That was so weird to me that I couldn't even think. Why were people applauding for a super-expensive home???

Then it was time for the public comment period. I stood up right away and said, "My name is Amy Johnson-Martinez and I have a public comment!" A man said, "You're the girl that stopped that development in Oaks Bottom!" and gave me a look which indicated he will probably never be my friend. It turned out that he's a developer.

I said that my public comment was that affordability should be part of sustainability, and that in fact I built my own sustainable home for only $2,000.

People were shocked at the low price. One man said, "People could save up that much money very easily. They wouldn't have to go to the bank for a mortgage!" I said,

"Isn't it GREAT?" and he said, "No, it's terrible!" It turned out that the man works for a bank.

I explained that making sustainable housing super-affordable is great for people, because they wouldn't have to work so much and they would have more time for meaningful things.

Then it was my turn to be shocked when a woman yelled out, "LIKE H*LL IT IS!" (She actually used profanity in front of the mayor!) She said, "Do you have any idea what affordable homes would do to my property value?"

She explained that she and her husband bought their house 20 years ago for "only $40,000" (which sounds like a FORTUNE to me, but that's way cheaper than houses now). She said the house was recently appraised at $400,000 which is 10 times as much.

Then everybody applauded again because the house is now 10 times less affordable! I couldn't believe it!

I said that this means young people buying a home have to pay 10 times as much as you. That means a lot of people can't afford a home at all, and the ones who can afford it are stuck with a huge financial burden. I said that to keep this up, the NEXT generation of young people would have to pay even MORE, so then each generation has to go MORE into debt.

The man who works for a bank said, "Woo-Hoo!" Somebody said, "That's why we need more economic growth." I said, "But economic growth is destroying the earth!" and somebody said, "I read that all we need to do it put the word 'sustainable' in front of 'economic growth.'"

Then the woman (the one who used profanity) sort of "exploded" with anger and yelled, "My husband and I didn't put up with 20 years of jobs we hate to have our profit wiped out by some hippies moving in next door and living in a hut and tearing up the lawn to plant tofu!"

Everybody was shocked into being quiet. I was thinking of telling her that tofu isn't something you plant, and that it's made of soybeans but they don't grow very well in Oregon. But I decided that was sort of not important at this point.

The mayor said, "Well, I believe this is a good time to end the public comment period." I said, "Mr. Mayor, I sure hope you take my public comment into consideration," He said, "Oh, this must be your first time to one of these," and I nodded yes. He said, "We actually already made up our minds before the meeting. We just have these public comment periods so people can feel like they have a voice in government. Thanks for coming!"

I'm VERY disappointed. In school I read many books about democracy, but none of them said anything about this.

October 20

I just saw the revised version of my presentation, "Out of Sight; Out of Mind." I have VERY mixed feelings about the new "more positive" version. For one thing, Katherine said the title needed a little work, so now it's called "There's Hope with HomeEarth."

The graphics are still really amazing, but now there's less "bad" news, and most of the bad news it shows are things that HomeEarth is working on. For example, after the part showing how forests are declining there was an image of a HomeEarth coffee cozy.

For endangered species, instead of a realistic image of the animal it was a "cartoon" image. For example, when the passenger pigeon went extinct, it said, "Hi, I'm the last passenger pigeon!" and then sort of "waves" and flies away. It doesn't exactly say that the passenger pigeon has gone extinct, but Katherine said, "Our audience is educated enough to understand."

She said the first version was upsetting to child test viewers. Some of them cried when it was explained they can't ever see a passenger pigeon, not even in a zoo.

In this new version, kids waved at the screen and said things like, "Bye-bye passenger pigeon!"

Katherine could tell I wasn't very "happy" with this new version. She explained that the idea is to inspire action, and the first version only inspired action if you consider "giving up" a form of action. She said people aren't inspired to do action without hope, and this new version offers hope. It shows that HomeEarth is working on their behalf, so the more they donate to HomeEarth the better they can feel.

As proof of this, she showed me the audience responses with comments such as "great graphics" and "my kids loved the vanishing species" and "I'm glad that HomeEarth has things under control."

I guess I'm glad for the positive reviews, and I sort of see Katherine's point about people needing to feel "hope." But somehow I feel like something important was lost in this new version. I really don't like the idea of kids not realizing that when they wave "bye-bye" to the passenger pigeon it means forever.

The "Creating a Sustainable Future for our Children" conference is TOMORROW. But the organizer never did get back to me like she was supposed to. That makes it really hard for me to know what to talk about. I guess I'll give sort of my "standard" talk about saving the earth, but throw in lots of stuff about "for the sake of our children" and "for future generations" and stuff like that.

October 21

I just finished my presentation at the "Creating a Sustainable Future for Our Children" conference. It did not go well. I'm not pleased with the organizer who never got back to me. It would have avoided the whole mix-up, including the man who looked like a college professor who had to go to the hospital after the fight.

I brought my PowerPoint slide show of beautiful nature photos, and every now and then I would refer to the photo and say, "See how beautiful nature is? We should save it for the sake of our children and future generations."

But I noticed a lot of people getting sort of "restless." Eventually somebody stood up and said, "Excuse me, the photos are quite beautiful but what does all this have to do with sustainability?"

I thought maybe I made a mistake and went to the wrong place. I asked, "This is the conference 'Creating a Sustainable Future for Our Children' isn't it?" Somebody else said, "Yes it is, but what does saving nature have to do with sustainability?"

I think the first person could tell I was confused, because he said, "You look confused." I nodded yes, and then he said something about tough times are ahead and it's very important to prepare our children to be sustainable. That totally made sense to me. I said, "Exactly! That's why it's so important that we save the earth."

Then HE got all confused and said, "What are you talking about?" Then another person said, "Amy, didn't anybody tell you what this conference was about?"
I explained that the organizer never got back to me, and she said, "Well that explains it!"

Then she told me that the conference is not about ECOLOGICAL sustainability but about ECONOMIC sustainability. Or in other words, preparing children by making sure they can compete for careers in what's left of our collapsing economy. It wasn't about environmental survival; it was about economic survival!

I felt it was my duty to point out that without environmental survival we can't have economic survival either! They have to go together! THANKFULLY somebody agreed with me! The man who looked like a college professor stood up and said, "We cannot afford to deplete the resource base on which the economy is dependent."

Then a woman stood up and said, "Go ahead and have your kid work on saving the birds. While your kid is doing that, MY kid will be preparing for a good-paying career."

What I said next turned out to be a little controversial. It's weird what people are "sensitive" about. But everything I said is based on scientific facts and I don't understand how people can get mad at facts.

I said, "Overpopulation is one of the major things destroying the earth, so to create a sustainable future for our children we'll need to have a lot less children."

Then there was this weird sound of a hundred people not breathing all at once, like their lungs sucked in a breath then got stuck. So I decided to keep talking. I remembered the conversation at the strawbale workshop, so I talked about how we have 300 million people and we're using resources 10 times too fast. Therefore the American lifestyle could only be sustainable with 30 million people. We have too many people for our lifestyle, so either we have to lower the population or reduce our lifestyle.

Then this lady held up a baby and said, "If Little Britney could talk, she would say she wants a future where she can have a higher standard of living." I said back, "Are you sure Little Britney wouldn't rather have a future with clean air and healthy ecosystems?"

Then the man who looked like a college professor said, "Perhaps we should wait until Little Britney is able to give her own opinion?" which is when he got slapped by the woman holding a baby.

A very shy-looking woman said something, but instead of yelling she said it quietly. She said that having a child is a deeply meaningful thing, and that for her "Faith in Life" translates to "Faith in Children." She said, "One of our children could grow up to be the genius that figures out how to solve all of our problems, so the more children we have the better our chances."

Then the man who looked like a college professor said, "So the more kids we have, the better chance we have to solve the overpopulation problem?" And she said, "Exactly!"

I said, "But we know how to fix our problems NOW! We don't need more people to figure it out!"

Then the man who looked like a college professor said, very proudly, "I have chosen to abstain from creating another child." This was VERY shocking to everybody. Then he said, "I do not wish to add another child to this troubled and overcrowded planet. To me, bringing a child into this world constitutes child cruelty." That resulted in him getting slapped again, not by the woman holding a baby but by another woman holding another baby.

Somebody yelled at him, "You don't love anybody except yourself!" He answered, "Is it 'love' to leave a child a degraded world and an economy on the verge of collapse?" One woman yelled, "How dare you imply we don't love our children!" and somebody else yelled, "I do everything I can to provide a good life for my child!" The man who looked like a college professor said, "What about leaving them a healthy planet?"

After the ambulance left, I finally found the organizer. I said, "My message did not fit very well with this conference, so why did you invite me?"

She said the "environmental stuff" actually had nothing to do with it. They just liked that I was a 14-year-old girl with a successful career. They thought I would be an inspiration to other teenagers.

October 22

Big economic news today. The president says that the economy is "stronger than ever" but we have to take desperate measures to save it. So today he announced an act that I'm thinking is a short-term solution to keep the economy from collapsing until the Save the Earth Act can take effect.

President Announces "Save the Economy Act"

Washington, DC – White House spokesperson Lloyd Jones prefaced the announcement of a new economic bill by reassuring Americans that the economy in no danger of collapsing. The act proposes that we keep the economy from collapsing by enacting the following measures:

- Initiate tax rebates for the super-wealthy in order to encourage investment to increase economic growth.
- Streamline nuclear power plant safety regulations to get new plants contributing to the electrical grid by a week from Thursday.
- Phase out Medicare, Medicaid and Social Security gradually over the next month.
- Initiate a "mandatory shopping tax" in which U.S. Citizens spending less than 30 percent of their net income on consumer durables will face steep income tax penalties.
- Immediately liquidate what's left of the country's natural resources.

In an emergency meeting of Congress, the act inspired a rare example of bi-partisan agreement and was enthusiastically passed in 17 minutes, a new record for a congressional bill.

I guess the "positive" thing about this is it shows that Congress CAN agree on things and can act quickly when the issue is important. This is encouraging because I am looking forward to this happening when the Save the Earth Act comes up for a vote.

When I got home tonight I discovered that the totally nice neighbor Carol left me a bag of spinach and a note:

> Hi Amy, I was shocked to hear that you actually live in that shed you built with those "people." I don't understand why a nice young lady like you wouldn't rather live in a proper house. Isn't it against city regulations to live in such a thing? ~Carol

I guess part of being a "radical" is being a pioneer for new ways that people don't understand. For example, people used to think recycling was "crazy" but now it's totally mainstream. Someday this will also be true for strawbale homes!

The conference "Environment and Religion" is in one week, and tomorrow morning I meet with the organizers so I can prepare (so there won't be any mix-ups like with the children's conference). I'm excited but I admit also a little nervous!

October 23

I'm afraid the meeting didn't exactly go as well as I'd hoped. I'm not sure what happened, it got off so such a great start.

I met with Reverend Robert McCallister and Reverend Susan Angleborg. They told me right away to just call them Bob and Sue, and not to be nervous because they're just regular people even though they talk to God.

Reverend Sue asked me, "Amy, would you call yourself a religious person?" I had never thought about that, so I said just what came into my mind.

I explained that I'm not exactly "religious" in the sense of going to church. But I'm not "spiritual" like Tiffany is, because the word "spiritual" makes it sound like there are "spirits" running around, and I'm too scientific to believe that. But I don't believe that molecules bouncing around somehow created life and all the beauty of the world and the universe. Everything is so amazing and beautiful that I know it's kind of a miracle.

Reverend Sue said, "That's a good start." Then Reverend Bob said, "Don't worry Amy, we're not a 'judging' church, we're an 'accepting' church." Reverend Sue said, "In fact, Reverend Bob is gay."

I looked at him and he was smiling and nodding. He said, "It's true! I am!" Reverend Sue said, "We're probably the most progressive church in Portland!"

I admit that this all made me feel a LOT better!

Reverend Bob asked me if I knew what the word "religion" means. I was excited that I could answer! I told them what I knew, about how it's a Latin word that means "re-link," and how religion started when humans got separated from the Garden of Eden, which is a metaphor of when we lived in harmony with nature. That meant we lost our connection with life and the universe and everything, so religion is how we "re-link" to that connection.

They looked at each other with very surprised expressions! Reverend Sue said that was a very advanced answer. She said most people define "religion" as an organized church that offers a community of people guidance in their relationship with God and a place to hang out on Sunday.

Then Reverend Bob said, "Well, Amy, we're here to discuss the conference 'Environment and Religion.' What would you hope for the conference to accomplish?"

I said that I hoped the conference would encourage religion to become more "activist" in environmental issues, just like they were active in the fight to stop slavery and promote civil rights and all the other social justice issues they've helped with. Reverend Sue said, "Of course! How can we, as stewards of God's creation, sit back when 'God's Country' is destroyed?"

I was SO EXCITED at this point in our meeting. I said that since millions of people are religious, it would be great if all religious people became activists for the earth. I said it would be amazing to see huge marches of religious people demanding that we live sustainably and stop destroying 'God's Country'!

Reverend Bob asked, "What do you plan to discuss in your presentation?" I said that I wanted to talk about the

Save the Earth Act and encourage all religious people to totally support it.

I was very surprised that they didn't know about it! So I tried to tell them about it in a short amount of time which is not easy. But I was able to include the really important stuff about how we need to stop our addiction to economic growth, because there are many ethical religious reasons that the church would agree with, including things from the Bible.

I explained about how money isn't evil, it's the LOVE of money. Before our meeting I even researched exactly what it says in the Bible. It's from 1Timothy 6:10: "For the love of money is the root of all evil: which while some coveted after, they have erred from the faith, and pierced themselves through with many sorrows."

I said that those words are very wise, because they predicted thousands of years ago what is coming true now, that our addiction to economic growth is piercing ourselves with many sorrows, such as destroying the earth! We are forced to "covet after" money or else our whole economy will collapse!

I also explained about how for hundreds of years the church has been against loaning with interest, or what it calls "usury." But then I realized how silly I was being. I said, "Oh, but of course you already know all that! It's so good that you're against it, because it's the root of our addiction to economic growth."

I also talked about Jesus being against the "money changers" which in the parable was just a few people destroying a temple in Jerusalem, but in modern times is the big banks that are destroying the temple of the entire earth. Back then, Jesus used a whip to "cleanse the temple." Of course, now we can't use whips - but we can use the Save the Earth Act.

I was very proud of myself for being so prepared!

Which is why I'm so confused that while I was saying all this, Reverend Bob and Reverend Sue had worried looks on their faces. Reverend Bob was the first to talk. He said, "Well Amy, I want to let you know that we are very committed to sustainability. For example, here at the church we've switched all our lights to compact fluorescents."

I asked about supporting the Save the Earth Act, and they stopped smiling and started acting "weird." Reverend Bob said, "If I understand you correctly, for the church to condemn usury now would be to basically condemn the entire economic system. Is that right?"

I said, "I'm so glad you understand!"

Then he said, "And ending economic growth would end speculative income, right?"

And I said, "Yes!"

Then Reverend Bob started talking and he KEPT talking. (I think he was doing a "sermon.") He was saying that the name of their church is "LifeFaith Church" because they are a church of faith, He talked a LOT about faith, and said they have faith in earthly things but ultimately their faith is in God.

I asked, "What about if you need to get surgery and it's a very dangerous operation, then wouldn't you have faith in the surgeon?" He said yes that's an example of "earthly faith," but ultimately our faith is in God to guide the hands of the surgeon. I asked, "Then why do surgeons go to medical school?" He thought that was funny, which made me sort of mad. I thought my question made a lot of sense.

I said that I couldn't understand how having "faith" could help fix the economy.

This time Reverend Sue gave a sermon. She said it's kind of the same thing with the "faith in the surgeon" idea. They have earthly faith that people will figure out how to get the economy growing again, but we must pray for God for guidance on how to do it.

That made me VERY CONFUSED, because I just explained how economic growth is based on usury which the church is against! So I said, "What about passing the Save the Earth Act so we don't need to depend on economic growth?"

Then both reverends were quiet for a minute and bowed their heads, like they were praying. Then Reverend Sue said, "I just asked God for guidance on that question, and God said he didn't think so."

Reverend Bob said, "Look kid, I'll give it to you straight." He explained that a reverend trying to be too radical has the same problem as a politician trying to be too radical. In both cases, people won't vote for you. With a church it's not exactly the same, since people don't actually vote for you. But they can vote "against" you by walking to a church that's less radical. He called it "voting with your feet."

I said, "I have the solution to that. If all the churches of your religion agree to be radical, then people can't just walk away. He said yes they can: They can walk to another religion.

I figured out there was one more thing I could say that I was SURE would convince them to support the Save the Earth Act. I said it had to do with the name of their church, LifeFaith Church. We already talked about the "faith" part, but we didn't talk about the "life" part.

Reverend Sue said they put a lot of thought into the name of the church. Including the word "life" was very important, because one of their core values is "to preserve the sanctity of life."

I said I was SO GLAD to hear that, and I explained how the definition of "natural" is "according to life" therefore saving NATURE is actually saving LIFE because they're the same thing. So all the churches that say they're "Pro-Life" also have to be "Pro-Nature" because that's two ways of saying the same thing.

As they were backing me out the door, they said they weren't sure there was actually enough time for me to give my presentation in the conference, because suddenly the schedule got all full, but if there was a last-minute opening they would let me know, but they were pretty sure there wouldn't be.

I've thought about this over and over, but I STILL can't figure out what happened. I did my research and presented my ideas very clearly. What went wrong?

October 24

I told Katherine that HomeEarth needs to make a powerful stand against all the crazy stuff going on, with so many people wanting to sacrifice the earth to save the economy, such as the president. We need to re-affirm our motto of "No Compromise in Defense of Mother Earth!" She said that if I want I can write up something, but try not to "ruffle any feathers."

Katherine was NOT in a good mood. I asked Tiffany what was going on, and she said it's because the numbers are WAY down.

I just realized that "ruffle any feathers" is a weird metaphor, as if people are chickens.

I saw a new poll. It's hard to believe, but the support for the Save the Earth Act dropped even further down.

I think I know what's happening. I didn't want to believe it before, but I realize that I was in denial. But once you know it then you can't be in denial anymore, because knowing is the opposite of denial.

Katherine is always saying not to use the word "sacrifice" (which she usually refers to it as the "S-word," as if it's a cuss word).

What I have to admit to myself is hard to believe, but it seems like people are thinking that a more simple and meaningful life with less affluence is a "sacrifice" for some reason. Even though it's practically impossible for me to figure out how they're thinking that, it seems to be true.

I think support is dropping because I'm not admitting this "sacrifice" thing that's a big deal to them. So instead of not admitting it, maybe I need to take the totally opposite strategy of admitting it. Actually, maybe not just "admitting" it (like it's an apology) but making it sound awesome.

I know what I need to do. I need to write the most incredible inspiring speech that anybody has ever written. It has to be so true and inspirational that people will be deeply moved and inspired to save the earth. Maybe even make people cry, if I can make it inspirational enough.

I just called Representative Bozzio and actually reached him! I told him it's an EMERGENCY. Support for the Save the Earth Act is not looking great, so I'm working on the most inspirational speech in history and he has to arrange a press conference so I can share it with the world. And he needs to also think of inspirational things to say.

He thought that was a good idea, he'll have Montia arrange it. Then he had to get back to a meeting. I guess he was talking to some lobbyists from the lawn equipment industry about the "Peace and Quiet Act."

I called Juvie Starr to see if she's had time to read about the Save the Earth Act and is ready to give public support. I was also really excited to tell her about my speech, and I thought maybe she could also give me some acting lessons on how to be especially inspirational.

Unfortunately something is screwed up at the phone service. I got a recording, "The number you are trying to reach has been disconnected." I'll try back later when the problem has been fixed.

October 25

I am NOT happy with Katherine! She edited my press release (a LOT) and published it without telling me.

> **FOR IMMEDIATE RELEASE:**
>
> **HomeEarth Annoyed With Increasing Destruction of Earth**
>
> *Portland, OR* – HomeEarth, the nation's fourth-largest environmental organization, has been observing recent events with a feeling of disappointment.
>
> HomeEarth wants it to be known that the unrelenting war on the environment to destroy what's left of the earth's productive capacity in a futile attempt to save the economy makes us mad.
>
> "It makes me want to stomp my feet in anger," said HomeEarth President Katherine Bliss.
>
> Ms. Bliss added that if anyone would like to join HomeEarth and support our mission of "No Compromise in Defense of Mother Earth!" please visit www.HomeEarth.org and visit our "New Member" page. Join now and receive a complementary re-usable coffee cozy!

October 26

Writing a speech is HARD! Also, when the purpose is for the speech to inspire humanity to change the course of civilization... Well, that's a lot of pressure! I've given many presentations about things like recycling as one part of saving the earth, but not to change EVERYTHING to save the earth. (Am I asking people to recycle our civilization?)

I did an Internet search for "How to write an inspiring speech to save the earth" but nothing good came up.

Well... here goes! I have a few notes of some ideas and I'm ready to start on my speech. This first draft is going to be VERY ROUGH.

AMY'S INSPIRATIONAL SPEECH
By Amy

(Somebody introduces me and says my accomplishments and the audience claps)

~~My fellow Americans~~, ~~My fellow human beings~~, Hi, I'm Amy. I'm here to talk to you about saving the earth.

I offer you the wise words of Abraham Lincoln: "I am a firm believer in the people. If given the truth, they can be depended upon to meet any national crisis. The great point is to bring them the real facts."

One fact is: If we win against nature, we lose. Another fact is: To save the earth we'll have to sacrifice. There, I said it.

(audience is shocked but they don't go away)

I'll say another thing that people have been afraid to say: Our lifestyles are unsustainable, and to be sustainable we have to change our lifestyles.

Yes, there will be sacrifice for this generation, so there can be future generations. It's like the "Greatest Generation" of World War II that sacrificed to save us from the tyranny of fascism. Now, THIS generation has the opportunity to be the next "Greatest Generation" by saving us from the tyranny of environmental destruction. We must do it for future generations for the sake of our children.

The Save the Earth Act will get us out of the economic growth addiction without collapsing the economy and also save the earth while we're at it.

Yes, it's true that no more economic growth means no more "money from nothing." We'll have to make money a very old-fashioned way: By earning it and saving it. That's something the first "Greatest Generation" understood, and will also have to be understood by this one.

We thought it was a good idea to base our society on fossil fuels that are now running out. We also thought it was a good idea to spray poisons on the food we eat ~~which sometimes gets spilled and results in sick babies~~. These are two of a whole lot of problems based on not living sustainably.

Now we have the chance to correct these problems. It will be hard for a while. But it will be a lot harder if we don't correct them soon and let them get way worse.

I've learned from a wise person ~~named Coyote~~ that addictions are not just to drugs or alcoholic drinks.
I propose to you that we're addicted to destroying the earth. Since we're addicted, the only way to stop is what addicts call "cold turkey." That means it's hard at first and requires great sacrifice, ~~but you are a lot better when you get sober~~ but later you are glad you went through it.

I offer you the wise words of the Cree Prophecy, which warns us of our perilous path:

> Only after the last tree has been cut down,
> Only after the last river has been poisoned,
> Only after the last fish has been caught,
> Only then will you find that money cannot be eaten

So yes, we will have to sacrifice. But it's for ~~an awesome~~ a noble purpose.

Recall from ~~the~~ history ~~book I read in school~~ the example of World War II. It was an inspiring example of what we can do when we set our minds to it. We turned the whole economy and our factories toward the effort. It didn't take years to do this, it only took months. And this was back before the Internet!

This example demonstrates the spirit we need today, a worthwhile goal to channel our energy, except not in a destructive war but toward something more positive than that. And I can't think of a more meaningful goal than creating a sustainable civilization that honors and preserves life and promotes human well-being. ~~If you think about it, having any other kind of civilization sounds kind of stupid~~.

In other words: We can do it! Those words came from our effort to win World War II from posters of Rosie the Riveter ~~who is a great feminist icon I learned about in school~~.

Perhaps some people think it would be too hard, or it would cost too much.

One answer is to consider another example from ~~my history book~~ our history. The arguments against slavery were always counter-argued with statements like, "We can't afford to stop slavery!" or "Without slaves the economy will collapse!" But Lincoln ~~who in my opinion was the best president~~ had the courage to say, "That doesn't matter. Slavery is just wrong." His philosophy was that you start with the question, "Is it right or wrong?" Then you act on the answer. Just think if we hadn't banned slavery. And to end our discussion of history and lead up to right now, consider what will happen if we don't ban destroying the earth.

Let us not fool ourselves; it will not be easy. But that's what grown-ups do: Accept their mistakes and do what it takes to correct them. My mom called it "taking responsibility for your existence." It's like if I didn't clean up my room she would yell at me to do it "for my own good." I didn't like to do it, but afterwards I was glad I did it. That's kind of where we are now, except it's the whole planet earth. And there's no mom to yell at us to do it. It's time now that we have to yell at ourselves.

There's a lot of agreement on the definition of "the meaning of life" as "leave the world better than when you found it." I think we can all agree that "better" does NOT mean more cars, or a bigger house, or more TV channels.

But we have a chance to be "better" in the IMPORTANT ways. We can measure our "standard of living" as having the most happy and meaningful life and the satisfaction that we are living in harmony with nature and not at war with it.

Hey, it sounds to me not like a "sacrifice" but an "opportunity"!

It would give our country such a great sense of renewed purpose, instead of everybody ~~just being selfish~~ seeking only personal satisfaction ~~and they don't care about anything else~~ and no larger meaning for their life.

We have two choices: We can accept the sacrifice as a challenge to forge a new and better world, or we can continue to deny the problem and put it off so it gets worse and some future generation gets stuck with it and thinks of us as a bunch of jerks.

It's like we're on a road that we're SURE is going over a cliff, and I'm asking people to change to a road that's curvy and we can't exactly see where it's going. But at least it's not over a cliff. ~~It will probably be bumpy though~~.

What are we going to tell our children and grandchildren when they ask what we did to stop the destruction of the earth?

I have an idea: Instead of destroying the earth, let's save it! Thank you very much for letting me talk ~~at~~ to you today!

(end of speech, then audience claps
and is inspired to save the earth)

I called Montia and told her MY SPEECH WILL SOON BE READY FOR THE WORLD! She said she found a "unique setting" for the press conference. It will be on the top of Mount Tabor, which is the only volcano within a city in the entire country. We can have the conference right in the old crater, where you can see lava rock. She said as far as she knew it would be the first press conference ever held inside a volcano!

Maybe I can think of some metaphors to include in my speech, such as we need to make "volcanic changes" to our lives, or we need "an eruption of ideas like hot lava."

Montia just called me back. She said the press conference will be TOMORROW! That's so quick! But we can't do it next week because the annual Mount Tabor Soapbox Derby is happening then.

October 27

The speech went GREAT! I was VERY nervous before it started. But my nervousness went away because

Representative Bozzio went on first, and I had to deal with a crisis situation that took my mind off the fact that millions of people were watching me and listening to me.

When he went on, all I could think was, "Please don't say anything about that badger you saw in Eastern Oregon!" He started off great. He talked about how sacrificing nature to save the economy is "suicide" because we depend on nature. But then he started talking about how amazing nature is, and about all of nature's amazing creatures.

And I thought, "Oh no! Don't do it!"

Then he started saying how one time he was in Eastern Oregon, and I knew if he started on that stupid badger story he wouldn't talk about anything else. So I was forced to act. I rushed up to the stage and told him, "Thank you Representative Bozzio for your great speech!"

Then I gave my speech, and I think it went really well. The people even clapped in the spot where I put "audience claps," even though they didn't have a copy of my speech.

Then I remembered that millions of people were watching me and listening to me, which made me unable to think or talk and made my brain fuzzy. I'm very glad I didn't remember any sooner, for example in the middle of my speech.

October 28

I checked online to see the comments to my speech. As usual there were a few "weirdos" who wrote things like, "When you want us to 'sacrifice' why don't you just say you want us to kill ourselves?"

But it's easy to ignore those when I got so many positive comments! Such as, "Amy has grown into such a fine speaker" and "Very intelligent for a teenager" and "It was cool that you were inside of a crater."

Although the comments were positive they didn't exactly seem to have the exact effect I wanted. But that's only the first time I gave the speech. I'll keep working on it and I'll give it everywhere I can.

Weird. I tried to call Juvie Starr again but the phone company is still screwed up.

I heard back from the book editor at HarperCollins. It was a letter and very formal - not friendly at all. It's very sad, it turns out they aren't going to publish my book after all. The letter said, "Due to a recent assessment of projected sales, we do not feel the proposed book would be profitable. If your approval rating improves in the future, we would be happy to re-visit the project."

So the book will cost too much to make a profit. I totally understand that businesses need to make money - that's how they stay in business! Maybe the cost for paper has gone up? When the Save the Earth Act passes, it will mean worthwhile projects like this will be VERY profitable. After it passes I'll call the editor again.

More non-great news. But it's important to keep my eyes open to the truth and not shut them.

Climate "Tipping Points" Trigger Irreversible Change

Stockholm – The "nightmare scenario" most feared by climate scientists appears to be well underway, according to the Global Climate Institute in Stockholm, Sweden. Two "tipping points" have been positively confirmed by head scientists Sven Olifson and Oly Lindquist.

Olifson confirmed the tipping point he calls the "Olifson Effect." Global warming has led to the collapse of Arctic sea ice, which has started a thawing of the Siberian permafrost. This led to a massive release of methane that will trigger further warming and further melting of polar ice.

The other tipping point was confirmed by Lindquist, which he calls the "Lindquist Effect." Global warming has caused massive droughts which have led to dying forests.

As a result, these forests absorb less carbon dioxide, which leads to further warming, and therefore more dying forests.

Lindquist and Olifson are currently arguing over whether the "Lindquist Effect" or "Olifson Effect" came first, as each scientist wants to be the one known as the scientist that predicted the upcoming downfall of human civilization. "There might be a Pulitzer at stake here," explained Lindquist.

China Demands U.S. Agricultural Output

Washington, DC – In a perfect example of the interconnected nature of the modern world, an agricultural crisis in China is set to exacerbate economic problems in the United States.

Global warming has led to diminished snowfall in the mountains of China, and the rapidly shrinking water supplies have devastated their grain harvest. As a result, China has turned for assistance to the United States, which is by far the greatest grain-exporting nation on earth.

However, the timing is less than optimal since U.S. agricultural output has dropped to the point where we barely have enough for domestic needs. Heightened demand for the limited supply is expected to drive up costs, adding to our own economic problems.

In response, the president initially declared an immediate ban on all agricultural exports. However, the Chinese government reminded the president that China currently holds $900 billion of United States debt.

The president responded by authorizing the export of 90 percent of the total U.S. grain harvest to China. As for the effects on citizens of this country, the president suggested, "This would be a really good time to go on a diet."

October 29

Great news! There was a new poll about the Save the Earth Act after my speech. Support has gone up 2%! That means "the tides are turning" to use an ocean metaphor. Actually, maybe "the tide is rising" is a better metaphor. Except maybe it sounds like ocean levels rising due to global warming. So I guess "the tides are turning" is better.

More great news! An editorial by the governor of Indiana that urges the president to take action to save the earth.

EDITORIAL: Where Are You Mr. President?

By Governor Eliza Martindale

Mr. President, where are you when we need you? I just left the Annual Meeting of the National Governors Association, and we have a message for you. The oil shortage and subsequent price escalation has put this great nation into a serious crises.

Because of urban planning based on unlimited cheap energy, our people can no longer afford to live.

We have spread everything out with suburban sprawl, and now driving has become a necessity that we can no longer afford. For many Americans, the cost of driving to work is almost as much as their job pays them. There is hardly money left over to purchase consumer goods from China so they can buy the Treasury bonds that keep our economy from collapsing.

In addition, suburban families can't afford to drive to the mall. They have been forced to remain at home and spend time together.

Mr. President, these are problems that require solutions at the national level.

Americans are traditionally leery of government interference, preferring laissez-faire capitalism and the "invisible hand" to choose wisely. Well, Mr. President, the "invisible hand" is now giving us the middle finger.

The time has come for government to step in and take control. It is time to return our government to its traditional role of getting us out of the messes that big business gets us into.

Mr. President, we're counting on you. The future of our great country is resting on your shoulders. And also on the rest of you.

This is GREAT! This means that the president has the support of all the state governors to start an emergency program for things like smart urban planning and energy conservation and converting to renewable energy.

I think what's happening is that things had to get REALLY bad before people sort of "woke up." It's kind of like how an alcoholic has to "hit bottom" and lose their job and home and family before they start thinking maybe they are drinking too many liquor drinks.

I can't believe what I just saw on the news. There was a big press conference, and the big banks are demanding another huge bailout. Actually, they're calling it a "keep the economy from totally collapsing plan." They say they need $900 billion of taxpayer money. This makes a lot of people mad, because we're still paying off the last bailout of $700 billion.

A reporter asked one of the bankers, "Are you holding the economy hostage?" The banker said, "Yes." The reporter was shocked. He said, "I didn't expect an honest answer." The banker said, "You can sit down now."

Then another banker said to the whole audience, "Don't worry, as soon as the economy gets growing again we'll pay you back." Then both of them started laughing for some reason.

Well, I laughed at THEM because as soon as the Save the Earth Act passes we won't need them, and they can't hold the economy hostage anymore.

October 30

A weird thing just happened. Katherine walked in and asked if I saw the latest poll about the Save the Earth Act. She wanted to make sure I was feeling okay. I said that I was feeling GREAT. She said, "I just want to make sure when the vote happens that you're not devastated."

Weird! I guess she meant "devastated by happiness." It's like when you're so incredibly super happy that you cry because it goes over the top and comes out the other side.

I asked if there were more speaking engagements for me. She said there haven't been a lot of requests lately because people are more concerned about the possibility of "total social collapse."

That's how she put it! So dramatic! I told her that's what happens when you watch too much TV. They make everything overly-dramatic. It's like the last time it snowed in Portland. It was only an inch of snow, and they acted like it was the biggest crisis in the history of the earth. One TV station even called it "Snowmaggedon"!

Katherine should be more relaxed, like Tiffany. Yes, it's true that me and Tiffany have some "philosophical differences." But there are many things about her that I admire, such as how she stays peaceful even when things are going crazy. She told me that it helps if she "remembers to breathe." I don't understand that, because if you forget to breathe your brain just makes it happen anyway.

October 31

The president responded to the editorial about the oil crisis! Tiffany brought me this article, which explains how the military is trying to pressure the president to start a war, but he is totally resistant to that idea.

President Responds to Oil Crises

Washington, DC – In a press conference today, the president responded to the widely-circulated editorial by Indiana Governor Eliza Martindale, urging a national response to the devastating oil crises. "The people have spoken," said the president, "and I have listened to it."

The president agreed that designing our entire national infrastructure around an unsustainable source of energy has had dire consequences. "I have had extensive meetings with experts in sustainable energy," said the president. As a result of these meetings, the president identified three core conclusions:

- It would take decades to make the transition to sustainable energy.

- We would basically have to tear up the entire country and start over.
- We can't afford it.

"Therefore, our course is clear," said the president. "The only question is: Which country do we invade?"

The president explained that he has consulted with the Joint Chiefs of Staff in a thorough cost-benefits analysis to identify the least problematic target that would provide the greatest petroleum returns.

Our neighbors Canada and Mexico both have substantial oil reserves. But the president pointed out, "Canadians are too much like us, and invading Mexico would lose me the Hispanic vote."

The current top contenders are Nigeria and Angola.

"A final decision will be made very soon," said the president.

The president was asked how the invasion would be justified. Would it be a "war on terrorism" or a "war on drugs" or a "war to advance democracy"? The president replied,

"Oh none of that. We're just attacking them so we can take their oil."

Tiffany asked me if I was OK. She said she was concerned because it seemed like I was feeling "too good, considering everything." Weird! How is it possible to feel "too good"?

Speaking of "weird"...

I just saw a big article in Newsweek called "Escaping the Trap." It has many scientists with ideas on how we can solve our environmental problems. Here are some of the ideas. They're so strange that I feel like I have to write, "I'm not making this up!"

- Genetically alter agricultural plants to grow in places they don't normally grow, such as deserts. One scientist thought he could engineer sagebrush to grow tomatoes.

- Genetically alter humans to make them super small, such as an inch tall. That way we would use only a tiny fraction of our current resources and not have to change our lifestyle. For example, cars for people an inch tall would get about 10,000 miles to the gallon. One drawback would be that all people would have to agree. Because if anybody stayed at our current size, they would be huge Godzilla-type monster humans that could step on the rest of us.

- We could abandon our bodies and have our minds converted to digital form and live in a virtual reality with no physical restrictions. Everybody could live in huge mansions and drive cars made of solid gold and waste as many resources as we want, because it's all in our imaginations.

- We could abandon earth and move to Venus, as soon as we figure out how to survive on a planet with a surface temperature of 872 degrees and has clouds made of sulfuric acid.

These ideas are so strange that they are actually kind of funny. I don't even think the scientists realize that these ideas are not "solving" the problems at all! The real solution is much easier and simpler: Just reduce our consumption and live sustainably.

Dad said a very surprising thing. He told me he's thinking maybe we should move to Mexico. I told him I couldn't believe he's thinking about giving up his good job and our nice home. But he said he has a "very bad feeling" about what is happening in America, and the good thing about living in poverty is that it's better than not living at all.

Now Dad is being dramatic! I'm surrounded by drama addicts!

November 1

Bad news, but it's only temporary. The latest poll shows that support for the Save the Earth Act has fallen again.

I know what I have to do. It's like what happened in the old movie "Mr. Smith Goes to Washington." It's the part at the end, when James Stewart goes to Washington DC when everything seems lost. Then he delivers a big speech to Congress which barely saves everything just in time.

I happen to have a very inspirational speech that is all ready to give. Probably a lot of people in Congress didn't see my speech on TV. Well, they're going to hear it in person!

Representative Bozzio just stopped by for a surprise visit. He was all nervous and looked scared and told me, "We have to talk. Just you and me." So we went to Jamison Square Park.

He said, "Two very large and scary men had a conversation with me." I asked if that made him lose his sense of fun, and he said yes the two men scared it away.

When he asked who they were, all they would say is, "We are representing several interested parties." He's pretty sure that means some of the big banks sent them. The one with the scar (I forgot to write that one had a scar on his face) said they wanted to discuss what happens to people who try to change things that don't need to be changed. Then the one with the eye patch said, "Such as how money is introduced into circulation." Then scar-face said, "Of course, there have been presidents who had the silly idea to try to change that."

I said, "Oh, like with President Lincoln who introduced debt-free 'greenback' money!" Representative Bozzio said they started to explain it to him, but of course he already knew about it.

But then eye-patch asked if he knew about President Kennedy and Executive Order 11110. (I think that's right.)

He told them he'd never heard of it. I told Representative Bozzio that I hadn't heard of it either.

Apparently it was a very radical thing. It was similar to what President Lincoln tried. It took the power to create money away from the private banks, and gave the Treasury Department the power to create debt-free money. Some of the money even got printed while President Kennedy was alive. But the weird thing is that soon after President Kennedy got assassinated the money disappeared - just like with President Lincoln's "greenbacks."

I didn't know President Kennedy was so radical, which makes it extra sad that he was assassinated before he could finish his plan. So all we need now is another president to finish what Lincoln and Kennedy started.

When I suggested this, Representative Bozzio got VERY nervous. I asked him why he was so nervous, and he said that the large and scary men made a very interesting point.

Scar-face asked, "Now, what is it that happened to President Lincoln after he tried to take the power to issue money away from private banks?" Eye-patch answered, "Shot in the head." Then scar-face asked, "That's interesting. So what happened to President Kennedy after he tried to take the power to issue money away from private banks?" Eye-patch answered, "Shot in the head." Then scar-face got really close to Representative Bozzio and sort of "petted" him on the head. Then he said, "It would be a real shame, you have such a nice head."

Representative Bozzio was actually shaking when he told me that part. I said I would have been nervous too, because I also hate it when strangers touch me. You never know if they washed their hands last time they went to the bathroom.

He said no, that wasn't it. He was afraid for his LIFE!

I said, "You're not thinking about falling for those scare tactics are you?" But I could tell from his expression that he was thinking about it very much.

He said he was having second thoughts about this whole "running for president" thing. I told him he HAS to be the next president because he's the only one with the vision to save the earth. He asked, "How much good could I do as a president without a head?"

For some reason I thought that was hilarious. I imagined him in the White House, sitting in the Oval Office at his desk signing legislation without a head. I told this to Representative Bozzio and he didn't think it was hilarious.

I said that once the Save the Earth Act passes there will be nothing to worry about. Scar-face and eye-patch would have to get jobs doing something besides scaring people, such as maybe they could work on an organic farm.

Representative Bozzio said he did not even want to think about the Save the Earth Act right now. But he wanted me to know that the Peace and Quiet Act has a very good chance of passing. The lawn equipment lobby promised its support if he made some minor changes. I asked what kind of changes and he said, "Very minor, just bumping up the noise limit a little bit, up to 95 decibels."

I just looked it up online, and according to the chart 95 decibels is equivalent to "subway train at 100 feet." Representative Bozzio must have been mistaken about the number!

Katherine just had a little meeting to tell me some non-great news about HomeEarth magazine. There wasn't enough time to make the special issue devoted to the Save the Earth Act. So the special issue has been cancelled.

She could tell I was non-happy, but she said it was OK because they had another "back-up" issue ready to print.

She thinks it will be very popular. The theme of the issue will be "50 Really Easy Things You Can Do To Save the Earth." She said that the first item will be, "Have a nice glass of local organic wine." I told her that I can't legally take that advice for another 7 years. She said, "I guess you're right." I also can't do the advice of the second item which is, "Have a nice shot of local organic whiskey."

November 2

Somebody played a joke on me! Tonight when I got back to my lovely strawbale home I found this note:

CITY OF PORTLAND

NOTICE OF CONDEMNATION

This property has been found to be in violation of code:
VTK-028

Specific violation:
Assessed property value below $400,000 minimum

Corrective Action required:
Remodel property to increase value by $398,000

If the corrective action has not been completed within 60 days, the property will be condemned and destroyed. Have a nice day.

That's pretty funny! I can't imagine who would play such a trick. Whoever it was did a really good job, though. It looks totally official.

November 3

NOW I KNOW!!! It must have been nice neighbor Carol who played the trick on me! It's VERY OBVIOUS because of this note I just found.

Hi Amy, it's such a shame that the city condemned your shed. But in my opinion that was not an appropriate living situation for such a nice young woman as yourself. Now you can go back to living in a real home and property values won't go down. ~Carol

The cover story in the Oregonian says that even with all the bad economic news, there is at least some good news. For example, Andy & Bax had to hire extra salespeople and is having trouble keeping guns and ammunition in stock. They also interviewed somebody from a fence company who is doing "very well" selling razor wire. THIS IS GOOD NEWS?

Well, one thing that I think is very optimistic is that even though there's a lot of non-great news out there, people haven't lost their sense of humor. One example is the fake condemnation notice. Here's another example I saw today.

HOW TO SURVIVE A TOTAL SOCIAL COLLAPSE

Any student of history will tell you that societies don't last forever. The society you are in right now could collapse in 100 years…or in 10 minutes! Are you prepared? Here are helpful steps you can take to survive the initial collapse and re-build a new society later on.

1 – Before you start going all "Rambo" on your neighbors, make sure that society is truly collapsing and it's not just a block party that got out of hand.

2 – If you have an emergency radio, listen for government announcements telling you that this mess was caused by the previous administration.

3 – Don't try to be a hero and risk your life for stupid reasons. Get somebody else to do it.

4 – Every social collapse in history has resulted in cannibalism. If the idea of eating other people sounds unpleasant, ask yourself if you'd rather have somebody else eat you.

5 – Many fearful and confused people will be in search of a natural leader to become willing subjects in exchange for

security. This is good news is you've always wanted to be a revolutionary leader or benevolent dictator or wacky king.

6 – Resist the urge to declare war on neighboring tribes, which will create an atmosphere of fear and escalating violence, unless they can be easily defeated.

7 – Stray animals will become an important source of dietary protein. Instead of thinking of pigeons as "winged rats," think of them as "petite chickens."

8 – Wear comfortable clothes.

9 – Prepare for a future Renaissance by preserving the best of our society. You can be the nucleus for cultural rebirth after the chaos and Dark Ages by saving all those DVD box sets of "Friends" and "Everybody Loves Raymond." It may not seem important now, but future generations will erect statues in your honor.

10 – Also preserve a large library of books which are excellent for starting fires for cooking and heating.

November 4

My life is setting a new record for weirdness! There are times when it feels like my life is really a dream. And instead of me dreaming it, it is dreaming me. Does that make any sense?

I definitely felt like this when I was in my office and Tiffany called me and said, "You have a special visitor." When I went out to her desk I saw a unicycle leaning against a wall next to an bagpipe, and she was talking to a Scotsman which I realized was DEEP ECOLOGY!

Then Tiffany said to me, "I think you've met my friend before, yes?" He turned around and said, "Hi Amy, how's it going?" But it wasn't a Scottish accent, it was a regular voice that sounded very familiar.

Then he said, "Oh, I forgot I was wearing this silly costume!" He took off the red wig and beard and fake eyebrows, and underneath all that was Anthony Iron!!!

DEEP ECOLOGY WAS REALLY ANTHONY IRON!!!

But Deep Ecology gave me secret information that helped me to defeat Anthony Iron! But they're the same person! So that means Anthony Iron gave me information to help me defeat Anthony Iron???

Then he said, "I was in the neighborhood to visit my girlfriend, so I thought we could have a nice chat. Can I buy you lunch?" I don't remember what my mind decided for my voice to say, but we ended up at this super-fancy restaurant. He ordered a drink for me, a "virgin chocolate martini" which was very delicious but that's not important.

He said he thought he owed me an explanation. He wanted me to know it was "nothing personal." I didn't understand, and I asked him why he gave me information that I used to defeat him. He laughed and said, "Do I look defeated? I don't feel defeated!" I admitted that he didn't look defeated at all.

He asked me, "Do you remember a while ago, when you asked me to debate you? Do you remember what I said?"

I answered that I did, and it didn't make any sense to me. I remembered that he said, "If I win against you, then I will lose."

He said that is correct. "Therefore, in order to not lose. I had to help you win. Obviously you wouldn't accept any assistance from me, so I had to create an alter-ego."

I guess I looked confused (because I was). He said, "You wanted the truth about the roots of environmental destruction, right? Have you ever heard of the expression, 'Be careful what you ask for because you might get it'?"

Naturally I was confused, because don't you want what you ask for? I told him that and he laughed. Then he said something that made no sense at all. He said, "Rather than defeat you, I merely led you to the truth so the public could do it for me."

I couldn't figure out why Anthony Iron thought that HE won.

I told him, "But you're the one that lost! It was your information that helped create the Save the Earth Act that will stop all those terrible corporations you worked for."

He acted shocked and said, "I am truly offended. Those companies paid me extremely well for my services. In fact, I can now afford to retire comfortably. And the way society is heading, I think I need to begin my retirement immediately. Did I tell you that I bought an island?"

I tried to tell him that we won't have a collapse because of the Save the Earth Act. He thought that was funny, and went back to talking about the collapse he thinks is going to happen. "Of course I saw it coming," he said. "I mean, I was working for the people causing it!"

Then he went back to talking about how he was able to finish his little "retirement cottage" just in time. He said, "Actually it's more of an 'island stronghold' but I prefer not to call it that because it makes me sound like a villain in a James Bond movie. I spent pretty much everything I had on it. But as you so wisely pointed out, after the earth's resources are gone, we'll all find that money cannot be eaten."

I couldn't believe it! I said, "You heard my speech?"

He said, "Of course! I have followed your career with fascination. You've taught me more than you realize. You are correct that after the collapse you can't eat money. But you can eat from the stockpile of food you bought with money. But man cannot live on caviar and a large variety of canned delicacies alone. He needs fresh fruits and vegetables, too. Which is why I hired a landscaper to build me a Permaculture garden."

I couldn't believe it! Anthony Iron made a permaculture garden!

He said, "Do you remember something else I said a while ago, about that I never stay with a losing team? Well, right now civilization is a losing team. I'm leaving tomorrow, and I suggest for your own sake that you do the same. I'd invite you to stay on my island, but unfortunately there's not enough room."

We were done and he left a HUGE tip for the waitress. She held it up and said, "Wow, $100!" He said, "It's no big deal. I mean, you can't eat it." She gave him a very strange look.

I went back to HomeEarth, and Tiffany said, "Isn't Anthony special?" I didn't know how to answer that, so I changed the subject to admiring how she was staying so calm and peaceful with so many other people going crazy. I said it must be because she's deeply spiritual and remembers to breathe.

She laughed and said, "I guess that has something to do with it. But mostly I'm peaceful because I'm leaving all the craziness behind!" I asked her what she meant. She said, "Anthony is taking me with him!"

I couldn't believe it! I said, "You're his girlfriend?"

She said that while society is collapsing they'll be snuggling on a warm tropical beach sipping ice cold champagne. She said if I'm wondering how the champagne can be ice cold, it's because they have a solar-powered freezer.

I asked her, "What about saving the earth?" She said that the Buddhist aspect of her spirituality teaches "non-attachment" and also "the only thing that's permanent is change." So what use is it to save the earth since it's just going to crash into the sun in a few billion years?

Am I the only non-insane person left? I feel like I'm in that science fiction movie, I can't remember the name of it. It's the one where gradually everybody is infected with space germs (or something) and turns into a zombie until there's only one non-zombie left. Is that me?

November 5

I can't believe it! There was an email sent to all employees of HomeEarth. It said the organization is "evolving its mission." And to go with that, they're changing their motto from "No Compromise in Defense of Mother Earth!" to "Slightly Less Unsustainable." I'm going to talk to Katherine about it.

Well, that conversation was less than great. I said (very excitedly) "What about our mission to save the earth?" She answered (very calmly) that she has seen the feedback from the membership survey, and over 90% of the people thought the old motto was "too extreme." She said it's very challenging competing for membership dollars when people are also buying generators and stocking up on canned food.

She could tell I was not happy, so she asked me a question: "If our membership numbers tank, how can we fulfill our important mission to save the earth?" I said, "But you just said that isn't our mission anymore." She said, "Yes, in order that we can retain our membership." I asked, "We have to change our mission so we can keep our membership so we can do what isn't our mission anymore?"

She couldn't answer that because she remembered that she had an important phone call to make.

Oh no! Representative Bozzio decided not to run for president! I just saw the press conference. He said he decided not to run for "health reasons." When a reporter asked him if he was willing to say what kind of health reasons, he said, "I'm trying to keep bullets from entering my head." The reporter didn't have any follow-up questions.

Representative Bozzio just called me to say he was very sorry. I said it was OK and he's doing great work in Congress. Maybe as a representative he can be more effective than he would have been as president.

He said he wasn't calling me so much about the "president thing," but mostly he was calling to say he was sorry about the Save the Earth Act. I said I had no idea what he was talking about. He said that he wanted to make sure I knew it was a great try, and who would have thought a 14-year-old girl could have gone so far co-writing a major bill. I STILL didn't know what he was talking about, and he finally said that in congressional language the bill "died in committee." I thought that was ridiculous because the vote is happening in a few days and I haven't yet given my "Mr. Smith Goes to Washington" speech to save everything at the last minute. He just said, "I'm very sorry," and hung up.

Personally I think it's very strange that a member of Congress has so little understanding of how Congress works.

November 6

Katherine said she needed to discuss something "very important." When I got to her office the door was open a tiny bit. I could see she was putting water on her face to make her mascara run. It was kind of weird, but when you have a life like mine you get used to seeing many strange things.

When I walked in she said, "I'm sorry, Amy, but my emotions are making me cry." Then she wiped the mascara and kind of "sniffled" a little and made a sad face and looked at me to make sure I saw.

I said she was probably sad about the condition of the earth. But she said no she was crying for my career. She said, "I'm sorry Amy, but we're going to have to let you go." She said the membership survey showed that our members identified me with the old motto that they were 90% resistant to, so the organization needed to "distance itself" from me. And since it didn't make sense for the organization to leave me, then I would have to leave the organization.

Katherine asked me, "That makes sense, right?" At that time I was kind of in shock, but I admitted that it was logical.

She also said it was very obvious that I wasn't "on board" with the new motto and the new evolved mission. I wouldn't be behind it 100%, which wouldn't work because HomeEarth needs "team players."

Then she kind of went into a speech about thanking me for my time at HomeEarth, and how I really helped get the numbers up because of my "youthful multi-cultural appeal" and "high sympathy value." I asked what she meant by that, and she said, "Oh, it has to do with being raised by a struggling single dad and having a dead activist mom."

She kept talking on and on, but I'm not sure what she said because a very interesting thing was happening in my mind. I could tell that Katherine was still talking because I could see her mouth moving, but instead of "words" I was hearing kind of like "background music" or something. It's very hard to explain. And suddenly I stopped being in shock and felt very peaceful. Then I wondered if Tiffany's saying "Everything happens for a reason" is true, even if we don't know what the reason is.

And then I realized I knew the reason! For being "let go" from HomeEarth, I mean. The reason is now I would have time to go to Washington DC and rush up the steps of Congress. And then burst in and give my big speech to pass the Save the Earth Act at the last minute. In my mind I pictured it, and it was REALLY dramatic. It came down to the last SECOND. Just before the gavel came down when all hope seemed lost, I burst in the doors and said, "Wait, I have something to say!" A bunch of people said, "No, it's too late!" But a bigger bunch of people said, "We can wait for another few minutes, let her speak." It was like a movie playing in my mind!

By then Katherine had finished her speech. She said, "I'm so sorry, you must be devastated."

I said, "Nope. Thanks for hiring me, it's been a lot of fun!"

Then SHE looked very shocked! She said kind of to herself, "Poor girl is deluded," like she didn't think I could hear. But I said back, "I think it's everybody else!"

So what I need to do now is to get all packed for my trip to Washington DC!

November 7

I remembered the name of the science fiction movie I was thinking of before. It's called "The Invasion of the Body Snatchers." I thought of that movie because I'm getting that feeling again of being the last non-crazy person on earth.

Everybody is going totally crazy because of some economic news. The media as usual is being overly-dramatic. The articles have HUGE headlines of things like "THE BEGINNING OF THE END" and "ECONOMIC DEATH SPIRAL." Fortunately, I'm aware that it's all an example of "sensationalism."

The "big news" is that China has announced it isn't going to buy any more U.S. debt, and in fact wants to cash in all their Treasury bonds. I guess it's a lot of money, such as hundreds of billions of dollars. One article said, "China has lost absolutely all faith in our ability to get out of debt, or to accomplish pretty much anything." Lots of articles are talking about a "domino effect." This will start all the dominoes falling, and the dominoes are the economy.

I'm not too much of an "economic expert" about what all this means, but it's probably not very good.

When they finally reached the president for comment, his response was that he has resigned so he can spend more time with his family.

I found some good news! I found it in the Oregonian. I got past all the "doomsday" economic news and found a very good editorial. The title is, "Perhaps it's Time to Re-Evaluate Our Relationship with the Planet?" I'm so glad that humanity is finally figuring it out JUST IN TIME!

November 8

I'm writing while on the road to the beautiful Oregon high desert! It was a result of getting some surprise visitors at home. I gave them a tour of my eco home and garden, even though I had to apologize for the garden being kind of messy.

Oh - the visitors were a couple people from EarthSage. They seemed kind of in a hurry. They said they had a message from Coyote, who would like very much for me to come for a visit.

I got a "tingly" feeling (but kept it secret) and said I would be honored and it sounds very nice, but that I was actually in the process of packing for a very important journey. I told them I was going to Washington D.C. to make a big speech like James Stewart in "Mr. Smith Goes to Washington" to get them to pass the Save the Earth Act at the last possible second.

One of them - Robyn ("like the bird" she said, but with a "y") told me I didn't need to do that because she heard that Congress had voted for the Save the Earth Act that morning.

I COULDN'T BELIEVE IT! I told them it was strange that I didn't hear about it, but maybe the media didn't report it because they're going crazy with this China thing. She shook her head "yes" very enthusiastically, and so did the other friend - Chris ("just Chris, not like anything" he said).

Then Chris said we had to leave immediately. I said that it would actually be nice to take a rest break after all the craziness. Then I remembered I would have to tell Dad, but he wasn't home. So I made him a note while Robyn and Chris loaded my bags into the car. I left a note for Dad: "I'm spending some time at EarthSage relaxing in the beautiful high desert. Don't worry, I'll watch out for rattlesnakes! "

Of course, I'm aware of what this invitation means. It means that Coyote really likes me and is willing to wait until I'm old enough to be his girlfriend. He's not the type of man to say this with words, but he's saying it with his actions. Some men are like that.

We're totally out of Portland now, and the traffic was CRAZY! People were driving like maniacs, and all the grocery stores were packed. I don't know why, but it was like everybody was doing all their shopping at the same time and filling up bunches of shopping carts. I thought it was a little early for Thanksgiving shopping, but I guess not.

When we were still in town I heard a lot of explosions that I thought sounded like guns. But Robyn and Chris said not to worry, because actually they were fireworks to celebrate that the Save the Earth Act passed.

Now that the struggle is over, I'm realizing how tired I am. It's all catching up with me, all at once. I feel like I could sleep for a YEAR. I told Robyn and Chris that I'm going to take a nap, and to wake me up when we get to EarthSage.

November 15

I can't believe I haven't written in my diary for an entire week! Part of the reason is because right after I got to EarthSage I slept for a looooong time. I could not believe when I finally woke up it have been FIVE DAYS! I knew that I was tired but I didn't know that I was THAT tired!

November 19

Has it really been three days since I wrote anything? It doesn't feel like three days, it feels like much less. But it also feels like a lot longer. Time is getting very weird. I've also been having many dreams about dolphins, even though there are no dolphins out here in the desert.

Coyote checks on me often. He doesn't give me hugs like many other people do. That's because he needs to keep our relationship top secret. I think of him as my "secret boyfriend." I guess that makes me his "secret girlfriend." It's kind of fun, in a way, even though it's also a little frustrating. Such as because of no kissing, except for in my imagination.

November 20

I overheard something that at first I didn't understand. Some people were asking Coyote why he brought me here. I couldn't hear everything clearly because they were on the other side of a big stack of firewood. But I heard things like, "Why did you break the 'no additional people' rule?" and "Will food production cover an additional person?"

Coyote answered something like, "I have no sympathy for the rest of the human race, but I feel like she was the only one who didn't deserve it. If they would've listened to her, there would have been no collapse."

I didn't understand this answer at all. But then I realized it was a "pretend" answer. He couldn't say the "real" answer about me being is "secret girlfriend" because then it wouldn't be a secret.

I'm sure glad I figured that out!

EMERGENCY! I'm writing from inside the main house, where Coyote told me to stay and do not go outside for ANY reason until he gets back. There were explosions not far away. Then there was a bunch of panic. People were running around saying, "Defend the perimeter!" Coyote and a bunch of other guys ran off - and they had guns! Real guns! I was VERY worried but Coyote said not to worry, they were totally prepared for this.

It looks like the emergency is over. I asked who was attacking us. Jeff (one of the guys who ran off with a gun) said, "Cannibals, just as expected." I said that doesn't make sense, because there would only be cannibals if society collapsed. Then Coyote got mad at Jeff and said, "Not cannibals, remember?" and Jeff said, "Oh, I forgot. I meant to say zombies."

I couldn't believe it! I've never heard of an actual zombie attack. But Jeff said, "Oh, we get them sometimes out here." I said I didn't realize zombies could shoot guns, but Jeff explained that "country zombies" can, and I was thinking of "city zombies" that have no experience with guns.

I tried to go online for news about the zombies, and also I was curious to see how much the Save the Earth Act passed by. Unfortunately, the Internet connection isn't working. Coyote explained that zombies like to chew on wire, so they probably broke the connection to the Internet provider. Stupid zombies!

Coyote said the zombie problem is only temporary because eventually they'll starve to death and won't bother us anymore. But for now it's not safe to travel, so we're "on our own" for a while.

I actually don't really mind, since I could use more relaxation. I'm so tired! I feel like I could sleep forever!

November 21

I was talking to Robyn and I mentioned how it's very strange how there are dolphins out here in the desert. She acted all concerned for me and even started to cry a little, which I thought was strange because I'm doing OK. She should really be more concerned for the dolphins, which are going to get all dried out. She gave me a big hug and said, "You just need a lot of rest and you'll get better eventually."

This is crazy! Now it seems like EVERYBODY is giving me hugs and telling me it's okay and I'll get better eventually.

November 22

I saw a badger today! It was the first time I saw one in person. Representative Bozzio was right, because I think it's the strangest creature I've ever seen.

Or maybe it was a dream. It's getting hard to tell the difference. If it was real, I hope it leaves the dolphins alone!

Well, my diary is almost full. So I think this would be an excellent time to reflect upon the extremely interesting things that have happened since I started this diary.

Saving the earth from ecological destruction sure wasn't easy! Nobody had ever done it before, so there were no instructions. There was no book such as "Saving the Earth from Ecological Destruction for Dummies"!

I'm WAY too tired to write a "real" book about how I did it, but it's a good thing I kept up my diary the whole time. There's a lot of good information in here, in case people wonder how a 14-year-old girl saved the earth.

Or maybe in many years people will "forget" and the earth will need to be saved again. Or if anybody knows any other planets that need to be saved from ecological destruction, my diary could come in VERY handy!

If my diary ever gets published, I think it should have a very simple title, something like: "The Diary of Amy, The 14-Year-Old Girl Who Saved the Earth." In fact, I'm going to put that title on my diary right now!

This diary is dedicated to the earth
which is very beautiful and in fact is
my favorite planet.

~ Amy Johnson-Martinez ~

Acknowledgments

Huge thanks to the friends who agreed to give valuable feedback on early drafts of this novel: Kristen, Julia, Ceiridwen, Lahni, Jessica, Sara, and Tonya. Your advice turned that embarrassing first draft into something I'm actually proud of. I couldn't have done it without you.

About the Author

Scott Erickson is a writer of humor and satire. He is a two-time winner of the Mona Schreiber Prize for Humorous Fiction and Nonfiction. One of his stories was included in the book *Laugh Your Shorts Off*, a compilation of contest winners from the website *Humor and Life in Particular*.

He honed his humor writing via his long-running zine *Reality Ranch*. This led to the publication of his first book, *The Best of Reality Ranch*.

He has done some interesting things in his life. He spent 5-1/2 months backpacking around the biggest lake in the world, lived for 1-1/2 years at a rural not-for-profit institute teaching sustainable living skills, and spent a summer helping friends establish an organic farm.

He feels at home in Portland, Oregon, which has the largest roller skating rink west of the Mississippi River and the highest concentration of craft beer breweries in America. He is possibly the nicest curmudgeon you'll ever meet.

More information can be found at
www.scott-erickson-writer.com

Printed in Great Britain
by Amazon.co.uk, Ltd.,
Marston Gate.